Twin Sins

Book 3,

The Sins Volumes

Fiction by

Mary Elizabeth Gaines

Mary Gaines Books

© 2018 by Mary Elizabeth Gaines

Published by Mary Gaines Books

First Printing February 2019

Printed in the United States of America

Library of Congress Control Number: 2018905285

Mary Elizabeth Gaines, 1950 –

Book 3, The Sins Volumes

ISBN 978-1-7320026-2-3   Paperback

ISBN 978-1-7320026-3-0   E-book

This Book is Dedicated to

<u>Sandra Forguson Crowell</u>

My Best Friend, Valued Critic, and Beach Buddy

I am thankful for the many blessings bestowed

Upon me by God, Our Heavenly Father.

This book would never have been written without

His spiritual guidance and inspiration.

— Mary Elizabeth Gaines

Also By This Author

<u>Buried Sins</u>

(Book 1, The Sins Volumes)

Mystery & Suspense

<u>Sacrificial Sins</u>

(Book 2, The Sins Volumes)

Thrilling Suspense

Available through notable booksellers

or directly from the author at

<u>*MaryGainesBooks.com*</u>

PROLOGUE

He lay naked and afraid, unaware of what was ultimately going to happen to him. It was bad enough that his body ached and cramped, causing sweat to pool beneath his tightly constrained body. He was positioned on his back atop a thin vinyl pad. He couldn't move, or at least not enough to matter.

There was no hope for escape. Even if he could miraculously break free of his shackles, his weakened body wouldn't support him. He thought he'd never make it out alive.

The people who took him were monsters. He never saw their full faces, only slivers of exposed skin. The worst one was the big man with the red glaring eyes. He was pure evil. He was the devil incarnate. He had been so cruel.

Swirls of bright colors pulsated behind his closed eyelids and ricocheted inside his head in time with the pounding loud music that blasted against his eardrums.

Please. Let me die. Let me die now!

The monsters would entice the Grim Reaper to come for him, but then the monsters would send the Reaper away before releasing him from his nightmare. Death was always close but not within reach. He couldn't grasp onto it long enough for the Reaper to work his black magic. And why? For amusement. Just to see him suffer for the hell of it.

Why me? Isn't that what everybody always wants to know? Because I've disappointed the man who spawned me? Because I'm still me? But why do I deserve this tormenting cruelty?

For a fleeting instant he lost consciousness as the loud music and searing pain battered his delicate body. When he fluttered his eyes open once more, his one and only thought was about the object of his desire. His dry lips formed a strange smile.

Please...could I just have another helping of the devil's powder?

When he completely passed out, he dreamed of Hell.

CHAPTER 1

It had been almost 24 hours since she had felt his touch, but her skin still tingled when she thought about their spontaneous moments of intimacy. Her tummy did a "thrill flip"—the same feeling induced by the sudden plunge of a steep roller coaster—when she relived the thoughts of the pleasure he had evoked within her.

Sophia Giordano tried hard to concentrate on the drive ahead, but she found her thoughts wandering back and forth between the road and the unexpected sexual encounter of the night before.

She drove the classic Jaguar that had once been her late father's. It had been kept covered and in pristine condition while parked for years in the garage at the DeLuca mansion where she and her brother, Ricky, had grown up under the care of her step-mother, Juliana DeLuca Giordano. When Sophia turned sixteen, the car was offered to Sophia. She readily accepted, choosing her father's cherished Jag over a brand new car for her birthday.

Sophia, too, had kept the Jag in mint condition. It had been driven, of course, but it also had been garage kept and maintained as if the car was a cherished family heirloom. Perhaps it was, in a sense. She had so few tangible reminders of her father, and she certainly didn't remember him clearly. Only that he had died when she was very young.

Trying to reign in her meandering thoughts, she squinted and focused on the Southampton roadways ahead that led to the DeLuca mansion. Her brother, Ricky—or Rick as he preferred to be called now—was hosting a re-election fundraiser for the distinguished incumbent Senator from New York, Sid Taylor.

* * * * *

Sydney Warren Taylor, known as Sid by his friends and widespread constituency, had occupied his Senate seat for decades. The upcoming election was only a formality as far as the Senator was concerned. He believed he had no viable opponent who could possibly jerk the senatorial rug from beneath him.

Besides, Sid had the power of the DeLuca name and the family's infinite funding to keep him seated for however long he wished to retain the federal position.   It was a win-win for everyone as far as the Senator was concerned. He kept his government job and DeLuca Enterprises retained his "service and protection."

 It certainly didn't hurt that he was married to Lucinda DeLuca Norton's distant cousin, Valentina.   "Blood Ties," he liked to call it.

* * * * *

Famous for being the largest mansion in Southampton, the DeLuca estate was bustling with activity and noise.   Its exterior seemed extraordinarily bright, with every window illuminated just enough to reflect the festive activities inside. The combined effect of the beaming landscape lighting and gas lamp posts cast an eerie artificial daylight glow on the expansive grounds.

The evening's soiree was in full swing when Sophia pulled the Jag around to the back of the house and parked it in its traditional spot. She climbed out of the car and approached the door of the familiar sunroom, the room that had once held enough sprawling plants to resemble a jungle room. There were still some palms and large potted plants scattered in the far corner of the room; but, now the room was classically decorated and mirrored the more elegant style of her step-grandmother. Lucinda DeLuca Norton had always had a flare for interior decorating, and her subtle touch was evident in every renovation that the mansion had experienced over the years.

The mansion's primary household staff members who Sophia knew as a child had long since moved on. Instead, the servant known to them as "the butler" had been replaced with a middle-aged man named Thomas. "The cook" position was now occupied by Maureen, an older lady who had a flare for Italian dishes and lush desserts. The two, along with a multitude of other servants, had loyally served the family for many years and dutifully executed the responsibilities of their employment.

Waiting at the interior door of the sunroom was Thomas, ready to greet Sophia and provide an insider's update on the party mood thus far. "Welcome, Miss Sophia. May I take your things?"

"Thanks, Thomas. Looks like everyone's deep in the swing of things, huh?" she chuckled as she handed him her purse and wrap. The racket coming from the other rooms was boisterous and gleeful.

"Yes, ma'am. The guests have been enjoying a great deal of entertainment this evening. The Senator seems full of himself. He and Mr. Rick have been enthusiastically debating the pros and cons of legalizing marijuana, and neither of them seems to be making a very good case either way. Most likely, alcohol consummation has something to do with it," Thomas smiled as if he had just shared an inside joke.

"Oh, Lord. Do I need to intervene?" Sophia chuckled as she watched Thomas's smile change into a broad grin.

"Not if you value your reputation," he sniggered. With that, he dismissed himself to find a safe spot to store Sophia's belongings. Sophia proceeded to the formal living room to join party central.

"Look who finally made it!" an exuberant Rick announced as Sophia made her way toward the Senator and her brother. "Tell me, dear Sis, don't you think it's time to pass a bill to legalize marijuana?" an inebriated Rick blurted out.

Lowering her voice, Sophia was quick to address her brother's question. "Rick, I think that's a discussion for another time, don't you? I'm sure the Senator needs to make the rounds and shake some hands while he has a captive audience. Besides, something as controversial as legalizing marijuana is probably a conversation best held in a more private setting. Don't you agree, Senator?" she asked as she took Sid's arm and began steering him toward the other side of the room.

"I agree, Sophia." As they walked away from Rick, the Senator patted Sophia's hand that gently gripped his arm above his elbow. "Thanks for rescuing me. I always said you were the smartest one of the damned bunch. You have a real feel for assessing a situation and handling it with finesse and authority. That's why you've been so successful in making DeLuca Enterprises the powerhouse that it is today. You're the complete package: brains **and** beauty. Now, if you could just keep that loudmouth brother of yours under control...," Sid said seriously while trying to act as if he were joking.

After a brief pause, Sophia answered. "Don't worry about Rick. He enjoys a good time, but he has the company's best interests at heart."

The Senator studied Sophia's face. "Of course. I didn't mean to offend. I've never doubted your brother's interests in the company's success." He paused for an awkward moment before continuing, "Maybe you and I should regroup for a chat a little later. I have some business ideas I'd like to share with you. DeLuca Enterprises could grow exponentially during my next Senatorial term if you're interested—assuming, that is, that you retain your role as the President of DeLuca Enterprises. And you should also know…I've always enjoyed taking orders from beautiful women."

The Senator smirked and gulped down the drink he held in his hand. Setting the empty crystal glass down hard on a side table, he smiled at Sophia. "Now if you'll excuse me, **Madam President**, I have a few hands to shake and ladies to kiss."

Sophia watched him stroll across the room and grab the hand of a handsome young campaign contributor. Just as Sid was about to kiss the contributor's pretty companion on the cheek, his wife, Val, emerged from the middle of the crowd and hastily took her place at Sid's side. Instead of kissing the young woman, Sid awkwardly recoiled and hesitantly took his wife's arm. "May I introduce you to my inspiration? This is my wife, Valentina. Val, this charming couple has a vested interest in my reelection. Darling, meet Carmen Ryan and Adam Woodson."

* * * * * *

Teddy Brantley had never been one to enjoy cocktail parties or meaningless chit chat. He was more relaxed when he was in his own apartment, his office, or during those rare occasions when he visited his parents' country home in Lenoir City, Tennessee. He felt anxious and cornered when he made appearances at social gatherings like the one this evening at the DeLuca estate.

He had watched eagerly for Sophia to arrive. Whether she realized it or not, she had always been his anchor. Sophia had an instinctive calming effect on him and kept him balanced when he felt lopsided.

His feelings for her were mixed: he always thought of her as the sister he'd never had, but lately he was viewing her in a different light. His admiration and respect for her had grown through the years, but he was beginning to feel something special toward her now. Could he be falling for her? That certainly wouldn't play out very well with Sophia's family. He wasn't sure why, but he always believed Sophia was off-limits to him.

It didn't matter, really, since Sophia was more interested in running DeLuca Enterprises than making a commitment to any personal relationship. Teddy would continue to keep his feelings to himself. He knew his place, and it was somewhere beneath the DeLuca/Giordano rung on the corporate ladder.

* * ***

"Where have you been hiding?" Sophia said mischievously when she found Teddy standing in the foyer. "You avoiding me?"

"Well, yes. I mean…no. I'm avoiding the crowd. You know how I feel about these kinds of things. They make me nervous that I'll screw something up and say the wrong thing," Teddy admitted.

"You're a lawyer, for goodness sake. You don't ever seem nervous about courtrooms or judges or legal arguments. Seems like you'd have conquered that social awkwardness by now," Sophia teased.

"Those things are different. I'm confident when I'm working, but I barely know a handful of these people and none of them that well. I'm not good at schmoozing just for the sake of making conversation. I'd rather stick to talking about the facts of law. If I have to make small talk, I try to only do that with people I'm comfortable with," he retorted.

"Well, talk to me then. You know me better than anyone, and I could use a little break. Let's take our drinks out by the pool and reminisce about the old times, shall we?" Sophia didn't wait for him to answer. She moved swiftly through the crowd toward the kitchen, then slipped through the sunroom out the exit to the backyard.

At poolside, she made herself comfortable in a chaise lounge and sank back into the plump cushion. Kicking off her shoes, she breathed deeply and took in the brisk air. "I so love this cooler weather. Don't you?" she said before she realized Teddy hadn't quite made it to her side.

"What did you say?" he asked as he finally caught up and approached her chair.

"I said I love this cooler weather. Don't you, Teddy?"

"It reminds me of Tennessee. When the leaves change from green to red and bright yellow, it makes me think of the mountains. My parents used to take me driving through the Great Smoky Mountains National Park several times a year, but fall was my favorite season. I watched for bears along the roadway, but never saw very many. There were always lots of deer though, especially in the fields around Cades Cove."

Sophia closed her eyes and tried to imagine the scene Teddy was painting for her through his memories. "Sounds so nice. Maybe you can take me there someday."

He seated himself on the foot of the adjacent chaise lounge before he answered her. "Sure. Everybody needs to experience the full effect of the Smokies. It's not all just about Dollywood, outlet malls, and candy shops. It's scenic and majestic and ... breath-taking." Teddy looked awkwardly toward the pool, trying not to let his perplexed feelings for Sophia show.

A momentary flashback of her own memories overtook Sophia. Her mind wandered to the time spent the evening before when she had surrendered herself to her physical desires. Blushing, she tried to change the subject.

"What do you think about Senator Taylor? I don't believe you've ever voiced an opinion to me or anyone else about him. I'd like to know what **you** think, Teddy." Sophia took a sip of her drink.

"I haven't done enough research on his record to provide any real input. But, to me, most politicians are just pawns. Their opinions are really the opinions of other people who want to gain something in return for the politician's power. I don't think much of politicians in general. From a personal perspective, I think the man might be an egotistical blow-hard. Keep in mind that I haven't been around him enough to say that with absolute certainty." Teddy smiled.

"Wow, do you always have to qualify your answers? You really are a practiced attorney," Sophia laughed while outstretching her hand to poke Teddy's shoulder.

He winced and leaned away before she had the chance to do it a second time. "I'm just trying to be honest. All I know about him is what my gut tells me."

"Well, for our company's sake, I hope your instincts are wrong." Even as Sophia said those words, she wanted to retract them. After her encounter with the Senator a few minutes before, not to mention all the distasteful things she had previously heard about the Senator's past, she had conjured up her own negative feelings about Sid Taylor.

Sophia couldn't understand her current internal turmoil, especially since the last words Sid had directed toward her were inappropriate and bordering on lewdness. She still hadn't decided if he was a power-hungry narcissist or simply a loose-mouthed sot who couldn't hold his liquor. She was leaning toward narcissism, although Sid's affinity for alcohol tarnished his reputation years before. He was the proud owner of a mixed bag of transgressions.

* ** ** *

Rick Giordano was leading a sing-along, standing next to the grand piano in the formal living room where the majority of the guests had congregated. The pianist—a good sport if there ever was one—tried to keep tempo with the out-of-rhythm and off-key host while Rick loudly sang *"Piano Man,"* a song originally made famous by Billy Joel, a Long Island resident and musical legend. The crowd didn't seem to mind that Rick couldn't carry a tune, but instead cheered him on as he murdered the song.

Teddy eased himself into the corner of the room, smiling across the crowd at his best friend while Rick made an absolute idiot of himself. *I'd never have the nerve to pull off something like that. Either Rick doesn't have any social inhibitions, or he's deliriously stoned.*

With everyone's attention focused so intently on the outlandish host, no one—not even Teddy—immediately realized that Sophia remained absent from the room.

CHAPTER 2

Barefoot and pensive, a relaxed Sophia stood at the edge of the Olympic-sized swimming pool watching the moonlight catch the ripples in the water. Deep in thought, she didn't realize someone was standing behind her until she turned her head and gasped in surprise.

"Oh! You scared me. I thought you were Teddy. Where is he, anyway? He was here a minute ago," an apprehensive Sophia asked.

"Disappointed, Madam President?" the tipsy Senator inquired.

"Uh, no...I just thought he was still here." Sophia resumed her stance—a little too stiffly, perhaps— but continued looking out across the pool. "We were talking about how the change from scorching hot weather makes us both happy in different ways," Sophia volunteered.

Until she spoke the words aloud, she hadn't realized she was making an excuse for being alone with Teddy Brantley. She blushed. She had always been strangely drawn to Teddy.

Still behind Sophia, Sid took a step forward. He was close enough to her now that she could smell the stale liquor on his breath.

Stepping to the side and turning to face him, Sophia anticipated the conversation she knew Sid planned to start. She was in no mood to talk to a drunken man—Senator or otherwise—about future business ideas that evening. Her plans for the evening were different.

"Sid, I think I'd like to go inside. I'm getting chilly out here. Why don't we talk later, okay?" she declared as she reached to pick up her shoes from the pool deck.

An annoyed Sid responded. "Sophia, why don't we talk now? I may never get your full attention again tonight. Of course, that wouldn't be an issue if I were *Teddy* ... "

Sophia stopped Sid in mid-sentence. "Leave Teddy out of this. You're out of line. He's been a family friend since we were all kids, and he's the Chief General Counsel of DeLuca Enterprises. Show some respect, Sid."

"Respect? Is that what you want?" Sid's drunken laughter sounded evil and threatening. "What about me? I'm not seeing any respect from your side of the table. I am well aware of what you "kids" say about me behind my back. I'm not the asshole you think I am." Sid pointed to his own chest. "If it hadn't been for **this** Senator, your company would have failed years ago."

"I highly doubt that, Sid. My grandfather ..."

"Your **step**-grandfather was the boss of an organized crime family, and all of his so-called legitimate businesses were tainted by that fact. He wasn't a model citizen. Far from it. The DeLuca family lifestyle that you, your brother, and your step-mother have always enjoyed was funded with blood money—DeLuca **business** blood money. I know, because I helped protect those businesses and kept them sheltered from unnecessary scrutiny. You can **all** thank me for that, and I expect your continued loyalty in return. Your grandfather understood the value of my assistance."

Sid took a long drink from his cocktail glass. "I demand some respect, too, dammit." He flung the heavy crystal glass into the pool, scattering ice cubes and rapidly staining the water with scattered pools of brown liquor.

For a moment, Sophia was stunned and speechless. When she regained her composure, she addressed the Senator as calmly as she could. "Senator Taylor, I believe it's time for you to leave. I'll find Val and see that you get home safely. You're in no condition to drive." As she began to step away from the angry man, Sid grabbed her forearm and jerked her back.

With beady eyes and a furious expression, he addressed Sophia as if she were a child that needed to be punished. "How dare you take that tone with **me**! I'm a distinguished Senator from New York, and no little 'girl' is going to tell me when I need to leave or what I should do. You're nothing but a snotty-nosed brat who's had everything handed to her on a silver platter. You show me the respect I deserve, you little bitch!"

Sophia looked around frantically, but no one was nearby or within ear shot. Even if she screamed, the loud ruckus from the party inside would have drowned out her voice. Thinking quickly, she tried to stall the irrational man. She wanted to calm him— maybe even reason with him.

"Sid, please. The house is full of your constituents and donors. We can't get into this now. Certainly, not with tempers riled. Please let go of my arm—you're hurting me— and let's sit down and attempt to have a calm discussion."

The Senator's eyes seemed to soften as if he understood exactly the vast damage such a scene could cause to his reputation and his coffers, not to mention to his marriage. He relaxed his grip, inhaled deeply, and dropped his hand from Sophia's arm. Backing up to let her pass, he bowed theatrically.

"I'm sorry, Sophia. I got carried away, and my emotions got the better of me. Let me escort you back to the house to warm up. I seem to recall you said you were chilly. I was selfish to ignore your discomfort. Here. Take my jacket," he said as he started to remove his coat.

"No, thank you." Sophia didn't want anything from Sid, much less the jacket he had been wearing that reeked of dry cleaning fluid and spilled bourbon. "I'll be fine once I get inside. Thank you for the offer, though."

Poised and with head held high, she moved deliberately toward the sunroom doorway. She would perform a damned good imitation of bravery, even if it wasn't something she was feeling at the moment.

* * * * * *

"So who's up next?" Rick enthusiastically asked the crowd. "I can't carry this singing gig alone. My voice is getting scratchy, and I need a drink. How about you, Adam?"

The piano crowd cheered and tried to coax Adam Woodson to take the lead in the next round of sing-along. Looking at Carmen for help, she only shrugged her shoulders and laughed. "But I can't sing in front of people," he whispered to his fiancé. When Carmen rolled her eyes in response, Adam knew he could sing better than Rick. Amid the cheers and encouraging shouts of the crowd chanting, "Ad-dam, Ad-dam, Ad-dam," he slowly made his way up front to stand next to the pianist. Rick clapped and punched Adam's arm before he passed the microphone to him and sauntered toward the bar.

"Okay, Okay," Adam said in his soothing Southern accent as he tried to calm the crowd. "I know two songs. One is called *99 Bottles of Beer.*"

The crowd booed as they unanimously dismissed his first suggestion. "All right. Forget that one. How about *Our Song* by Elton John?"

The response was an overwhelming chorus of whistles and applause. When the pianist started the intro, the group silenced. What followed was a beautiful solo sung by an accomplished vocalist. The captivated audience never sang along; instead, they were mesmerized by the delivery of the poignant lyrics by the unexpectedly talented young man.

When Adam finished, he couldn't budge from his spot. The crowd stood in silence until a solitary person started clapping, then another, until the entire audience erupted in loud applause shouting, "Bravo, Bravo," in loud voices.

Adam stood rigidly, acting as anxious as an auditioning hopeful on *American Idol*. His knees felt weak, and there was a glistening line of sweat beading above his upper lip. The moment the audience began to applaud, he managed a slight smile. Eventually a broad grin appeared across Adam's face as an excited Rick rushed to his side.

"Good job, man! We'll have to book you at our next function, but you better have more songs to choose from by then!" Rick clasped Adam's hand in his and raised them victoriously in the air. The crowd continued their applause and chants of "Ad-dam, Ad-dam" as the shy young man made his way through the crowd. "Let's hear it for our Southern Gentleman, Adam Woodson!" Rick exclaimed as Adam tried to make a quick exit from the stage.

Carmen smiled knowingly as she watched her fiancé rush past her. *Poor Adam,* she thought. *He'll get his nerves under control after he throws up and settles down.*

She turned her attention to the front of the room and raised her cocktail glass in Rick's direction. They both mouthed the word "Cheers" right before taking their next sips.

* * * * * *

Being no stranger to the DeLuca home, Valentina Bellini Taylor made her way to the kitchen in search of a cup of strong coffee. She had long ago decided she couldn't control Sid's intake of liquor, so she voluntarily assumed the designated driver responsibility when the couple didn't use a limo service for transport to evening engagements. Tonight was one of those rare occasions they had decided to drive their vintage Mercedes SL500, a car too dear to them both to allow anyone else to take the wheel. Sid had driven them to the fundraiser, but clearly he was now so drunk he couldn't be trusted to get them or the car safely home.

"Maureen, do you mind if I sit with you a few minutes? I need some of your coffee to counteract the only glass of wine I was allowed to have tonight. Looks like I'll be driving us home, as usual." Val took a seat at the glass-topped table situated in the kitchen's bay window nook.

"Absolutely, Mrs. Taylor. We women have to keep ourselves ready to take over for the men who need us, don't we?" Maureen chuckled. "Want some dessert to go with that coffee? I have a pineapple upside down cake I was saving for the kids, but they always seem to be on some kinda diet nowadays. There's plenty, even if they decide to have some later."

"No, Maureen. I think I've had enough to eat today. And what do you mean, 'the kids?' Are you still calling Sophia and Ricky 'kids?'" she teased.

Maureen smiled as she poured Val's coffee. "Old habits, Mrs. Taylor. When I came here to work for Mrs. Giordano, those two were just teenagers.   They still seem like those same awkward kids to me. Sometimes I think I love 'em as much as my own. I'd do anything for those two— and Teddy, too— if it'd keep 'em happy."

"I'm sure you would, Maureen. I think they feel the same way about you," Val replied as she sipped the hot coffee she had just been served.

Suddenly, Maureen snapped to attention. "Did you hear that?"

* * * * * *

She stumbled into the doorway, forcing herself to put one foot in front of the other. She wasn't exactly sure what had just happened, but her face hurt and her body screamed at her in pain. There was something wet and sticky between her legs, but she wouldn't look down.

Sophia was hardly keeping herself upright as it was. If she had to exert much more effort, she would surely faint. She tried to concentrate on getting her uncooperative body inside the house to get some help. *Just make it a few more steps.*

As she managed to grip the door facing that led into the kitchen from the sunroom, she felt herself drifting. Her eyes rolled back into her head, and all she managed to get out of her mouth was a single word: "Maureen."

By the time Sophia collapsed on the floor, the loyal cook was already running toward her, with Val Taylor following closely behind.

Sophia heard someone's fading scream as she blacked out and embraced the comfort of darkness.

CHAPTER 3

Not long after Teddy resumed his inconspicuous position in the corner of the living room, he felt a sharp nudge on his shoulder.

"Teddy, you're needed in the kitchen," an obviously shaken Val announced. "Hurry," she demanded and dashed away before he had a chance to respond.

"What …?" he started to utter, but realized Val was now out of ear shot. *What the hell? What's wrong with her?* Finding an empty tray in the corner cluttered with abandoned glassware and hors d'oeuvre plates, he set down his full cocktail glass and hustled to the kitchen.

As he neared the kitchen doorway, he could see someone lying on the floor with legs splayed and posed in an awkward position. He noticed bare feet before he saw anything else— Maureen's wide body blocked his view as she knelt on the floor over the person. He saw a fidgety Val now standing next to Maureen. When he made it fully inside the kitchen, he felt his fearful heart jump into his throat.

"Sophia! Sophia, are you alive? Open your eyes!" he blurted out a little too loudly.

"Shush, Teddy. We've got to handle this low-key. Help me get her into the sunroom away from prying eyes. She blacked out just a minute ago, but I suspect we can bring her around. She's moaning," Maureen explained.

Without further comment, Teddy gently lifted Sophia and carefully delivered her to the sofa in the dimly lit sunroom. Kneeling on the floor next to her, he took her hand and squeezed it tenderly. Tears were pooling in his eyes as he kissed her fingers, watching intently for Sophia to open her fluttering eyes.

Maureen hurried back to the kitchen in search of ammonia while Val grabbed wet paper towels and hastily wiped the floor where Sophia had lain unconscious only moments before.

 By the time Maureen reentered the sunroom, Val's careful cleanup left no sign of any previous incident in the kitchen area.   Val stood guard, respectfully shutting the sunroom door behind Maureen to help ensure the privacy Sophia deserved.

"Move aside, Teddy," Maureen commanded as she made her way to Sophia's side. "Here, darlin'. Take a whiff of this," she continued as she waved the ammonia bottle under Sophia's nose.

Sophia gasped…then coughed…then put one hand on top of her head. She tried to focus her vision. It took a moment for her to clearly see Maureen's face looming over her.   Next she spied Teddy standing stiffly behind the sturdy cook. "Why does Teddy look so upset? What happened?" she murmured.

"Thank God, Sophia. You're alert!" a concerned Teddy said as he pushed Maureen aside and grabbed Sophia's hand once more.   He knelt where he could see Sophia's face clearly. Only inches apart, they both smiled weakly as he squeezed her hand.

"Is the party over? Did I drink too much?"

Teddy smiled through grateful tears. "No, silly. You didn't, but it looks like you must have fallen out by the pool. I shouldn't have left you out there alone."

Suddenly, Sophia reached for her crotch, indicating that perhaps something more sinister than a mere fall had happened to her. Sophia started breathing very rapidly, alerting Maureen to take control once again. The hefty cook leaned in front of Teddy, causing him to lose his balance and nearly topple over.

"There, there, darlin'. Let Maureen make you feel better," she cooed as she wiped a cool wet cloth across Sophia's forehead. "Let's get you upstairs away from all this hullabaloo so we can figure out what made you fall, okay darlin'?"

Sophia looked terrified.

A host of horrid thoughts stampeded through Teddy's mind as he watched his friend grimace. "I'll help you, Maureen," Teddy eagerly offered.

Realizing that moving Sophia was going to be a two-person job, Maureen nodded. She wished she had the brute strength to do it alone. Reluctantly, Maureen allowed Teddy to assist her with Sophia's relocation to a more secluded part of the house.

The two carefully guided the unsteady Sophia through the kitchen and down the back hallway. Without detection from anyone except Val, they made it to the rear elevator that would deposit the three on the private second floor bedroom wing of the DeLuca mansion.

* * * * * *

Val stood guard by the foyer's entrance to the kitchen while Teddy and Maureen half-dragged, half-walked Sophia hastily through and down the long back corridor. She knew within minutes that Sophia would be securely upstairs, lying in a comfortable bed with all her injuries attended with care.

Finally, the stumbling parade had passed her by, and the kitchen was yet again a welcome area for anyone who ventured in.   She gazed slowly around the room, eyes stopping at the very spot where Sophia had collapsed not ten minutes before.   She wondered if anyone might have glimpsed Sophia lying on the floor before Val had taken her sentry position at the door.   She hoped that everything had transpired fast enough for that to be highly unlikely.

Should I go tell Ricky what happened?   And where exactly is Sid?   I really don't want to start a panic.   Val knew she would be expected to protect Sophia's privacy, but she also knew Rick would be furious with her if she didn't let him know his sister had been taken upstairs after collapsing. Val tried weighing the pros and cons of remaining silent, but it was a challenge to patiently wait for word from Teddy or Maureen. Rick's temper was unpredictable, to say the least.   Sid, of course, was so drunk it wouldn't matter what she tried to tell him—it probably wouldn't register in his befuddled mind.

She decided to warm up her coffee, retake her seat at the table, and try to appear as calm as she could. Perhaps it was Teddy's place to alert the family of the mishap. After all, she didn't want to step on anybody's toes. It was much safer that way.

* * * * * *

While Maureen gently stroked Sophia's temple, Teddy anxiously paced back and forth by the side of the bed. "You're gonna wear a hole in that rug if you don't settle down, young man. Take a seat over there so our girl can see you without having to move her head. And stop fidgeting. You're upsetting Sophia with your constant pacing." Maureen had taken command of Sophia's old bedroom where the young woman now rested.

"I'm sorry, Maureen. I just want to make sure she's all right."

Sophia lifted her head off the pillow to make eye contact with Teddy who now sat nervously in a nearby chair. "I'm all right, Teddy. I just can't remember much about the last little while."

Maureen gasped as soon as Sophia's head moved up off the pillow, noticing the blood stains that now smeared the white pillowcase.

"Let me help you hold your head up for a minute, girl. Looks like there might be some bleeding coming from your scalp. Whatever your head hit, there must be a big dent in it now." Maureen tried to joke to mask her alarm.

She attempted to scan the back of Sophia's head without luck. "I can't see back there well enough. Let me feel," she insisted.   Sophia painfully turned her head in Teddy's direction to give Maureen better access to the back of her head.

"Jesus, child.   You got a gash back there big as my thumbnail. No wonder there's blood on the linens. We need to get a doctor in here to see if you need stitches!"

"**NO**, Maureen. I don't want a doctor." Sophia reached behind her head and felt matted hair caked with blood. She pulled her hand away and focused on the red sticky mess painted over her fingertips.

Teddy jumped to his feet, racing to Sophia's bedside. "Let me see," he said as he leaned over her and parted her hair. He gazed closely at the gaping injury.

"Sophia, don't be ridiculous. I think you need a doctor. You probably have a concussion at the very least. Maureen's right—you might need stitches, too."

Tears began to roll down Sophia's face as she mentally reconstructed the events of the evening. "Teddy, I think ..."

"What, Sophia? You think what?" Teddy, breathing irregularly, was unaware of the emotional reaction he was displaying. "WHAT, Sophia?"

"I think I might have been raped," she managed to say, pulling up the bottom of her dress just enough for both Maureen and Teddy to see the blood-streaked substance encrusted on her inner thigh.

"WHO DID THIS, SOPHIA! I'LL KILL THE FUCKING BASTARD!" Teddy shouted through clenched teeth. His hands formed tight fists, fingernails cutting crescent moons into the skin of his palms.

Shocked and enraged, Maureen didn't attempt to calm Teddy or make him lower his voice. Instead, she screeched in anguish and buried her head in her hands as she moaned in pure grief. Her whole body shook as she cried for the little innocent girl who used to trade kisses on the cheek for extra cookies.

"Where's Thomas? Maureen, where would Thomas be right now?" Teddy snarled impatiently.

With tears streaming down her puffy cheeks, Maureen answered in a low voice. "He should be overseeing the caterers. He carries a cell phone, though. We can text him if you need him. That's how we stay in contact."

Still staring at the distraught Sophia, Teddy replied without breaking his gaze, "Tell him to send Ricky up here. Now."

* * * * * *

Except for passing catering employees coming in and out, plus a few stray guests searching for the bathroom, Val had seen no one of interest come through the kitchen while she sat impatiently with her drained coffee cup.

When she saw Rick pass by on the way to the elevator in the back hallway, she finally rose from her chair. *I guess Ricky knows about Sophia now.*

Placing her empty coffee cup next to the sink where other dirty party dishes had been stacked, Val wandered back to the living room where the singers and pianist were still performing. Glancing around the crowd, she didn't see her husband anywhere.

That's odd. Sid should still be where the liquor is—or near the bar trying to look down some young woman's dress. She smirked and continued the hunt for her husband.

After several trips around the first floor of the mansion, Val exited the front door thinking Sid might be outside smoking. He said he'd quit months before, but she knew he still sneaked a cigarette once in a while. He craved smoking when he drank heavily, and tonight was such an occasion.

Surprised that Sid was nowhere to be seen, Val re-entered the house. She kept her eyes peeled for signs of Sid as she passed through, thinking she might have overlooked him before. Perhaps he had been in the bathroom, or maybe their 'timing' had been off, and they had somehow missed each other. Either way, he was conspicuously absent from his own fundraiser. She was feeling more and more determined to locate him.

Val had been stuck in the kitchen for what seemed like hours, so she never thought to look in the sunroom or backyard for her husband. In a final attempt to cover all grounds that could have been accessible to the guests, Val approached the sunroom door.

Upon entering, she felt spooked by the looming palm tree in the corner and the eerie shadows playing in the dimly lit room. She spied a dark stain on the sofa pillow where Sophia's bleeding head must have lain. She quickly turned the pillow over to conceal the spot before taking another step forward.

Val shuddered but tried to put the image from her mind. At last, she reached the door to the backyard and the swimming pool area.

Val stopped a few steps out the door and looked behind her. She felt a second shudder run through her body. *I feel like someone's watching me…this is insane! Maybe I should turn around and go back inside. To hell with Sid.*

Standing rigidly, she decided she was being silly. She may as well walk to the swimming pool and check the last area. Gathering her courage, she marched forward.

She could see chaise lounge chairs lined up neatly on both sides of the long pool. The dim light on the water reflected like a prism on a sparkling object rolling spasmodically on the bottom of the pool. A closer look and she could identify the crystal cocktail glass as an exact duplicate of those she had seen the guests drinking from in the house. *Humph, that's strange.*

Ready to go back inside the house, Val's peripheral vision caught a glimpse of something shiny at the far end of the row of chairs. Approaching slowly, it only took a moment to realize Sid was lying there, sprawled on his back between two chaise lounges with one arm limply lying across one chair's edge. His gold Rolex watch had caught the light from a gas lamp post several feet away, creating the glinting signal that had drawn Val to look in that direction.

She hurried to stand next to his outstretched form. "Sid, you piece of shit! Wake up! You're sloppy drunk again, you asshole!" Val kicked Sid gently on his calf. He didn't move.

"Bastard, wake the fuck up! I'm not going to drag you inside and give you coffee this time. You can lie there until you rot!" Val kicked him again, this time harder. He still didn't move.

"ASSHOLE!" she shouted over her shoulder as she flipped him a bird behind her back. "Pathetic!" she declared as she crossed the threshold of the sunroom and slammed the door behind her.

CHAPTER 4

"What's so damn important to interrupt ..." Rick blurted out as he pushed open the door to Sophia's old bedroom. He stopped in mid-sentence when he saw his injured sister lying on the bed, a blood-stained pillowcase under her disheveled hair.

"Good God! What's happened to Sophia?" Rick stopped in his tracks, eyes wide with alarm.

"That's what we're trying to find out, but we wanted to wait until you got here to start asking serious questions," Teddy volunteered from the chair he now occupied. Maureen nodded agreement from her seat on the foot of Sophia's bed.

Setting the stage, Maureen began the conversation. "While I was in the kitchen with Val, Sophia stumbled in from the sunroom and collapsed on the floor. I sent Val to get Teddy, and together we got her to the couch. She had fainted, I guess, so we never really knew what we were dealing with. We just thought she must have fallen."

Rushing to his sibling's bedside, Rick leaned over to touch her hand. "Sis, what's going on? What's happened to you? Are you able to talk?" He swiveled his head toward Teddy for a brief second, displaying a look of confusion and concern.

A steady stream of tears rolled down Sophia's red cheeks. She nodded and looked toward Maureen for encouragement.

"Go on, child. Tell us what happened to you," Maureen whispered as she gingerly patted Sophia's thigh.

Clenching her eyes shut, Sophia struggled to recount the evening's events. "Well, I remember that Teddy and I talked for a few minutes by the pool. Next thing I remember is Sid sneaking up behind me. He scared me at first because I was expecting it to be Teddy—I didn't realize he had already gone back inside the house. I think Sid and I argued about something, but I can't remember what. Next thing I know I'm on the couch in the sunroom, and Maureen's face is hovering above me. Teddy was standing behind her. I remember how my head was throbbing, and then the other pain hit me so hard, I … I just wanted to die. I knew something awful must have happened, but I never imagined …" Sophia started to sob loudly as she turned her head into the pillow and wept.

Rick's eyes darted back and forth between Sophia and Maureen watching both women weep. Still puzzled, Rick turned to Teddy for answers to the many questions he still had.

"Teddy, help me understand. What other pain is she talking about? Help me, please."

Teddy lowered his head, squeezed the bridge of his nose between his thumb and forefinger, then exhaled loudly. "She thinks she was raped, Ricky," he murmured as he finally looked up into Rick's eyes.

"You think WHAT? RAPED? HERE? How in God's name could you let that happen?" An enraged Rick was moving briskly toward Teddy.

In a defensive move, Teddy jumped from his chair and grabbed Rick around his chest, pinning Rick's arms tightly to his side.

"I wasn't there, man. If I had been with her, nothing would have happened. I swear. She wanted to stay outside a while longer, so I went back inside. She was alone when I left her.

I never saw anybody out there besides the two of us. Believe me, Rick. I'm just as upset about this as you are!"

Teddy held Rick tightly for a few more seconds before he started to relax his hold. Rick broke free as soon as he felt Teddy's restraint ease. He glared intently at Teddy; angry daggers flying from his eyes.

Realizing what was happening, Sophia tried to calm Rick. "Ricky, don't blame Teddy. I invited Teddy out to the pool, and it was my choice not to go back inside with him. Please don't be angry with him."

The sound of her weakened voice prompted both men to regain their composure. Teddy slowly returned to his chair, but Rick moved quickly back to his sister's bedside.

"Soph, how do you know you were raped? Are you sure?" he asked gently. He was too embarrassed to make eye contact with his sister.

Once again, Sophia lifted her skirt just far enough to expose her thigh and the red-tinged residue on her skin. "The other pain I was talking about came from between my legs. Whoever did this to me wasn't trying to be gentle."

Maureen reached over to pull Sophia's skirt back down to cover her exposed leg. No one said anything for a little while, but everyone's thoughts were whirling.

Finally a livid Rick broke the silence. **"I'LL KILL THE FUCKING BASTARD,"** he roared, unknowingly repeating the exact words Teddy had bellowed less than thirty minutes before.

* * * * * *

Adam and Carmen looked for a place to stash their empty glasses while trying to make their way out the door of the DeLuca mansion. They had a long drive ahead of them to their apartment in Manhattan.

The couple scanned the still-crowded room but didn't see their young host or the Senator anywhere. They were near the front door when Adam spotted a frowning Val Taylor moving in their direction.

Adam stepped into her path to get her attention. "Mrs. Taylor? We're heading out now. We just wanted to say our goodbyes and wish the Senator well with his reelection." Carmen nodded in agreement and smiled at the Senator's wife.

Automatically switching into the gracious mode of a political wife, Val's expression morphed into a brilliant smile. "Why thank you both for coming. The Senator's in the middle of a conference call—always busy, the citizens prevail, as usual—but I'll be sure to let him know. He'll be sorry he missed you, I'm sure." Val extended her hand for Adam to gently clasp, and leaned her cheek close to Carmen's as both women feigned air kisses.

"It was our pleasure, Mrs. Taylor. Please give the Giordanos our thanks for the invitation. This house is amazing," Carmen said enthusiastically.

Adam smiled and nodded as he lightly placed his hand on Carmen's lower back, ushering her out the front door. They walked hand-in-hand to the temporary valet station at the edge of the covered portico, smiling all the way. It had been a wonderful evening for them both, but for different reasons.

Meanwhile, with the door firmly closed behind the couple, Val's expression changed back into the grimace she had disguised so well only moments before.

She marched straight to the living room bar and ordered a White Russian—perhaps not a politically correct drink for a Senator's wife, but *what the hell.* She figured she and Sid could both sleep off their liquor in a spare bedroom in the gigantic manor. **We're** *family, too, for heaven's sake.*

She ordered a second drink, then a third. Eventually, the bartender automatically filled her standing order and "kept 'em coming."

* * * * * *

"Please. No police. No doctor. I'm fine. We can't risk having this house turned into a crime scene. Just tell everyone I went to bed with a migraine, the kind that comes on all of a sudden," Sophia directed.

"But what about your head wound? Shouldn't we get some help for that?" Rick asked. "People can die from those, you know. Their brains start swelling, and they don't even realize it until it's too late."

Sophia studied her brother's concerned face. "If it'll make you feel any better, I'll take a hot shower and try to assess my head wound myself. Or better yet, Maureen can help me. That way if I get dizzy again or start acting weird, she'll be there to alert you guys."

Teddy and Rick exchanged glances and simultaneously nodded their approval.

"Good. Maureen, let's get this done. I think the aspirin you gave me is already helping. I just need to get my head on straight again ... pun intended," she joked as she and Maureen made their way into the suite's private bathroom.

Some tension had been released when Sophia was off the bed and up on her feet. But the next mission for both Rick and Teddy was to find whoever so heinously violated Sophia.

The two young men waited until they heard the shower water running before they discussed their next moves. Rick cleared his throat and began. "We should go find Sid. If they argued, he can tell us what it was about. If he's too drunk, he might not remember anything. But I think that's the logical place to start."

Teddy agreed but voiced a concern. "The fundraiser is supposed to go on for about another hour. What do we do about the guests? Do we tell them Sophia has a headache or not mention her absence? I don't think too many people realized she had even arrived. Maybe we just don't say anything about Sophia at all."

"The piano player is here entertaining the guests. Let's grab Sid and start out with a few questions, then let him go back to his contributors. Maybe he's been shaking hands with his voters this whole time, and we've got nothing to worry about with him. Still, that's the obvious place to start, anyway. What'd you say? Sound like a solid plan?" Rick asked.

Teddy nodded. "Sure, let's find the pompous bastard. I told Sophia earlier I thought the Senator was an egotistical blow-hard. I'd like to prove myself right."

"Should we wait until Sophia's out of the shower before we go down to look for Sid?" Teddy mentioned as an afterthought.

"Nah. If Maureen thinks she needs help, she'll get word to us. We need to get to Sid while we still can, especially since he was the last person Soph remembers talking to. We need to get his story before he gets too drunk to remember anything."

Rick was adamant about tackling this task quickly. Any amount of time they wasted might be enough time for the attacker to cover his tracks or set up an alibi. Showing impatience with the slow-moving Teddy, Rick nudged his best friend. "Let's go, Teddy. Tick tock, man."

CHAPTER 5

"Your head doesn't seem to be bleeding so much, after all. It looks better now than when I first looked at it. I guess it seemed worse than it was, thank God," Maureen muttered as she parted Sophia's freshly washed hair. Peering closely at Sophia's scalp, Maureen saw a crescent-shaped gash much smaller than she'd first imagined. The cook sighed with relief.

Sophia smiled. "So you think I still need stitches?"

"Maybe I can rig a tiny butterfly bandage across the wound, but I'm not sure how good it'll stay. But, no, I don't think you'll need stitches. It'd still be a good idea for a doctor to look at you, though. You know what your brother said about head injuries."

Sophia thought about it for a few seconds, but shook her head. "I think I'll ride this one out without alerting anyone professional. I don't want a doctor, and I sure don't want the police involved. Our family takes care of our own messes, or so I've been told," she said with a tinge of sarcasm in her voice.

"Yes, ma'am, I understand. But you've got to stay awake and alert for several hours—you can't drift off to sleep, young lady. That's supposed to be the worst thing you can do," Maureen warned.

"Is that an old wives' tale, or is that for real?" Sophia inquired, catching Maureen's eyes through the reflection in the mirror atop the bathroom vanity.

"Don't matter. Just pay attention to it," the concerned cook declared.

Sophia smiled. "Yes, ma'am."

Both women remained silent while Maureen continued to comb Sophia's wet, shoulder length hair.

They both started to speak at the same time, then smiled at each other through the mirror. "You go first, Miss Sophia. I was just gonna ask if you wanted to call your Mama in Italy."

"Well, that's what I was about to ask. Do you think we should wait until they get back to let them know what happened? Telling them would only make them worry, and there's nothing that anyone can do about this now—they would just come home early. I don't want them to do that because of me. Besides, Grandmamma and Mama were looking forward to getting away together for a while. And Aunt Caroline had always wanted to visit Mama's family in Italy, and this was the first time she was able to work it out. I don't want to bother them."

Maureen shook her head. "Just wait until you're a mother. You'll understand why you ought to call her now. You think you're being a good daughter by keeping this secret from her? In a way, I can understand that. But as a mother, I'd be real mad at you when I DID find out. I'd want to tan your hide for shutting me out. When a woman delivers a baby, she earns the right to worry unnecessarily about that child for the rest of her life. Someday you'll understand. But for now, you better make sure nobody else lets her know anything about this before you tell her yourself."

Sophia turned away from the mirror to look straight into Maureen's round face. "You're a wise woman, Maureen."

Those simple yet earnest words sparked a bright flash of happiness in Maureen's lonely heart.

"Thank you, Miss Sophia," was all she could respond. Anything more might provoke another bout of uncontrollable weeping.

* * * * * *

When Teddy and Rick exited the elevator, they split up. Rick headed outside to search the grounds for Sid, and Teddy planned to look inside the house where the party was winding down.

Teddy spotted Val leaning over the bar, ordering the bartender to grab a towel and clean up her spills from her White Russian. Very tipsy herself, she had repeatedly splashed countless drinks on the counter as well as on herself.

Squeezing between Val and a boisterous party enthusiast, Teddy tried to whisper in her ear. "Val, do you know where Sid might be? I need to talk to him for a minute."

Loudly she answered, "That asshole? He's passed out at the pool. Go see if you can drag his drunk ass back inside. I'm officially disowning Sid Taylor as of right now."

Everyone within a radius of twenty feet clearly heard her declaration. Many guests immediately set down their empty plates and glasses, gathered their belongings, and made their excuses to leave.

Before Teddy got to the door of the living room, Val turned and exclaimed after him, "And let him know how **PROUD** we all are of our distinguished Senator tonight." She downed the last of her drink and turned to demand another.

* * * * * *

"What the fuck!" Rick exclaimed as he spotted the unconscious senator sprawled limply on the pool deck between two chaise lounges. He hurried closer to get a better look.

Rick stood astride Sid as he lay there comatose, then methodically leaned over to check for a pulse. "At least you're alive," Rick murmured as he tried to grab Sid under the arm pits to get him up and into a chair. "You're nothing but dead weight, you motherfucker," he lamented, unable to make upward progress with the clumsy body.

"Let me help," Teddy volunteered as he trotted up from behind. Quickly, the two managed to get the heavy man into the adjacent lounge. Now sprawled in the chair, Sid looked more like he had peacefully dozed off by the pool after a tough day at the office.

"Let's wake him up," Teddy said through gritted teeth as he watched the steady rise and fall of Sid's chest.

"Get some water from the pool. From anywhere. I'm gonna drown the son of a bitch," an angry Rick bellowed.

Teddy looked around, checking the immediate area for a receptacle that could hold enough pool water to douse Sid back into consciousness. Seeing nothing suitable, Teddy chose the next best alternative—a garden hose neatly rolled in a huge copper bowl. Conveniently situated only a few feet from the rear edge of the pool, Rick grabbed the connected hose quickly and aimed it at Sid's chest.

"Get outta the way, Rick. I want to get full view of his reaction when he gets plastered full in the face!"

"Not the kind of 'plastered' he enjoys so much, but let him have it—full force!" Rick moved carefully to the side to avoid the gushing water as he anxiously awaited the surge.

* * * * * *

It was nearly 4:00 a.m. in Italy when Caroline Norton's phone vibrated noisily on her bedside table. She flipped on the table lamp and tried to focus her sleep-filled eyes on the caller ID. When she realized the caller was Sophia, she grabbed the phone and quickly placed it to her ear.

"Sophia, what's wrong? What's happened?" Caroline barked, now suddenly awake and fearful of looming bad news.

"I'm all right, Aunt Caroline. But I wanted to talk to you before I talk to Mama," the young woman said. Instantly, Sophia lost control. "Oh, Aunt Caroline! It's been an awful night," she stammered. Her bawling revved up into full gear.

"Calm down, child! What on earth's happening over there? Talk to me!" Caroline demanded, sitting straight up in bed and already pulling back the covers in case she had to travel halfway around the world to Sophia's side.

* * * * * *

Sid thought he was drowning, and his arms flailed crazily in front of him. Teddy showed no mercy, continuing a steady stream of water aimed right at the Senator's nose.

Rolling off the chair and attempting to find his footing, Sid managed to get half-upright as he lunged forward in the dark.

He tried to evade the onslaught of water, but he couldn't escape. Within seconds, he had stumbled to the edge of the pool. A little extra whip of the hose caused him to trip and execute a perfect belly flop into the chilly water.

Neither Teddy nor Rick laughed at the water aerobics the drunken man fought so hard to perform. When Sid finally found the side ladder, he grabbed one rung and attempted to lift himself above the pool's edge. Teddy was there to provide a hand, and Rick stood by waiting for Sid to gain his footing and catch his breath.

"Jesus, Mary, and Joseph! What the hell was that all about?" a seething Sid yelled.

As Rick took his time approaching the soggy man, Teddy stepped backward out of range.

"This is for what you did to my sister, you motherfucker," Rick bellowed as his fist connected solidly with Sid's red alcoholic nose.

CHAPTER 6

After disconnecting from the distressing call, Caroline paced around her bedroom wringing her hands and silently cursing Senator Sid Taylor.   The fact that he was the last unsavory person Sophia encountered before the terrible nightmare made him an obvious target for suspicion and hatred.

She was wrought with worry about Sophia's state of mind. Physical injuries aside, Caroline's utmost concern was the fragile mental state of the young unmarried woman who had been assaulted and violated on the grounds of her own family's estate.   Sophia would eventually recover from her wounds and injuries—Caroline knew that.   But would the mental scars leave a lasting and devastating effect on the radiant young woman?

Sophia had been firm about not interrupting the three women's vacation in Italy; however, Caroline had been adamant that nothing was more important than being back in the United States during Sophia's time of duress. In the spirit of compromise, Caroline proposed a modified itinerary: she would get up early to meet Juliana and Lucinda for breakfast, as usual.   Afterwards, when they routinely took their coffee cups to the porch, Caroline would let them know that Sophia had been in touch overnight.   When they were all alone without other family members to hear, the story would be repeated.   No doubt, Juliana would reach out to Sophia immediately by phone, but by then she should understand that Sophia was physically faring well despite the tragedy. It would be left to Juliana as to whether or not the vacation would be cut short in favor of flying home immediately to Sophia's side.

With that decided, there was nothing left to do but wait until breakfast at 6:00 a.m. *Not exactly what I thought my last few days in Italy would be like,* Caroline thought as she picked up her cell phone to make a transatlantic call to her trustworthy 'go-to' private investigator.

* * * * *

"Honest to God! I don't know what you're talking about!" Sid Taylor bellowed after Rick pummeled him again. By now, Teddy was standing behind Sid, pinning his arms behind him so Rick had a clear shot at the senator's soft middle section. "PLEASE! Listen to me! I haven't done anything except fall asleep out here!"

"I don't believe you, cocksucker! Why did you assault my sister?" Rick drew back to swing again, but Sid started bawling like a baby.

Teddy braced himself for Rick's next punch to slam into Sid, but it didn't happen. Taking advantage of the pause, Teddy offered advice. "Maybe we should get him inside before you beat him to death. Let's take him up to one of the guest rooms through the back hallway. We can grab the elevator and put him in the opposite wing from the family rooms. I'm sure we can get Thomas to stand guard if we still need to get the rest of the guests out of the house."

Rick mulled over the idea and agreed. "Okay, nice and easy. We'll stop at the sunroom door, and you can scout the kitchen. If it's clear, we'll get the bastard upstairs before anybody knows where he is."

When Teddy released Sid's arms, the befuddled man tried to make a clumsy run for it. Rick was too quick, however, and jerked him backwards and down on the ground before Sid realized what had happened to him.

"Damn it, Sid!" Rick exclaimed as he backhanded the quivering Senator. "Are you gonna be good, or do I have to knock you out to get you inside the house without a fight?" Rick sneered.

"I ..I ... Uh, I'll go. I won't try to run. Just don't hit me anymore, Rick. PLEASE!" Sid whimpered as he uncontrollably began to urinate on himself.

"Good God, man. Don't make me have to carry you over my shoulder with THAT running down your leg! You walk nice, or I'll make it so you never walk again!" an angry Rick screeched at the broken man. "Now march and keep your mouth shut."

Teddy followed obediently, waiting for his turn alone with Sid.

* * * * * *

"What in God's name have you done to Sid!" Val stormed into the private upstairs bedroom known as the 'Gold Room' and sloshed her drink on the fine Persian rug. "What the hell, Ricky!"

Always seeming the compassionate one, Teddy eased to her side and took the drink from her shaking hand. "Val, calm down. I'm sure we'll get to the bottom of this, but it looks like Sid may have been the one who attacked Sophia."

"That's insane! He's a sot and a scoundrel, but he would never *attack* anybody! *Especially* not Sophia!" she pleaded. "Don't hurt him, he doesn't know what he's doing when he gets like that," she pleaded.

Teddy escorted Val to a chair and tried to calm her down. Meanwhile, the interrogation continued with Sid in the hot seat.

"So, Sid. If you can remember anything, you'd better spill it now. My patience is running very thin tonight," Rick threatened.

Before he spoke, Sid glanced at Val who appeared to have been shocked nearly sober within the last few minutes.

"I swear, I remember asking Sophia to listen to some business ideas. We were standing by the pool. The next thing I remember, she said she wanted to go back inside because she was getting cold. After that, it's all a blank. I swear to God!" The senator squirmed on the bunching towel placed beneath him in the leather club chair. He raised his wet leg and tried to reposition himself to spare the leather from more of the acidic urine and cold pool water still soaking his disheveled trousers.

"Can you explain why your fly is unzipped right now? Why your shirt is loose? And why you look like you might have attacked someone?" a seething Rick demanded to know.

"**You** attacked **me,** for God's sake! That must help explain why I look like this!" Sid whimpered. "Ricky, I swear! I didn't do anything except sleep in that God-awful chair!"

"You weren't in the chair, you bastard. You were lying on the ground passed out, as usual!" Val interjected from the other side of the room.

Rick turned to peer at Val. "What? You knew he was out there in this condition?"

"I told Teddy where to find him. When I found Sid earlier, he was unconscious on the concrete between the chairs. His shirt was out, but that's normal for this passed-out drunkard. I sure as hell didn't check his zipper, though." Val's concern for Sid's welfare was reverting to anger once again.

Teddy nodded. "That's right. Val told me where to find him…and then I found you already with him. Things escalated quickly after that."

Rick turned back to Sid. "Let me see your hands," he commanded.

Meekly, Sid held his hands out in front of him, palms down. There were bloody scratches on the tops of both hands.

"How'd you get these?"

"I guess when I fell on the pool deck or landed in the pool. I honestly don't know." Sid looked surprised when he saw the scrapes, as if he had felt no pain from the injuries until that moment.

Teddy stood stoically, arms folded across his chest, surveying the entire room. Finally he spoke up.

"Rick, why don't we leave these two here for now? We're not getting any closer to solid answers while Sid's memory is still vague. These two probably have things to clear up between themselves, anyway. I'm sure Maureen and Thomas would get them what they need to stay overnight. Maybe tomorrow we can be less emotional, and we can sort this out civilly. What do you think?"

Taking in a deep breath before exhaling through his flaring nostrils, a sneering Rick concurred. "No way this will be less emotional tomorrow, but maybe Val can get the bastard to talk." Rick turned, looked at Teddy with beady eyes, and stomped across the room to the door. He slammed it behind him as he made his furious exit.

Teddy looked at Val first, then made direct eye contact with Sid. "You two can expect someone here shortly to look after you tonight. Don't go anywhere. I don't think Rick is in the mood to have to chase you down again, Sid." Teddy watched them both nod their assent before he joined Rick waiting for him in the hallway.

Rick had already texted Maureen to have the necessary overnight supplies delivered to the Gold Room for the Taylors. He had received her confirmation text just as Teddy came out the door.

"Think they'll try to sneak out?" Rick asked.

"Nah. I think they're too scared to try anything. Besides, Thomas is a pretty stout guy. He'll make sure they don't go anywhere. You know how much Thomas cares about Sophia. He'd defend her to the death if he had to."

The two young men ambled down the hall on their way to join the fundraiser's last few lingering guests. It was time to clear the house and close down the estate for the evening.

They silently hoped a public relations nightmare hadn't already started brewing on the horizon.

* * * * * *

At the Bellini country manor near the vineyards of Marsala, Uncle Joe was hustling in the kitchen, weaving between the cooks and maids, and testing every dish before it was taken off the stove. "Perfetto," he announced as he tasted the eggs Florentine, adding an unnecessary dash of pepper before allowing the cook to transfer the steaming dish into a serving bowl.

Uncle Joe—born in 1934 as Giuseppe Alessandro Bellini— was the oldest living relative Lucinda still had who remained in the old country. Even at his octogenarian age, Uncle Joe was still spry, witty, and maintained a focus on the Bellini business that had outlasted his welcome, according to some. Regardless, Uncle Joe continued to manage the vineyard side of the business, consisting of vast acres of land that his Bellini predecessors had started snatching up during the 1920s.

As the years passed, the Bellini family continued to wisely expand their empires, supplementing valuable land purchases with smart investment diversification. Carefully and sometimes secretly, many of their dealings were made through shady 'partnerships,' often a little questionable but always lucrative.

As a result, the Bellini family was now worth billions, and the last man standing—Uncle Joe—had the power to bequeath generous (or meager) portions of the colossal wealth to anyone he chose. Bellini relatives traveled far and wide to shower him with their affections (and of course, impress upon the old man how much they deserved a big slice of the money pie). Even his own children and grandchildren didn't know where they stood in terms of the old man's affections and hopeful generosity. It was rumored that he didn't care for any of his offspring, and he thought his grandchildren had grown up with too much given to them throughout their lives. "Nobody works for anything anymore," he often lamented.

Thus far, Uncle Joe had given no hints to anyone as to how his wealth would be distributed after his death. To quote Uncle Joe himself, "That's none of anybody's business except mine."

But for now, breakfast was going to be late if the cooks didn't get the food on the table. It was already 5:58 a.m., *and cold food is spoiled food,* according to Uncle Joe.

The maid rang the traditional bell that was located at the edge of the front porch. Footsteps could be heard approaching on the wooden floors as the three American women hurried to take their appointed seats at the long table in the corner of the kitchen.

With heaping bowls of food in front of them, they bowed their heads as Uncle Joe offered a prayer of gratitude from the head of the table.

* * * * *

It was midnight in New York when Uncle Joe was offering the breakfast prayer in Italy. Sophia had been in bed for less than thirty minutes when she grabbed her head. She prayed through the throbbing pain. "God, please make this stop," she said aloud to the empty bedroom. "Everything's done now. There's nothing I can do to make things go back to the way they were. Please give me strength to muddle through all this," she prayed as she clenched her eyes together.

She heard the low chirp of her cell phone before she finished her prayer. Sophia reached for the bright screen and read the clandestine text message that shined like a beacon of hope in the dark.

"I want to see you. When can we be together again?"

Sophia smiled only slightly, recalling the request for strength for which she had prayed so fervently.

This gentle man *was* her strength in her weakest moment. She realized that more than ever as she reread the words on the screen.

She only needed to send him a brief but meaningful response for now.

"Soon, I hope. I really need to feel your strong arms around me again."

CHAPTER 7

Maureen was scurrying around the kitchen, putting the last of the freshly washed dishes back in the cupboard. It was past midnight already, and the evening had dragged by, hampered by lingering guests who wouldn't take the hint to go home.

The most difficult part of her entire evening had been trying to maintain a façade of pleasantness when her heart was trying to explode inside her chest. Even after Sophia demanded that Maureen go back downstairs to attend to the party, she had felt a sense of uneasiness about leaving the young woman alone. Since both her mother and grandmother were out of the country, Maureen assumed the protective, maternal role for Sophia that no one else was there to provide. She was taking her role to heart.

Thomas wandered into the kitchen and plopped down at the breakfast nook table. "Any coffee left?" he inquired of the bustling cook as he wiped his tired eyes.

"There's a little left in the pot. I was going to clean it out before I head up to bed."

Without hesitation, Thomas stood up from the table and retrieved the last of the strong brew. Automatically, he rinsed the pot under the tap and set it on the counter in front of Maureen.

"Be sure to wash that empty cup when you're finished. I don't want any dirty dishes laying around in the morning," Maureen warned as she picked up the drained coffee pot and started scrubbing.

"Sure," Thomas responded. "By the way, how is Miss Sophia?" he asked without volunteering any information of his own about the evening's events.

Maureen stopped what she was doing and gazed at Thomas with a forlorn look. "Poor child. We thought she fell outside and hit her head. But, it's more like somebody attacked her instead."

"My word! Is she all right?" he asked, surprise in his voice. Before Maureen could answer, Thomas absently mumbled, "So **that's** what the Senator was doing out there." His facial expression looked horrified.

"What did you say?" Maureen stopped what she was doing and moved to Thomas's side, coffee pot still in hand. "Tell me again…what did you say?"

"Uh-well. I came around the kitchen corner from the living room earlier this evening. I'm not sure where you were— maybe when you popped out to replenish the hors d'oeuvres or something—anyway, you weren't in the kitchen when I came through. I thought I heard some kind of ruckus coming from the pool area, so I went into the sunroom to look through the window. I saw the Senator, shall I say … having sex … with Sophia between some chairs on the pool deck. I was so totally embarrassed. I immediately left the window and trotted back to the living room where the guests were gathered. I was hopeful I could keep them from wandering toward the back of the house until the two were … uh, finished."

"Having sex with her? What are you saying? **Voluntarily**?" a stunned Maureen exclaimed.

"I … I don't know. She wasn't putting up a struggle and he seemed to be… well, he was certainly busy."

"Could she have been knocked out? **Tell me, Thomas**!" Maureen was agitated and incensed.

"I couldn't see. I don't know! I just thought it was a mutual ..."
Thomas tried to explain.

"For God's sake, man! THINK! Why would Sophia ever give
that man the time of day?"

"I wasn't thinking—I felt like I was intruding just by looking out
the window! Oh, God, Maureen. Did that man sexually
assault her? Oh, Jesus! Help us!" A frantic look crossed
Thomas's face as his hands began to tremble.

"Have you shared this with anyone else, Thomas? Did you
tell Mr. Rick?"

"No. I was aware the Senator had collapsed outside and that
he and Mrs. Taylor were spending the night here, but no one
has shared any details with me about anything so utterly ...
sickening, " he trailed off.

"We need to tell Mr. Rick. He'll want to hear about this right
away," Maureen declared as she picked up her phone to text
the man in charge.

* * * * *

Juliana's hair was pulled back in a silver-streaked ponytail,
her beautiful face still radiant with the healthy glow of the sun
and good genes. She looked much younger than her almost
58 years, thanks in part to a healthy lifestyle and the skillful
hands of some of New York's finest plastic surgeons. Though
she never remarried after 1997 when she lost her husband
(and her stepchildren's father), she remained quite the
sought-after society "catch" of the wealthy upper crust
bachelor/single crowd.

Juliana took her seat in an old wooden rocker next to her elderly mother, Lucinda, who would be celebrating her 80th birthday the middle of next month.

Lucinda Bellini DeLuca Norton had become a frequent visitor at the Bellini manor and vineyard. Since her second husband, Perry, died from a massive heart attack, she spent more and more of her time in the wine country of Sicily.

Their host, Uncle Joe— the youngest surviving Bellini brother who was less than six years older than Lucinda— always made his niece feel welcome on every occasion she showed up unexpectedly at his door. In contrast to most of his other relatives, Uncle Joe always loved to see Lucinda. She never asked for anything, and often asked to do whatever she could to pitch in. In fact, he sometimes put her to work on simple bookkeeping tasks. Occasionally, he would send her on an errand or two to keep her occupied. Regardless, she had been given her own room in the manor, decorated to her taste, and furnished with every comfort she could possibly want. She and Uncle Joe had formed a bond more like sister and brother than uncle and niece. It was a comfortable arrangement. She was happy there and felt at peace with Uncle Joe serving as her family touchstone.

Caroline lagged a few steps behind the mother and daughter, taking an extra second to refill her coffee cup. She tucked a napkin in her pocket and was about to move when Uncle Joe strolled in. Silently, Caroline hoped he wasn't planning on joining the ladies on the porch for their morning chat.

Thankfully, Uncle Joe kept moving, tipping his worn straw hat to the seated ladies. He scrambled past them, leaped off the porch, and made his way to the side of the house to repair a dripping spigot.

Caroline opened the door to join the two contented women as they took in the morning fresh air. She took her seat on the other side of Juliana, wondering how to bring up the upsetting news from the night before.

"I can't ever remember a time I've felt so serene," Juliana remarked. She leaned her head back on the chair and closed her eyes. She wore a slight smile of contentment as she gently rocked in the big chair.

Caroline glanced at her friend. *God, help me here.*

"This place brings that out in everybody. There are no pressures, no deadlines, and nothing to worry about except whether Uncle Joe will behave," Lucinda joked.

Lucinda and Juliana chuckled, but Caroline merely smiled weakly. Noticing Caroline's silence, Juliana spoke up.

"Don't you feel at peace, Caroline? This place is great medicine," she smiled.

"Well. Not exactly. At least, not today. There's something I have to tell you two, and it's not an easy topic to broach."

* * * * * *

Armed with new and revealing information, Rick stomped into the guest wing of the DeLuca mansion, looking for Teddy.

Since the tragic events had transpired so late in the evening, Teddy opted to stay the night there in case he was needed for any reason—and that included dealing with Sid Taylor.

Banging on the door, Rick shouted, "Teddy, are you still up?" He banged again.

When Teddy opened the door, he was still fully dressed. "Yeah, man. Something else happen?"

Bursting into the room, Rick began to blubber. "It **was** Sid. No doubt. Thomas saw him do it!"

Dumbfounded, questions swirled through Teddy's mind. "Wait … he saw him? Why didn't he stop him? That doesn't make any sense!"

"Thomas said that he glanced through the sunroom window and thought he saw them having sex. He said he was embarrassed and got the hell out of the sunroom."

Teddy looked vexed. "I don't get it. *Consensual sex*?"

Rick shrugged and shook his head, baffled by the new information he had shared with his friend. "Let's go wake up Sophia!"

* * * * * *

"How can you sit there and be so calm?" Juliana snapped as she peered into Caroline's sad eyes. "How can you tell us this horrible thing—so unemotionally—like you were reporting the evening news into a camera?"

Caroline looked down at her hands in her lap. The words stung, but she was trying to cope, too. It had been hard to keep the story to herself for all those hours before the ladies had a private moment together.

Juliana's heart hurt as she realized whatever innocence her sweet Sophia had been able to cling to would most likely vanish forever. "I can't bear the thought of my poor girl lying helpless at the hands of some … some MONSTER! Oh, Mama, I can't bear it!" She leaned over as close to her mother as she could get without vacating her seat.

Gingerly patting her daughter's leg, Lucinda tilted her neck so that the side of her head rested against Juliana's. They sat weeping in unison for several long minutes.

At last, Lucinda cleared her throat, raising her wrinkled hand to stroke her daughter's cheek. With their heads still touching in a bond of unified strength, Lucinda spoke to her daughter in a firm and steady voice.

"Be strong, child. If I've taught you nothing else in life, remember the universal force and justice of karma. Whoever the bastard is who has dirtied our girl's goodness will receive his just reward. I know this to be true, because I've witnessed such things."

Lucinda held up her chin boldly. "I swear to God Almighty: I will NOT go to my grave until my granddaughter's honor is avenged **tenfold**!"

* * * * * *

Rick and Teddy made a beeline toward Sophia's room, expecting to solve the evening's puzzle sooner rather than later.

A bold Maureen met the two in the hallway just a few feet before they made it to Sophia's bedroom door. Normally, she would have felt somewhat intimidated, but not at that moment.

"Please don't try to wake her up now. I know you're both anxious...we all are... but she's been through so much this evening. It has to be traumatic for her, not remembering everything and all. I doubt she'll remember anything about what you're planning on telling her, either. That's just gonna make her more upset, and she'll never get any rest tonight. Can't this wait until morning, boys? Just let your sister get a few more hours of sleep first, Rick. Please?" Maureen's face turned a bright red as she watched Rick's face change expressions while he absorbed what she had beseechingly requested.

"You're right, Maureen," Rick softly replied. "We aren't thinking clearly. We'll talk to Sophia first thing in the morning."

Not knowing how else to react, Maureen slightly nodded her head and stood in front of Sophia's bedroom door until the two men walked away. When they were out of sight, she grabbed her chest and closed her eyes. *That's a sure way to get fired, Maureen,* she thought as she leaned back against the wall and sank down to a squatting position. She took a deep breath before she sprang back up and hurried back to the kitchen to talk more to Thomas.

* * *　* * *

Say what you would about Uncle Joe's aging physique, his hearing and eyesight were extraordinary for a man of 86 years. His keen ears had detected the steady "drip...drip...drip" of the outside spigot when he had passed within fifty feet of it on his way to the shed to gather fresh eggs.

 It wasn't nearly as hard to make out the women's voices on the front porch, especially when they started to get so excited and upset. He decided whatever was bothering them was now his business, too. Instead of trying to move away to allow them their privacy, Uncle Joe crept to the edge of the house and listened intently to everything the women said.

His anger built as the unfolding story got clearer and more detailed. He realized immediately how hurt and upset Lucinda was. So was Juliana. He still had influence in the family, and outside the family, as well. It would do him good to be calling some heavy shots again, he figured.

Nobody would ever have to know, either. That was how it was with real power.

CHAPTER 8

Dropping his keys on the narrow table inside his front door, he looked at his cheap knock-off watch as he removed it methodically from his wrist. It was nearly 4:00 a.m., and the weary man had pulled another all-nighter. Considering he had been slouched down in the front seat of his non-descript sedan for more than ten hours straight, his back only felt a little bit tight. Usually, his spine screamed at him in pain after half that time during a stakeout. *Must be the Percocet,* he mused. *Gotta hit Leo up for another bottle of those miracle pills.*

For the past fifteen years, Raymond "Slick" Silvio had been working on and off as a private investigator for Walker, Harrington, Norton, Stone and Norton, a prestigious law firm located in his hometown of Syosset, New York. His point of contact there was Caroline Norton, and she was by far their sharpest lawyer. Not just in brains either, because she didn't look too bad for a broad her age.

She'd been working there for over twenty years, or so he'd been told. Rumors about her previous 'attachment' with her late boss, Perry Norton, ran the entire gambit from being his wife to adopted daughter. Crazy. Frankly, Slick didn't care how she got to be a law firm partner. All he cared about was how well she paid him to unearth unsavory things about people and keep his mouth shut.

He turned the light on in the bathroom and reached behind the plastic, partially ripped shower curtain to start the shower. Water in his cheap building barely crawled through the pipes, even in the middle of the night when everybody ought to be asleep. While he waited, he had plenty of time to undress and brush his teeth before the water would yield a lukewarm stream.

When the water was as good as it was going to get, he stepped inside the tub and stood directly under the shower head. As he began to recall the phone conversation he'd had with Caroline Norton only a few hours before, he shivered slightly. *Jeez, Louise. Felt like somebody walked over my grave.* He opened his eyes and peeked around the side of the curtain, ensuring he was still alone in the bathroom. *Good grief, Slick. Things must be gettin' to you.*

He chuckled to himself and did his best impression of shaking off the spooky feeling. *That idiot investment banker you been watchin' with his parade of prostitutes in and out of his downtown office—not to mention the mountain of cocaine he inhales before breakfast—damn if you're not actin' more paranoid than **him**.*

When Slick stepped out of the shower, he wrapped a large towel around his paunchy middle and headed straight for the bedroom. He casually dropped the oversized towel on the floor, crawling nude under the dingy sheet and light blanket he had used ever since his wife left him with only the clothes on his back and his imitation Rolex.

It was at the exact moment he closed his eyes that he saw the premonition.

SWEET JESUS! He sprang from his bed, tripping clumsily over the tangled sheet as he frantically tried to find the light switch.

* * * * * *

Augustus Alphonso "Big Al" Bellini was surprised when he heard Uncle Joe's voice on the other end of the overseas phone call.

"Uncle Joe! How are things at the winery?" Big Al asked once he identified the caller. "Long time, no hear. What's it been? Six, seven years? "

"Long enough you probably thought I was dead, you bastard. Sorry to disappoint you," Uncle Joe snapped.

"No, No! It's good to hear from you. How've you been?" Big Al tried to hide his disappointment that the undistributed Bellini fortune was still resting firmly in Uncle Joe's gnarled hands.

"Never mind me, goombah. How would you like to earn a few family points for doing a little job, eh?"

"Sure, Uncle Joe. What do you need me to do?" Big Al listened carefully, expecting to be delegated some minor task by the old man that wouldn't take much effort or time.

"I want you to dismember a senator," Uncle Joe said casually, in much the same tone he would have used to order a New York pizza.

* * * * * *

Sid opened his eyes and looked around the unfamiliar room. *Is this a hotel?* He couldn't place the setting, but he heard Val's soft snoring coming from nearby. At least he wasn't alone.

The hung-over Senator sat straight up in the middle of the massive bed and tried to locate Val. Once he realized she was sleeping peacefully across the room in an overstuffed chair, he relaxed. *Must have really tied one on last night.*

He pulled the covers back, quickly inhaling a repugnant stench rising from his lower body. "Val! Did I piss myself last night? Jesus, Mary and Joseph! Val, get up and help me!"

Startled by her husband's loud voice, Val jumped from the chair and hurried to his bedside. "What's wrong, Sid?" was all she could respond in her sleepy state.

"I smell like PISS, dammit! Did I wet the bed? Where in the hell are we?"

Memories of the evening's theatrics flooded Val's brain at once. "We're still at the DeLuca's. Don't you remember anything about last night?"

"Hell, no. Let's get out of here and go home. I need a shower and a change of clothes." He jumped off the bed and onto the floor, not slowing until he reached the bedroom door. "Grab my shoes, will ya' Val?"

He reached for the doorknob expecting the door to unlatch automatically. Instead, he felt resistance as he jarred the locked door repeatedly.

"The damned door's locked! What the hell?" he muttered.

"Great. Just great. Sid, you really fucked up this time. I can't believe even YOU would stoop so low as to hurt Sophia!"

"What? What are you saying?"

"I'm just saying that **this** family is known for taking revenge and asking questions later. You're a fucking idiot, you know that? I can't believe I've stayed married to you for all these years. If it hadn't been for Brent —and thank God he was born when he was—you and I would have parted ways a long, long time ago. You're pathetic!"

Still confused and standing barefoot next to the door, Sid dropped his hand from the doorknob. His thoughts wouldn't gel, and he remembered only the early parts of the evening before.

"Go take a shower, for God's sake. You reek. Thomas brought up some clean clothes for you last evening, but you were too far gone to move out of that bed. They'll probably have to bag up all the sheets and bedspreads and burn them. Otherwise, these linens will probably always smell like your piss!"

Embarrassed, ashamed, and apprehensive, Sid moved slowly toward the suite's private bathroom. Before he closed the bathroom door behind him, he turned to ask his wife for a favor.

"You won't tell Brent I pissed myself, will you? I couldn't stand him knowing that."

"I don't think your son is who you should be worried about right now," she scowled.

* * * * * *

By 7:30 a.m., the employees of the DeLuca household had been busy for two hours preparing a lavish breakfast buffet and making sure multiple urns of hot coffee were ready for the awakening house guests.

Both Maureen and Thomas had been closed-mouthed, keeping their thoughts to themselves. Each wondered anxiously if the morning gathering would be civil or explosive. Neither had slept well for the few hours between cleaning up after the soiree and rising for the morning's duties. Both looked as though they were walking on eggshells as they took their places on either end of the overflowing buffet.

Sophia entered first, looking fresh and confident. Business as usual, she poured her own coffee and slid a piece of buttered toast on a small plate before she found her usual seat at the side of the dining table. Then came Rick and Teddy, already having met briefly in Rick's bedroom to speculate on how the morning's questions should be presented.

The two young men were surprised to find Sophia alone at the table, a newspaper spread before her as if the stock market status was the only interest she had. Teddy touched her shoulder gently to let her know he had entered the room, and Rick kissed the top of her head as he passed her chair. "Ow," she said and reached up to feel her sore head.

"Oops, sorry. How'd you sleep?" Rick asked her as he moved to the buffet to fill his plate with Eggs Benedict. Teddy went straight for the coffee.

"How do you think I slept, Rick?"

Rick nodded as Teddy joined Sophia on her side of the table. Rick sat across from them both.

"Maybe we ought to privately discuss a few things before Val and Sid come down," Rick said as he shoved a grape in his mouth.

"I don't want to talk about it, Rick. I've already told you what I can remember, and I still don't know anything else." She picked up the paper and moved it closer to her face, blocking her view of Rick.

Teddy cleared his throat. "Sophia, I know this is hard, but we've found out more information about what happened last night. You need to hear it, and then we need to plan how you want to proceed."

Slapping the paper down on the table in front of her, Sophia turned to glare at Teddy. "Why can't you two just leave me alone? I don't WANT to know what happened. As far as I'm concerned, it NEVER happened! Just drop it!"

"But …" Rick started.

"No **BUTS**. It's over and if I can put it out of my mind, you two sure as hell ought to be able to. Keep your mouths shut, and don't bother me with this anymore." Sophia picked up the newspaper again, signaling her dismissal of the conversation.

"But we know who did it," Teddy murmured. "There was a witness." He took a sip of coffee, hoping Sophia would pay attention to his comment.

"So kill the bastard for all I care. I'm not interested," she nonchalantly remarked as she flipped to the society section of the paper.

* * * * * *

"Val, I don't want to have breakfast with anybody. I'm embarrassed enough. If what you told me is true, it's better to just avoid those people altogether," a jumpy Sid announced.

"The door's unlocked now. Go for it, you coward. I'm staying for breakfast if for no other reason than to see where we stand with this family after the stunt you pulled last night. I swear, if we've lost our footing with the DeLucas and Giordanos because you can't control your liquor **or** your prick, I'll …," Val didn't finish her empty threat, opting instead to vigorously shake her head in silence.

"Val, that couldn't have happened. I'm not a violent man, even when I've had too much to drink. I can get a little surly, maybe…but I've never hurt anybody in my life."

"There's always a first time. You were blacked out for too long, and you don't have anyone to vouch for you. You're screwed, for lack of a better word," she said as she sauntered out the door to join the group for breakfast.

Sid stood alone in the Gold Room, contemplating his choices. Even if he found his car keys, he didn't know where the valet had parked their car. It could be anywhere on the grounds. He didn't want to wait for Val to come back and inform him, either.

"Fuck it," he said to himself. "Seeing as this might be my last meal, might as well enjoy it."

* * * * * *

Adam Woodson pulled out his phone and checked his messages while Carmen was still in the shower. He reread the response he'd received from his midnight text. *She wants to see me again. I feel like a school boy—toying with the forbidden.* He smiled as he tucked his phone inside his jacket pocket. *When I get to the office, I'll try to reach her to arrange a meeting.*

As Carmen turned off the water and reached for a towel, she heard Adam calling her name. "What did you say?"

"I said I'm taking off now. I'll check in with you later, and maybe we can meet at that Chinese place for dinner. Sound good to you?"

"Sure, Adam. Whatever. Have a good day," she shouted as she wiped condensation from the bathroom mirror. She hoped to have a good day, too. If she played her cards right, she'd be having lunch with Rick Giordano—and maybe she'd be joining him later in a decadent dessert.

CHAPTER 9

Slick Silvio couldn't shake the uneasiness he'd been feeling since the wee hours of that morning.

His premonitions had always been both a curse and a blessing. He remembered what his mother used to say to him when he'd tell her about his childhood intuitions: "Raymond, pay attention to your gut feelings, not your wild ideas. Sometimes those are just bad thoughts that flood your head, and not really signs of anything except your vivid imagination. The real ones? They can be evil or good. But you gotta learn to tell the difference in paranoia and prophecy. It'll come easier to you as you get older." But it never really did.

In his opinion, his mother had been a master in analyzing and vetting her own premonitions—psychic events that she'd had ever since she was a girl; but even now, Raymond still had a lot to learn. Over the past thirty-five years, his visions occasionally terrified him; but, the ones she had experienced and selectively shared with him had never failed to enlighten him. That's why—without fail— he immediately tried to reach his mother whenever a particularly jarring premonition shook his core.

This time, though, after his hurried summary, she wanted to know even more about what he had seen. Instead of the usual, "Raymond, go back to sleep. You'll feel better tomorrow when you've had time to clear your head," she remained noncommittal for too long.

"Moms, you there?" he remembered asking.

"I'm here, Raymond." She was still pondering what he'd just described in vivid detail. His mother took him by surprise when she suggested he visit her later that morning to discuss the details. Apparently, Mrs. Silvio required face time with her son to absorb the "sighting" he had explained. She would need even longer to help Raymond decide how to deal with it.

* * * * * *

Sophia sat in the dining room with her nose in the newspaper while Teddy and Rick finished their coffee.

"Oh, no!" she exclaimed and smacked the table, jarring silverware and rattling dishes. "Did you see what's in the paper? In the society section? Someone wrote a story about the fundraiser. I can't believe what the article says!" Eyes wide as saucers, Sophia passed the paper to Teddy and looked at Rick with mouth agape.

"What does it say?" Rick asked as he looked back and forth between Teddy and Sophia.

Teddy scanned the article and rolled his eyes before responding. "Someone tipped off the paper that the Senator only attended the first half of the party—at least he was sober enough to make it that long. It says Sid was unconscious by the pool for most of the evening, and that he was planning to initiate legislation to legalize marijuana. This makes it sound like Sid is an alcoholic pothead. Plus, they aren't sure which, if not both, he was stoned on when he passed out during his own campaign event. Whoever wrote this either had an inside source or was at the party uninvited." Teddy passed the paper across the table to Rick.

"At least Sophia's attack isn't mentioned. Maybe that part will stay buried for now," Rick murmured sarcastically.

Sophia tossed her napkin on the table and abruptly stood. "I'm going to work. DeLuca Enterprises doesn't run itself."

"We're right behind you."

In one synchronized movement, the two men followed Sophia's lead, leaving the events of the evening behind them and the embarrassing newspaper article face down on the table.

* * * * * *

"Where in the hell is everybody?" Sid asked as he entered the empty dining room. He saw dirty dishes and empty coffee cups still cluttering the table. "Val?"

"How should I know?" she answered curtly as she turned toward the breakfast buffet. "Maureen, where are the others?"

Maureen was still standing in the same spot she had occupied for the past thirty minutes. "Mrs. Taylor, they left minutes ago to go to the office. All three of them. Thomas and I, well, we were just about to clear the table when we heard you and the Senator coming down the hall." Thomas nodded his agreement.

Val looked suspiciously at the two servants. "Had they been in here very long?"

"No, ma'am. Mr. Rick looked like he was gonna eat a bit, but then he pushed his plate aside. Truth be told, they barely had a bite and only a little bit of coffee. Miss Sophia said she had things to do at the office," the cook told her.

Still standing in the doorway, Val turned to Sid and gave him a surly look. "Let's go home, Sid. I think we've overstayed our welcome. "

Following obediently like a scolded puppy, Sid followed Val to retrieve their personal belongings and to find their car. From what Sid could tell, it was going to be a long and torturous drive home.

* * * * * *

During his commute to the import/export business he ran with Carmen, Adam Woodson couldn't help but smile. He had purposely placed his cell phone in the driver's seat between his legs so he could answer it quickly. For some reason, he expected to hear from Sophia Giordano that morning, and his anxiety was overwhelming.

He wondered where she had disappeared to earlier last evening. Knowing her and how she prioritized "business first— everything else second," he supposed she had been drawn into an impromptu meeting with her brother and Teddy Brantley. The three of them were always together, making Adam wonder just how close the trio really was.

Regardless, it didn't matter nearly as much to him as it did when he first began the clandestine mission to infiltrate DeLuca Enterprises. He had fallen hard for Sophia which was never his intention. Regardless of how or why those feelings for Sophia had developed, he feared his business relationship with Carmen would be irreparably damaged. He knew their personal relationship was at risk.

Unfortunately, having romantic feelings for Sophia would make his ultimate goal harder to attain. He needed to adopt Sophia's business philosophy: 'business first, everything else second.' Adam wasn't sure he could follow through with the original plan now that he cared so much for the woman who was in charge of DeLuca Enterprises.

* * * * * *

Raymond Silvio waited patiently for his mother's interpretation of his shocking vision. Perhaps he would have to lead her through it, because apparently, he believed it would be an uncomfortable discussion.

"So, Moms? I gotta get some answers, here. This time, everything looked so real! I could feel things around me, and I could see details I don't usually see. And I could smell things! Geez, Moms. I need some help figuring this out," he pleaded as he felt his anxiety mount. No response.

"Why aren't you responding, Moms? Am I supposed to figure this one out myself?" he moaned. "Come on, Moms! Don't do this to me again!"

Finally, Slick started pacing. "Okay, I can see you're gonna make me do this all by myself. All right, fuck it…oops, sorry Moms." He hung his head as if he expected a good tongue lashing for swearing.

"I'm gonna go through it once more out loud, just to make sure I haven't missed anything." He looked upwards and stared at nothing while he tried to recreate the memory. "I wish it had lasted a few seconds longer, but I guess I have to just work with what I have. Okay, here goes." He closed his eyes tightly.

"I'm in a crowd. We're outdoors, and I smell cornbread. Cornbread? Hhmm, that's a new memory. Ok, cornbread and ...now... grease? I smell grease frying? Somebody's up on a stage, and there's applause. Then...boom! Sounds like a cannon or something. I look up and whoever was on the stage isn't there anymore. Somebody yells to call an ambulance. People scream and scatter. Then somebody fleeing the scene knocks into me so hard I fall to the ground. Somehow my watch gets broken. When I look at it, the hands are stuck at 2:27. Has to be afternoon, right Moms?" Eyes still closed, he continues. "I think whoever was on the stage has something to do with Caroline Norton because I was thinking about a new job she gave me right before I saw all this." Finally, he opened his eyes and another shiver went down his spine. "Yep, it's connected to her somehow. I gotta talk to her, Moms. I gotta talk to her real quick like."

* * * * * *

Rick Giordano's cell phone rang, and he answered through the hands-free system in his Mercedes.

"This is Rick," he said without looking at the caller ID.

"Hi, Rick. This is Carmen Ryan." She waited with anticipation for his welcoming response.

"Carmen Ryan? From last night at the fundraiser?" he asked.

Clearly disappointed, she lost her smile on the other end of the line. "Yes, that's right. I was hoping perhaps we could set up a meeting to discuss Senator Taylor's upcoming campaign events ... remember, you gave me your cell phone number so I could reach you directly?"

Rick briefly considered what she said but couldn't remember doing that. However, she did have his cell phone number. He wouldn't have handed that out to just anyone unless he had agreed to be contacted.

"Oh, yes. Carmen. How are you this morning?"

"Great, I ..."

"Listen, Carmen. Could we discuss this a little later? I'm late for the office and have a packed schedule the minute I walk in the door. I don't mean to be rude."

"Oh, no, no, no. I totally understand," an acutely disappointed Carmen replied.

"Thanks, and I'll be in touch," Rick said as he ended the call. He shook his head in disbelief. *Funding leeches coming out of the woodwork. Every election brings them out in swarms.*

After the brisk phone disconnection, Carmen had her own unique impression of Rick Giordano, as well. *Pompous Asshole,* she thought as she realized he must have been too drunk the night before to have been serious about their lingering eye contact and silent toasts.

CHAPTER 10

Uncle Joe never fully explained what he really wanted to happen to his target. Once the name on the contract was disclosed, all Big Al was supposed to do was make a plan and execute it. He didn't take what Uncle Joe said literally. Dismembering someone was a gruesome task, and that particular scenario took a lot more effort to cover up than a simple assassination.

Still, Uncle Joe was the patriarch, and when he gave an order it was supposed to be carried out. *Maybe I can kill the bastard, and then cut off his dick and stick it in his mouth or something. Maybe that would be good enough for the old man.*

Big Al sat at the neighborhood diner that he visited everyday for lunch and watched as the cook flipped over the sizzling burgers on the steaming griddle behind the counter. His thoughts were preoccupied with the new and difficult assignment.

Big Al felt excitement and anticipation, which hadn't been something he'd experienced in quite awhile. It was exhilarating to make tactical plans again. He had been complacent far too long behind the business end of the crime family. This time, he was going to personally handle the important job.

It should be easy enough to find this Senator, but getting him alone might be a little tricky. A big public area might be less risky to manage… Lots of frantic confusion and even more diversions. Everybody will be trying to run for cover to keep from getting killed themselves.

When his burger and fries arrived, Big Al turned his attention to his growling stomach. Next up on his agenda was eat a satisfying lunch and to familiarize himself with Sid Taylor's daily routine. Figuring a senator would never step foot in a place like the diner, Big Al was pretty sure this would be the last burger he'd get to enjoy for a while.

* * * * * *

Sid Taylor sat in his home office, still recovering from his lingering hangover from the night before. As expected, Val had given him a sermon during the long ride home from the DeLuca estate, and he knew he deserved it. He also knew better than to argue with his wife, especially when she thought his actions reflected poorly on her family status.

He tried to review paperwork and get his mind on business, but his head still throbbed too hard. Instead, he opted to watch the local news on the large plasma television that was mounted before a plush couch and matching leather chairs in his office.

By now, the news at noon was featured. The weather report had just wrapped up, and the scene switched to stock photos of Sid and Val. He grabbed the remote and turned up the volume, now taking a seat on the sofa to get a central view of the screen.

The anchor began to cover the fundraiser held the evening before. Next, the anchor switched to a close-up of Sid as he blurted out, "Why the hell not legalize marijuana?" The clip abruptly ended after Sid's one question, but not before the clip revealed him smiling broadly before taking a big gulp of his cocktail.

"Oh, God," he murmured.   The anchor then reported that their 'anonymous source' stated that shortly after the clip was recorded, the Senator disappeared from the crowd. He was later found passed out near the estate's swimming pool.

The veins on Sid's head were pulsing as he stood angrily and lobbed a box of tissues across the room at the television. He growled loudly, sounding more like a wounded bear than a furious man.

At that instant, Val burst in the room, hands clenched into fists at her side and rage engulfing her.   "You may as well kiss your Senate seat goodbye, you idiot! Who the hell recorded you making that ridiculous statement? And who knew you were passed out by the pool? Who? Sophia? Is this how she gets back at you for hurting her, you dumb ass?"

She rushed toward him, and he cowered as if he were about to be slapped. Instead, Val leaned in close to his face, noses almost touching. "I swear, if you blow this I'll divorce you and take everything you've got! **Everything**! Including Brent!"

"Don't worry, dear ..." he started, but Val glared at him.

"Just SHUT UP! I'll let you know when I want to hear your measly voice again. Stay away from me!" she screamed as she abruptly turned and left the room.

"Gladly," Sid responded, but in a very low voice.

* * * * * *

Brent Warren Taylor was the only child of Sid and Val Taylor, but he had never spent much time at home with them. As soon as he was old enough, he was shipped off to prep schools, military academies, and eventually graduated college across the country in California.

When it was time to commit to a career decision—and after all those years of being told where to go and what to do by Sid and Val—Brent declared to his parents that he had no desire to pursue a life in the military or politics, which had always been their preferences and not his. He wanted to help people, he said— not go off to war or get involved in the nasty business of big government. Instead, he planned to be a public servant.

It was no secret that his parents felt monumental disappointment in his chosen career path. Eventually though, Brent compromised and agreed to pursue a law degree, conditional on putting his license to good use as a Public Defender.

Both Sid and Val believed he would come to his senses someday, perhaps run for District Attorney or possibly Attorney General; but, for now they were satisfied that he was starting his second year at Georgetown, and doing quite well in spite of his parents' lack of involvement in his everyday life.

What Sid and Val didn't know (and if left up to Brent they would never discover) was that he had two secret vices that could hamper him from ever becoming successful in the public eye: (1) the heroin and pot addictions he had battled since he was a college sophomore on the west coast, and (2) his homosexual tendencies, which he had fully embraced when he was in prep school.

Unknowingly, his parents had provided the ways and the means for him to cultivate both of his choices when they decided that young Brent would benefit more from the finest education that money could buy. Unfortunately, that also meant that their son was left with no real-time parental guidance or loving affection.

Living in a variety of private boys' schools throughout his formative years, he became a product of his surroundings, trying to fit in and adjust the only way he knew how. With limited chances to mingle with the opposite sex, he began to form deep friendships with classmates, adopting them as his family of choice and convenience. Plus, it was never difficult to find affection at any school he attended—too many other young boys had been shipped off and had similar backgrounds as Brent. Those boys were automatically drawn to each other. It didn't hurt that most of the students had unlimited financial resources to support whatever recreational habits they decided to try—sexual or otherwise.

So far, Brent had done amazingly well scholastically despite his nonacademic indulgences. His intelligence level was superior, and he was able to make excellent grades with limited effort. His photographic memory relieved him from long study sessions while earning him a stellar grade point average.

The only real battle he openly faced was how to avoid going back to New York once his education was behind him and his law degree was obtained. If he was forced to change his lifestyle to accommodate his robotic, unemotional parents, he would surely die a slow and miserable death. He still had over a year before he would be faced with that, though. Until then, he planned to live his days to the fullest before life as he knew it would end.

* * *   * * *

Rick hurriedly entered Sophia's office without knocking.

"What the hell, Rick. You should knock, you know," she said as she glanced at him briefly. Turning back to her computer screen, she ignored her brother who now stood in front of her desk.

"What? What is it, Rick? I'm trying to work here." Her irritation was evident as she kept her eyes on the computer monitor.

"Sophia, I'm angry. I'm frustrated. I can't let this go. I don't see how you can, either," Rick growled, slamming his fist down hard on her desk. Paper clips scattered from a small pile she had pushed to the edge of her desk pad.

Startled at his outburst, she looked him straight in the eyes. "What do you want to do, Rick? Huh? You want to start a manhunt and crucify the bastard? What's that gonna do to resolve anything? You got any ideas about how something like that would play out?"

"Dammit, Sophia. I **told** you we have a witness! I want to pursue this—I can't drop it!" Spit was flying from Rick's mouth as tried to explain.

"You selfish prick!" she screamed out. Now standing behind her desk, she pointed to the door. "Get out of here, Rick."

"No. No, Sophia. I want to know why you want to let this go. I want to hear it from your lips. Who are you protecting, Sophia?" he demanded.

"I'm protecting myself! ME! I'm just as selfish as you are, Rick, except I'm smarter about it," she snarled.

* * * * * *

Big Al wasn't looking forward to the ninety minute drive from Brooklyn to Long Island. He knew the traffic on I-495 and the scheduled construction delays would probably double the time he spent cooped up in the car. It would most likely be hours before he could stretch his long legs again.

A half hour into the drive, his legs were already starting to tingle. *Damn diabetes.*

By early afternoon, Big Al had found what he had been searching for: a neighborhood campaign office sporting an oversized picture of Senator Sid Taylor's smiling face across the front window. "**Let's Keep Sid**" bumper stickers were plastered along the side windows, placed strategically around hanging banners declaring Sid's superior leadership throughout his long tenure as the incumbent candidate for Senate reelection.

When Big Al opened the heavy glass door, a small cowbell clanked to announce his entry. A perky young lady, complete with bouncing ponytail, smiled broadly from behind the front desk and greeted him enthusiastically. "Welcome to the Taylor Camp! I'm Lorie. How can I help you today?"

"Uh, well. I don't know exactly. I was wondering if maybe I could help out working rallies or speeches or something? I'm a security guard, and I'm between jobs right now." Big Al smiled shyly.

"We are a volunteer organization, Mr. ... uh? I don't think I got your name?"

"Name's Johnson. I wasn't asking for a paying job. I just thought maybe I could help out some until my company calls me back. I'm just laid off for a couple weeks."

"Excellent! That's awesome, Mr. Johnson," Lorie giggled. "Well, let's see where we can use you. And you can only help for two weeks?"

"Yep. But I'm a good worker and don't mind long hours or nothin'."

Picking up a roster of upcoming events, Lorie studied the agenda closely. "Well, we have an event scheduled in two days in Central Park. The Senator and the Mayor will be hosting a free concert at the Band Shell. But...the Senator won't be there very long, though," she said under her breath.

Her eyes got wide with excitement as she read further down the agenda. "But ... wait! Maybe you'd like to help out Saturday afternoon at the fish fry? It's going to be at Port Jefferson, and there'll be fireworks and everything. I think the Senator and his wife will both be there, and it should be so much fun! We'll need extra hands to fry the fish and serve, and I suppose we'll need extra security, too." She looked pleased with herself.

"Okay, I can work Saturday. What do I need to do to get signed up?"

"Let me get you a clipboard, and you can fill out your contact and background information, Mr. Johnson." The happy campaign volunteer left Big Al standing in the exact spot he'd occupied for the past ten minutes.

This is too damned easy. Big Al laughed out loud, prompting another campaign worker sitting a few desks back to look up and smile at the new recruit's enthusiasm.

CHAPTER 11

"I don't understand." Rick looked with amazement at his sister as he took a seat in front of her desk. He leaned back slowly in the leather club chair and sighed. "Please explain, Sophia, why it isn't important to you that you were assaulted and raped. Tell me why we shouldn't pursue justice or revenge." He closed his mouth tightly, holding back more frustration.

His sister stared at him for what seemed like minutes, then averted her eyes. Lowering her chin, she gazed at her clasped hands in her lap. Finally, she looked at her brother again.

"I know you don't understand, Rick. How could you? But I've thought of nothing else since it happened. I can't let go of the sick feeling of being violated. I feel dirty, and my self-esteem is nonexistent right now. I can never get back what that fiend took from me. I'll always be stained, and I'll always wonder what I must have done— directly or indirectly— to cause this horrible thing to happen.

"You couldn't possibly understand because no one ever challenges you. I'm challenged every day of my life. I have to live up to the DeLuca legacy...the Giordano legacy, too. I have to constantly prove that the presidency of DeLuca Enterprises wasn't handed to me because of my name alone. I have to be WORTHY every day I walk in this office, every time I open my mouth. Somebody's always going to say that I am just a female puppet, and that I have some brilliant but secret man behind me pulling my strings."

Rick wanted to interrupt and assure her no one ever questioned her business acumen, but he knew she was right. For once, he realized Sophia had struggled the whole time she had been in charge of the company businesses. Until that very moment, he never thought about how much stress and anxiety she had always been under. She had successfully hidden her apprehension under a thick mask of fake confidence.

"I'm so sorry, sis. I had no idea you felt this way," Rick muttered apologetically.

"Rick, that's not the half of it. For the past few years I've successfully run this company. We've been thriving and continue to be. But don't you see? If word gets out that someone raped me, the next things you'll hear will be that I asked for it, I dressed for it, I propositioned it, or I was too weak a person to prevent it. Whatever you hear won't be about my victimization, it'll be about a snooty, rich woman who finally got what she deserved ... or caused some poor bastard to go over the edge because I flaunted my success in his face. I can't win. There is no good outcome.

"And don't discount this, either: I don't remember what happened, and I certainly don't know who did it. But, if I knew, it would make it harder for me to shun questions when the time comes, **if** it ever comes. I'm better off not knowing. Right now, I honestly believe if any memory of this comes back to me, I'll try to block it. I don't want to play this out in the media. I don't want to be put on trial in the court of public opinion. I don't want to pick up a newspaper and be afraid of what I might read. I just want to forget it. I don't want to stain our family name any more than our predecessors already have. " She stood and turned to look out her office window.

Rick stayed seated, but still had concerns. "Sophia, that explains your feelings and your wishes. But this isn't settled as far as I'm concerned. I don't know how to put this aside. I'm your brother, and I failed at protecting you."

She turned and smiled. "Rick, thank you. But it's not your job to protect me forever. Please, let me move on."

He nodded slowly. "Okay, sis. But if I get the chance to get back at your attacker without repercussions, I'm going to handle it. You okay with that?"

 Sophia nodded and walked to the side of the chair where Rick sat. "Just so long as you don't wind up dead or in prison. You're a grown man. You can make your own decisions. But you have to promise me I'll never know anything about who it was or what you might do. From today forward, no more discussion about this subject. Agreed?"

 Rick stood and embraced his sister. "Agreed."

* * * * * *

Adam Woodson had waited as long as he could. He had struggled to concentrate on business, but all he managed to do was shuffle paperwork around. Accomplishing nothing constructive all morning because of constantly glancing at his phone, he finally gave in to his impulses.

Assuming that she should be back from lunch and settled back in her office, he took a chance and dialed Sophia's private number.

Please let her answer. Please let her answer.

* * * * * *

Slick sat behind a battered desk, leaning back in an ancient executive chair he had purchased at a thrift shop twelve years ago when he first rented his office space off a side street in Syosset. Glancing around his meager surroundings, he compared the condition of his used furniture and his rundown office building to the status of his life: *Rough around the edges, but not ready for the garbage heap.*

He occasionally thought about moving to a better location or to an upgraded building, but he could never justify the effort or the cost.. The two cozy rooms above the neighborhood deli felt more like home to him than his apartment did.

When he called Caroline Norton back that morning, she had given him no further insight into why she wanted background information on Senator Sid Taylor. He thought he could pressure her, or that she would volunteer more information about the impromptu assignment, but she repeated what she had said several hours before: "Dig up any skeletons you can find on Sid Taylor. If he has anything to hide, I want to know about it. And this is a rush job, Slick."

Usually, Caroline gave him the "why" behind her assignments, especially front-burner ones. This time, zilch—she provided nothing else to him except her repeated directions. He imagined it had to do with the Senator's reelection campaign, but Slick always assumed Caroline was a staunch supporter of the man. Now, he wasn't so sure.

During their brief second conversation, Slick tried but failed to find a way to steer the conversation toward his premonition. Believing it would be more of a detriment to his reputation than anything else, Slick always kept his visions to himself. But this time he was prepared to take the risk. He would have been willing to discuss it in detail with Caroline if she had provided the opening, but she never opened that door. Like all the previous times they had discussed investigative assignments, she was brief and to the point, leaving no opportunity to introduce a sensitive personal topic. So, as he had done on past occasions, he kept his mouth shut.

"Not for me to reason why..." he mumbled to himself. "Just for me to do or die," he said aloud, misquoting Alfred Lord Tennyson.

He booted up his laptop, put on his reading glasses, and scooted his chair up close to the desk's edge. *If the Senator has anything to do with my vision, I sure as hell hope I can figure it out before it's too late.*

* * * * * *

By dinner time, Juliana had decided to cut her vacation short and return the next day to New York. Neither Lucinda nor Caroline objected since they, too, had similar urges. Uncle Joe had kept quiet, pretending he had no idea why they had made such an unexpected decision to leave the sanctuary of the remote vineyard.

As the four sat on the porch watching the sunset streak in pinks and grays across the Sicilian sky, Caroline took a deep breath and sighed. "Uncle Joe, I hope you understand why we're rushing back to the states. Some urgent business came up, and it just makes sense for us all to travel back together, especially since we came here together." She looked sheepishly at her elderly host.

"Oh, that's all right. Business ran my life for many years, not the other way around. But, you do what you have to do. And come back anytime, Caroline. You're a part of the family, in my book, and you're always welcome here." Pointing at Juliana and Lucinda, he smiled and said, "I'm glad you will take care of these girls and watch over them when they get back home." His eyes held Caroline's a little too long.

What are you up to, Uncle Joe? Caroline wondered as she nodded her agreement. She maintained eye contact with him until the old man became uncomfortable and looked away.

* * * * * *

"I can't meet you today… uh, I've got too much going on here," Sophia said awkwardly into the phone. "I've got a lot of people around right now. Can we talk later?" she said in a barely audible whisper.

"I … well, I suppose so. It's just … I don't know. I was really looking forward to seeing you today. You were hardly around at the fundraiser. I never even got a chance to tell you how gorgeous you looked," Adam stuttered, feeling embarrassed and excited at the same time.

"I was called out of the party unexpectedly. But there's nothing wrong between us, if that's what you're thinking. I'm still happy we were able to … uh, connect." Sophia blushed slightly.

"Promise me you'll see me tomorrow? Somehow?"

"Maybe we can have coffee sometime later this week?" she suggested.

"If that's all you can offer, I'll take it."

"Okay, I'll call you soon, Adam." She hung up the phone before he had a chance to respond.

Sophia stared at the phone in her hand. *How can I face him and not tell him everything? We shouldn't be alone together for a while. What am I doing?*

She looked at her calendar and realized she was late for a staff meeting.

I won't think about this now.

* * * * * *

Port Jefferson, or Port Jeff as the locals liked to call it, had an abundance of great locales where a fish fry/political rally could be held. Luckily for Big Al, when he signed up as a campaign volunteer named *Gus Johnson*, the naïve Lorie disclosed the exact spot where the event was scheduled. He told her he'd like to preliminarily scout it out for potential security issues, and promised he'd get back to her with his report as soon as he could. It was simple to see how this young lady wanted to impress the powers that be, and she was all for agreeing to an independent assessment that **she** could proudly present to the office manager. Due diligence, she would call it later.

Big Al drove directly to Port Jeff from the campaign office in Melville, stopping only to get fuel and a soda. He was tempted to get a beer, but didn't want to take a chance of being stopped by law enforcement and questioned about his visit to Long Island.

When he located Waterfront Park, he drove around the turnabout to get a good view of the land. Once he parked, he scouted the public park on foot.

In some spots, he noticed waving sea grasses set in clumps to accent the landscaping. Planted roses dotted the promenade's landscaping, as well as grassy dunes filling low lying areas along its south perimeter. The entire park was prime real estate and a popular public area in Port Jeff for locals and tourists. Built to interact with the Town Center, the park was a great choice to hold such an event. Big Al could see where maintaining a secure setting here for the Senator and his staff would be a challenge even for the best professionals.

He spent another hour walking through the Town Center, visiting the unique shops, and getting the general lay of the land. Before he left, Big Al would memorize every nook and cranny that could possibly be used to his advantage when the time came for him to execute his assignment.

* * * * * *

Carmen Ryan was angry. She felt she had been semi-seduced by Rick Giordano during the campaign fundraiser…or at least, she was lead on by his perceived attention and behavior. She was feeling like a woman scorned.

Her business day hadn't gone any better than Adam's. Her failure to fully concentrate on their import/export business had directly and negatively impacted routine invoice approvals and shipment deliveries.

It was times like this that she envied Adam's role in the business arrangement. He was less hands-on than she was, especially when it came to daily operations. He was more like the face of the business, while she believed her butt was always on the line if she failed to be on top of operational details.

Mostly, she had been looking forward to sneaking away for a long lunch that day, but that plan went up in smoke. She was growing tired of the farce. Deep down, she was also growing tired of Adam, maybe even resenting him a little. They had been together too long, and she was craving a new adventure.

Maybe I should be looking more at Teddy Brantley. He's not a Giordano, but he's just as involved in DeLuca Enterprises. He doesn't go out much...seems private and keeps to himself. He might be easier to get close to, plus he's more handsome and approachable than that pompous asshole, Rick.

Forming a brand new strategy, she smiled for the first time since she'd been hung up on by Rick that morning. She remembered what Scarlett O'Hara would have said in such a harrowing situation: *"After all, tomorrow is another day."* She giggled to herself.

Carmen immediately dove into the paperwork she had allowed to pile up that morning on her desk. With a new outlook and fresh motivation, she plowed in and cleared her backlog. She managed to complete some of the next day's work before she left that evening to have a satisfying Chinese dinner with Adam.

CHAPTER 12

A burly man with a hairy chest stood at the outside entrance to the lounge called "Disc♂ Dude's." He wore no shirt. Instead he sported a fringed leather vest that was too small to cover his abundant belly hanging over tightly fitted black pants—also made of leather and adorned with various chains and safety pins. His hat made him look more like the fictional bus driver, Ralph Kramden from *the Honeymooners,* than the fierce doorkeeper image he tried unsuccessfully to project.

When Brent Taylor approached the lounge, the bouncer stepped aside, immediately recognizing the frequent customer. "Welcome, Mr. T," he nodded as he unhooked the purple velvet rope that obstructed the entry.

Brent nodded his hello, and quickly stepped inside the dark and cavernous club. He spotted friends and waved as he moved through the crowd to find his usual spot at the end of the polished bar. "The usual," he mouthed to the bartender who hurried off to fetch a cold draft beer for his best-tipping customer.

Scooting in beside Brent and the two men who made out to his left, a new face smiled broadly while trying to get the bartender's attention. "Hey, can I get a beer?" he shouted over the noise that engulfed him. "Hey? Over here!"

Brent caught the eye of the bartender as he turned, and raised two fingers to indicate he wanted two beers instead of one. Signaling acknowledgement, the bartender picked up another mug and filled it to the brim. When he delivered them, he set both in front of Brent.

"Wow, you must be a regular here," the new face told Brent.

"Here's your beer. You just gotta be more assertive to be heard in this place," Brent said as he slid the second mug to the stranger. "I'm Brent. Enjoy that one on me."

"Thanks. I'll buy the next round," he said as they clinked mugs.

'Never seen you here before," Brent began, moving slightly to his right to allow the new customer to have more room at the crowded bar.

"Well, I'm new in town. I'm attending a conference here at Georgetown University, and I'm just trying to find my way around. My hotel room is closing in on me."

Brent looked straight ahead, not turning to show any significant interest in what the man was saying.

"What's your name, dude?" was Brent's next question. He lit a cigarette and offered one to his new drinking buddy.

"Can you smoke in here? I didn't know you could do that inside businesses anymore. What about pot? Is pot allowed?" the new customer asked instead of answering Brent's question.

"Name? Or do I keep calling you 'dude?' It's a simple question." Brent turned to gaze at the man's face.

"Oh, sorry. You can call me whatever you like, but I usually answer to Chris."

"And yes, you can smoke in here. Pot is frowned upon, but people smoke weed in the bathroom sometimes. It's a private club. How'd you get in, anyway?"

"My dad is ..." he started to explain.

"I don't want to know about your dad or your family or your life. I don't share my story in here, and I don't expect you to do it, either," Brent interjected, ensuring his rules of engagement were spelled out early in the evening.

"Gotcha. Sounds great." Chris took a big gulp of beer. "Hey, you wanna dance?" Chris asked as he patted Brent's arm.

"Sure. Why not?"

The two left the end of the bar and headed for the dance floor. As the name of the lounge implied, only loud disco music was ever played there which made the nightspot extremely popular with a certain segment of the young gay crowd.

When the two began dancing to the 1980s' music, Chris leaned in toward Brent's ear and tried to whisper above the pulsating bass. "I've got some H out in my limo. Wanna have a private party later?" he smiled coyly. Chris leaned back to gauge Brent's reaction.

Brent's response was a wide grin and a wink at the handsome man he hoped would be a long-term friend—at least for the next day or two.

* * * * * *

The running of the DeLuca mansion was back to its normal routine. No parties were scheduled, no last minute overnight guests were anticipated, and no one roamed the home except for the live-in staff members.

Both Sophia and Rick had returned to their respective homes: hers, the penthouse in Manhattan that had been in the family for years; and his, the large home in Oyster Bay that had once housed the Giordano family at the time of his birth.

Maureen and Thomas had kept busy straightening the mansion in anticipation of the arrival of the two ladies of the house, Lucinda and Juliana.   Since they weren't expected until the next evening, the busy servants had plenty of time to make certain all the finishing touches were satisfactory.

Maureen had baked a coffee cake, and Thomas had taken his seat in the kitchen nook when she offered him a warm slice and a glass of milk. Gladly accepting, Maureen served him a generous portion, poured his milk, and sat down across from him with her coffee.

"We've sure had our share of excitement, haven't we?" she declared as she watched Thomas eagerly cut into his treat.

"Nothing I'd want to go through again, I'll tell you that," he responded without looking up. "I'm surprised the Senator and Mrs. Taylor showed their faces in the dining room for breakfast. That took a lot of nerve, if you ask me."

Maureen cleared her throat and cautiously asked, "Are you absolutely certain of what you saw, Thomas?"

He stopped chewing and raised his eyes to meet hers. "Yes. I know what I saw."

"But do you think she was voluntarily 'involved' in that...that...act? She can have any man she wants, but why would she want to be with **him**?" Maureen was clearly troubled.

"I don't know, Maureen. Who knows what goes through people's minds nowadays. Maybe he hit her, or she fell, or something traumatic caused her to black out." He paused thoughtfully. Thomas took another bite of his coffee cake.

Maureen shook her head, wondering if Sophia might have been unconscious when she was attacked. "Maybe you're right, Thomas. She doesn't remember how she got her head wound. If she was knocked out when it happened, that makes more sense." She gazed thoughtfully into space. "I'm surprised Rick let the Senator leave the house without confronting him."

Maureen abruptly left the table and rinsed her coffee cup.

Thomas took his last bite, carried his plate and glass to the sink, and left the kitchen without further comment.

* * * * * *

Judging from their hysterical laughter, the two men who were stumbling arms over shoulders down the sidewalk were having one hell of a good time. They approached the waiting limo, doors open in welcome, as if it was their fairy tale chariot.

"After you," Chris bowed, almost too tipsy to bend at the waist without falling. Stumbling backwards, he snorted, then broke out in full laughter again.

His laughter was contagious, and Brent guffawed in response. Trying not to fall, Brent grabbed the door of the car and attempted to slide into the back seat without success. Instead, he found himself sprawled on the damp pavement, legs spread wide, and seated awkwardly. "I can't get up," he said innocently as Chris laughed harder. "I'm serious. My legs don't work," Brent giggled.

"I'll get you, man," Chris offered generously. Positioning himself behind Brent, he tried to lift the helpless man by grabbing under his armpits and pulling upward. Instead, Chris lost his footing and collapsed backward, landing on his butt in a similar sitting position as the man he tried to help.

"Oh, no! Now we're both stuck!" Brent cackled. The two continued their hysterics until finally Brent rolled on his side and was able to position himself on his knees. Using the frame of the limo for support, he struggled to pull himself into a semi-standing position.

"Look! I made it! Come on, man. You can do it!" the drunken Brent cheered.

It only took Chris one more attempt to get himself upright. "Now, let's go party with a capital P," he giggled as he tried to initiate a "high five" with his buddy. They failed, and chortled again.

Somehow they managed to get inside the limo and close the door. The black, nondescript Lincoln pulled away briskly, leaving the two inebriated men alone in the backseat where the windows were shrouded with dark curtains and the doors were locked from the outside.

* * * * * *

Sid Taylor had tried to call his son multiple times that evening, but either Brent didn't have his cell phone with him or he refused to answer his father's calls. Sid preferred to believe his son had left his phone at his apartment before he went out for the evening.

He knew that Val had spoken with Brent earlier in the day, hoping to prepare him for the news reports and film clips he might see on television. What Sid didn't know was what Val had said to Brent during the impromptu opportunity to poison their son against his father. When she was angry, Val could be spiteful and vindictive. He wouldn't put anything past her; in fact, he'd caught her telling embellished stories of his less-than-perfect behavior to Brent several times before. Sid tended to believe all he was good for was doling out money to Brent and Val. *I'm their damned ATM. That's all I am to them. A motherfuckin' money machine!*

Cradling the phone receiver again, Sid considered the state of his family life. He wasn't happy—hadn't been in a long time. He knew Val was bitter and miserable. Brent didn't care about his father until he needed money.

Maybe it's time to change some things around. Maybe I should talk to my attorney to see what can be done. They'd both shit bricks if I left all my insurance benefits and estate funds to Alcoholics Anonymous!

Ironically, just as Sid started to laugh at his own vengeful thoughts, his only son was sprawled on the damp pavement of a Georgetown side street giggling with a stranger who was about to take him for the ride of his life.

Twin Sins

CHAPTER 13

Upon settling into the back of the limo, Chris had presented a grateful Brent with a bag of heroin to consume at his discretion. Chris had his own separate supply of powder, which he planned to use himself.

"Here, man. If you run out, that's on you. Don't ask for any of mine," Chris said, as he joyfully tossed the goody bag to his eager new friend. "Germs, you know," he snickered playfully.

Both simultaneously pinky-tasted their portioned product and settled into their seats for what Brent hoped to be the next phase of a long and satisfying evening.

Wherever they were headed, it had been a long drive. After twenty minutes of pot smoking and serenity, Brent reached for the bag of heroin powder.

"Yeah, go ahead man. We still got a little ways to go," Chris encouraged his new buddy.

"Where are we going, Chris? You never said. I thought we were going to your hotel room," Brent asked as he snorted the first full hit of his stash.

"No, man. I told you that hotel room was closing in on me. I have a friend who lives another twenty miles away. He's in Europe, but I know where he keeps his keys. We're gonna party in his penthouse!" Chris proclaimed exuberantly.

Brent smiled cautiously. "You sure it's okay with your friend? I mean, you bringing another guy in there and all?"

"Be cool, man! Of course it's all right. We do this stuff all the time. He's 'family,' man," Chris remarked and winked his assurance.

Brent nodded, but wasn't convinced that Chris was telling the whole story. Regardless, Chris had been true to his word so far: he had pot, he had heroin, he had a limo, and he was sharing it all with his new friend. What did he have to lose, anyway?

Eventually, Brent leaned back into the soft leather seat and let the heroin do its job, pushing him into the state of euphoria that he knew so well. His body relaxed, feeling the drug's full effects, still slightly buzzed from the marijuana. He dozed but woke quickly when he heard the rumbling roar of a metal garage door lifting.

"Welcome back. We're here," Chris smiled as the car slowed, accelerated forward, then stopped suddenly. The same sound of the garage door closing was even more jarring to the half-alert Brent.

He heard the click of car doors unlocking, and watched as Chris reached for the door handle to exit the vehicle. To Brent, suddenly Chris seemed no longer tipsy or stoned, but rather fully in control of his emotions and his body.

Brent peeked out the car door, scanning the sizeable empty area of what appeared to be the first floor of a warehouse. He looked questioningly at Chris who waited patiently for Brent to step out of the limo.

"I thought you said ..." Brent started.

"The penthouse is on the fourth floor. Let me go get the key from the hiding place, and you go wait for me over there where those chairs are," Chris instructed and pointed to a spot several yards in front of the limo.

Brent looked in the distance and saw two straight back chairs resting against a short dividing wall. Still unable to logically process his underlying thoughts, Brent did as he was told.

Chris stood firmly in place until he saw Brent take a seat in one of the chairs. Chris gave him a 'thumbs up' sign before he turned to exit the huge room.

Instead of looking for a key, Chris went directly to a door that would lead outside the building.   Finding himself only a few feet from the closed garage door of the deserted warehouse, he smiled to himself. He quickly got in the driver seat of an unlocked black van that had been stashed there for his getaway. He would be back in New York in no time, and his inflated bank account would reflect the success of his evening's activities.

* * * * * *

The limo driver watched through his tinted windshield, noting that Brent Taylor had now leaned across the second chair in a feeble attempt to take a quick nap.   His feet still touched the floor; but, with his head and torso bent sideways in the middle, he looked like the half-deflated balloon man that waved at customers from the edges of car lots. The driver scoffed at the pathetic image.

Just as Brent reached what appeared to be the depths of a peaceful sleep, a masked man descended from a metal stairway to the left onto the warehouse floor. He was tall and bulky, dressed from head to toe in the costume of a sexual dominator: full black shiny leather jump suit, knee high boots with large buckles, thin shiny black gloves, and a leather head cover that any superhero would have been proud to sport.

Not a speck of skin was showing, except for two eye slits above the nose—his eyeballs having been fitted with solid red contacts that covered even the whites of his eyes. Holes for the Dominator's nostrils were small, but provided enough space for breathing. Only a round • had been cut where his lips would meet, not conducive to talking so much as for breathing.

The Dominator dragged a cat o'nine tails across the floor as he approached the sleeping Brent. In his other hand, he held what appeared to be a duffle bag, setting it down quietly next to Brent's feet.

Shifting his head from side to side, he surveyed his prey, studying the position of his arms and legs.   Quietly, the Dominator reached into the bag and brought out a set of shackles—not ordinary handcuffs, but metal cuffs about two or three inches in length connected with a heavy chain—and easily secured them to Brent's wrists.   Within seconds, a dreaming Brent became his prisoner as he slipped another set of shackles on Brent's limp legs.

The Dominator turned toward the limo, bowing theatrically and waving his right hand toward the bound prisoner as if to give him accolades for his unconscious part of the performance.

The limo driver blinked his lights, signaling to the Dominator that he was to wait to be summoned before returning to the 'stage.' Nodding his understanding, the Dominator retrieved the duffle bag and his sex toy before ascending the metal stairway to a waiting area on the second floor.

Meanwhile, the limo driver placed a call to New York, saying only a few encrypted words before hanging up: "Ready for Phase 2, boss."

* * * * * *

"Val, where the hell is Brent?" Sid demanded to know when he burst into his wife's private bedroom. They had maintained separate bedrooms for years, but they had made it a practice to knock before entering each other's rooms.

Stunned that Sid had barged in without warning, Val's first reaction was defensive. "How am I supposed to know? Isn't tracking people your specialty, Mr. Senator? At least, newspapers always say the government can spy on anybody at anytime," she sneered.

"What's that got to do with anything? I don't spy on people, for God's sake, Val. I'm just trying to find Brent. He hasn't been answering my calls today, and I'm getting worried."

"Do you blame him, Sid? I told you this afternoon, he's fine. He was prepared for the media if they showed up. He knows how to handle them after all these years. Leave him alone, dammit." Dismissing her husband, Val picked up the magazine that she had been scanning before she had been so rudely interrupted, ignoring her husband who still stood inside her door.

Giving up, Sid backed out of the room, shaking his head.

I'm gonna try to call him once more before I go to bed. Eventually, he's got to answer.

Instead of using his cell phone, Sid went back to his bedroom and picked up the house phone on the bedside table. *Maybe he'll answer if he thinks it's his mother calling.*

On the fourth ring someone answered, but it wasn't Brent.

"Who is this?" Sid Taylor asked, puzzled.

"Jimmy. Who's this?" a man responded, slurring his words.

"Can I speak to the young man who owns this phone, please?" Sid asked patiently.

"I own this phone now," Jimmy said. "I found it. It's mine. Finders keepers," he snickered. "I gotta go ..."

"Wait! I'll give you a reward for that phone if you will tell me where you found it," Sid offered anxiously.

"How you gonna get me the money? How much?"

"Whatever you want, but I need to know where you found the phone. Please?"

"It was just laying on the sidewalk next to the alley. I almost took a piss on it, but I didn't," Jimmy seemed proud of his ability to shift his aim.

"What alley? What alley? Please?"

"Just a few doors down from that faggot disco place. You know the place?" Jimmy volunteered.

"Oh, Jeez," Sid exclaimed as he hung up the phone.

"Hey? What about my reward?" Jimmy said into the dead phone line. "Damn lying asshole!" he remarked with disgust the second he realized the caller had hung up.

Maybe when he got a little more sober he'd call the man back and get his reward. He slipped the cell phone into his tattered coat pocket and proceeded down the sidewalk toward what the local homeless crew referred to as 'the faggot place.'

They may have a strange habit or two, but those guys sure are nice to people like me. Always giving me a few dollars even when I don't hold out my hand.

I bet I'll get a good tip out of that kid who dropped his phone. He probably didn't realize he'd dropped it when he fell down trying to get into that big car.

CHAPTER 14

He laid his phone down on the coffee table. He would have to decide quickly, or else all their efforts would have been in vain. He was struggling with his conscience, and his surroundings weren't helping him get off the decision fence.

Rick Giordano sat solemnly in the immense palatial home that had once been inhabited by his mother and father, Lorenzo and Cathy Giordano. The emptiness of the house echoed with loneliness and sadness, as it did whenever he spent any length of time there by himself. He had no live-in help to combat the feeling of active spirits circling him when he was alone there in the evenings. The only way he knew to calm those spirits was with hefty and frequent gulps of straight whiskey.

Often he thought about selling the house and splitting the proceeds with Sophia, but she would never seriously entertain the idea. The deed to the house had been recorded in both their names when he and his sister became of age; so, without her consent the house couldn't be conveyed to a new owner. Then again, Sophia refused repeatedly to move into the house with him or instead of him. She claimed it was too hard for her to get to her routinely scheduled business appointments from Oyster Bay. "It doesn't take men nearly so long to get presentable, Rick. You should stay there," she had protested.

He had to admit, the place was stunning. Even in its original state, the decorating had been done so tastefully that it was still elegant and inviting to this day. The structure was almost thirty years old, but no one would know by just looking. The only changes made to the home throughout the years had been updating appliances or changing bedroom draperies and bedspreads. Other than that, the house was the exact same as when his parents lived there with their children.

Rick knew something in his parents' tragic background—including the circumstances of their untimely youthful deaths—had been kept as a secret from him and Sophia for many years. As far as he knew, only his step-mother, his step-grandmother, and Aunt Caroline knew the full story. It was too late to ask his maternal grandmother, Genevieve Parker McNeal, to reveal anything she might remember about it. She was currently in a nursing home in Nashville and couldn't recall her own name on her best days. But Aunt Caroline had promised them that by the time Sophia turned thirty, she would sit down with both of them and explain the back story. That wouldn't be for another three years.

He recalled how once he tried to Google his father's name to see if anything interesting popped up. It didn't. It was almost as if the man never existed. There wasn't even an obituary to be found. Many times before, Rick had tried to pry the information out of the three women who knew the story but refused to share it. His queries only seemed to make them all anxious and a little bit angry when he brought it up. He had finally learned to wait and stop asking.

But he had also learned that drinking helped quell his inquisitive nature, not to mention how it created a sense of bravado when he felt the eerie presence of his parents in the empty house.

Whenever he felt like he needed answers or confirmation of their past existence, he toasted his father and mother instead. "To Lorenzo and Cathy Giordano. Here's to your short lives. Wish I could have been a bigger part of 'em," he would say as he raised his glass to the only picture in the house of his parents.

The framed snapshot on the sunroom mantle never answered back, but Rick swore that once he heard a woman softly whisper, "here, here."

This time, however, he heard nothing of the sort, only another buzz from his silenced cell phone. Setting down his glass and glancing at the phone, he read the text message that displayed brightly on the screen.

"You there?" was all it said.

Rick picked up the phone and texted his reply. "Yes."

He raised his glass toward the mantle.

"To you both. Hope you're proud of your only son."

* * * * * *

"Tell us every detail. Take us through every minute of that night," Caroline asked Maureen while she, Juliana, and Lucinda sat staring at the cook from across the kitchen bar.

The women had arrived at the DeLuca mansion around 8 o'clock that evening. However, instead of resting or eating the dinner that Maureen had prepared, they immediately began asking questions. Caroline was the self-appointed leader of the inquisition.

"I will, of course. But don't you want to eat? I can serve your plates here on the counter, and I'll talk while you have dinner."

Remembering their last meal which had been served on the plane, their stomachs began to growl in unison.

Juliana agreed, also remembering her mother hadn't eaten much lately and hoping that Maureen's tasty food would remedy that.

While serving the food on the plates usually reserved for dining room events, Maureen began to voice her recollections of the fundraiser evening.

The ladies ate slowly, sometimes interrupting Maureen to get clarification, but they remained solemn and attentive during the cook's account of the evening.

"I swear, Miss Sophia was the bravest woman I've ever seen. Even through all that, she left here the next morning with the same dignity—the same confidence and grace—of a woman who had experienced nothing so horrifying and traumatic," Maureen sniffed and turned her head, trying to conceal the pooling tears that were trying to sneak out of her eyes.

Lucinda blew her nose and cleared her throat. "Thank you, precious lady. You took care of our girl when we couldn't. We won't forget this, Maureen. You've always been there for me and Juliana, and it's apparent you hold the same affection for our Sophia. Bless you, Maureen." Lucinda started to rise, but her legs felt weak. "Juliana, would you help me to my room, dear? I think I've heard all I want to hear of this for now."

"Of course, Mama," she responded as she glanced at Maureen and Caroline. "Don't you two eat all the tiramisu while I'm gone," she smiled. "Mama, I'll make sure Maureen saves you a big piece for later," Juliana assured Lucinda as she led her fragile mother down the hallway toward the elevator.

Caroline smiled and called after them, wishing Lucinda a good night. Not expecting Juliana to return for a few minutes, Caroline took the opportunity to ask Maureen a few more questions while they were alone.

"Did you see what Thomas described, Maureen?"

"No, ma'am, I didn't. Thank the Good Lord."

"Was Thomas drinking or could he have been wrong about what he saw?" Caroline asked.

"He said he knew what he saw, and he was sure of what was going on," Maureen nervously responded.

"Do you believe him?"

"Why wouldn't I, Miss Caroline? Miss Sophia stumbles in here, collapses, and her head's bleeding like she must have hit it on something. None of us knew about the 'other' until we got her up to her bedroom and she showed us what had run down her leg. We didn't know she had been attacked until that very second."

Caroline studied Maureen's face. "Maureen, why did Thomas wait until after you came down later to tell you what he saw?"

"Honest to God, Miss Caroline. I don't know. He just mentioned it like it was an oddity, not an assault."

Caroline nodded. "Don't you think it strange that he saw this happening just a short while before Sophia falls down in the kitchen floor? And still he never mentions it to anybody?"

"Well, Thomas was busy coordinating the caterers and making sure the party was running smoothly. I don't remember even seeing him before then, except to send him a text to ask Mr. Rick to join us upstairs."

Caroline reached across the bar to pat Maureen's hand. "Thank you, Maureen. You've been very helpful. Perhaps I'll try to talk with Thomas tomorrow."

"Well, ma'am, it won't be tomorrow. Thomas asked for two weeks' vacation to visit relatives in Colorado. He left about an hour before you ladies got home." Maureen looked apologetic.

"Who gave him approval to leave?" Caroline quizzed.

"I did, ma'am. Miss Lucinda gave me full run of the household years ago. She told me I could let people have time off without telling her, provided I maintained adequate household coverage. Randall will be covering for Thomas for the next two weeks." Maureen offered.

"Thank you, Maureen. I appreciate everything you do and everything you've done. Would you ask Miss Juliana to join me in the living room when she comes down? I want to talk to her before I leave to go home."

"Of course, Miss Caroline. I'll be sure to do that."

* * * * * *

Embarrassment and anger had caused Teddy Brantley to make a detour and spend the day working from his Manhattan home instead of his office. He didn't know if he could look Sophia in the eyes again without remembering how she had reminded him of a clipped-winged sparrow. He had never seen her look as vulnerable as she had when she lay wounded and stunned in her childhood bed—quite a contrast to her usual strong-willed self.

Teddy had never felt the urge to seek and destroy before, either; his guilt for leaving Sophia alone by the pool was only slightly eclipsed by the sheer anger he felt for the cowardly assailant.   Fortunately, it was hours later when Thomas revealed what he saw poolside.   Had the timing been different, Teddy would surely have killed the Senator as he lay unconscious behind the pool chairs.

Wondering if he could control his temper when he again met Senator Taylor face-to-face, he tried to recall what he had preached to his clients in the past: innocent until proven guilty. But it was hard to live by that rule when a witness had already identified the man to be the perpetrator.

Remember you've only heard a brief second-hand account of what Thomas saw. There are no details yet to back it up. Plus, you haven't talked to Sophia about this since it happened. You haven't spoken to Sid Taylor at all. How can you be so judgmental without hearing all sides of the story?

As if he were responding to another person in the room, Teddy stared at his mirrored image above the fireplace and answered aloud.   "I don't know everything, but I know enough. If Sid Taylor hurt Sophia, he's going to pay dearly for that mistake."

Twin Sins

CHAPTER 15

Cold water splashed over his face as Brent was urged to rouse from his sleep.

"Stop it, Chris," he said before he opened his eyes in the sterile white room. Blinking, he focused on the figure before him, dressed in turquoise medical scrubs with matching cap, including a surgical mask hooked behind his ears that covered his nose and mouth. Big green eyes beneath blondish eyebrows peered over the mask at the involuntary patient. His gloved hands held an empty small plastic bowl that had previously been filled with water from a nearby sink.

"What the...? Where am I? Where's Chris? Am I in a hospital?" Brent tried to sit up but was restrained by broad straps, similar to seatbelts, which stretched across the gurney in several places. As he strained to lift his head, he could see the shackles that gripped his hands and ankles. Feeling suddenly cold, Brent realized he had been stripped of all his clothing except his underwear.

The Doctor said nothing the entire time the patient was squirming and pleading for answers.

"What do I have to do to find out what's going on?" Brent begged. "I'll do whatever you want. **I can get money**! Is that what you want? Just let me go, please!"

The Doctor turned his back on Brent and walked out the door. The click of the door lock engaging was enough to make Brent start openly sobbing.

Within a few seconds the metal door opened, and the Doctor entered again. Still silent, he spread a thin blanket across the now shivering prisoner.

Whining softly now, Brent watched the Doctor as he pulled a surgical tray close to the gurney. The Doctor deliberately lifted a gleaming scalpel and several clamps, giving Brent a preview of the instruments of torture that were available for immediate use. When the Doctor reached for what appeared to be an electric bone saw, Brent fainted on the table. It was then that the Doctor allowed himself to respond to the prisoner's reactions: He doubled over in laughter.

* * * * * *

Not long after she arrived in her office, Caroline Norton's private office phone line rang. She waited until it rang twice before she answered.

"Caroline, it's me, Slick. You got time to see me this morning?"

"Yeah, but only if you can make it sooner rather than later. When can you get here?" she asked. She flipped her calendar to the current day to check her schedule, but a peripheral movement caught her attention. Caroline looked up quickly to find Slick standing in her doorway, cell phone against his ear.

"How 'bout now?" he asked with a sly smile, smacking his gum loudly as he stepped boldly inside her doorway.

* * * * * *

Val Taylor called the bank to get the current balance in the joint checking account she shared with Sid. She had no concept of how to keep a check register or balance a checkbook. She never took the time to learn how to access online banking—no, thank you.

So, she called the bank every day without fail and talked to the same representative who, by now, knew to have the balance ready for the Senator's wife at precisely 10:00 a.m. every weekday. In Val's mind, the quoted balance was equal to the amount available for her use that particular day.

Most days, she spent less than a thousand dollars. On rare occasions, Val would splurge and indulge in some ridiculously expensive bauble. Sometimes she didn't spend anything at all, but that was not the norm.

Today she expected to use as much of the entire balance as she could without alerting Sid to anything suspicious.

Today she intended to start building up the bank account she had kept hidden from Sid for all these years. Little by little, she planned to pump up the balance from the measly $500,000 it currently held to something closer to $5,000,000. It might take a year or two of carefully calculated withdrawals from their combined account, but she was patient. It would be at least that long before Brent would graduate from law school and could join her in the Caribbean to kick off her new independence.

She had incurred some recent unexpected debts, however. Those would have to be paid first; but, whatever was left at the end of two years should be quite a nest egg.

* * * * * *

Thinking she was probably making a big mistake, Sophia entered the Starbuck's and looked toward the back of the narrow room. She saw him sitting there, two cups in front of him, silently praying she would show up. She ambled toward his table, taking extra time to allow herself to calm a little.

She sat down across from him at the small table, relieved that she instantly felt the same joy as when they were last alone together. There it was—the familiar thrill in her tummy that she was afraid might never surface again. She was excited to see him, unexpectedly and thankfully excited. Anyone looking at her could tell she was relaxed and content in his presence.

There was no doubt he was overjoyed that she had agreed to meet him. It didn't matter to him that the meeting had to be so brief. All he wanted was another chance to look into her eyes, and maybe even tell her he loved her. And he did. He knew he did. But he didn't want to scare her off. He knew he had to tread carefully.

"Thank you for getting my latte, Adam," she said coyly as she moved the cup marked 'Adam 2' in front of her. She sipped the drink slowly as he watched her reaction. "Perfect," she said and leaned back in the straight chair.

Adam reached across the table and took her hand in his. "Sophia, when can we meet again? I don't mean for coffee, but really have some time together?"

Her smile faded as her gaze shifted from his boyish face to the rim of her coffee cup. She didn't want him to move this fast—not now.

"What about your fiancé, Carmen?" she asked, slowly sliding her hand away from his.

Adam's eyes darted rapidly from left to right, then up at the ceiling. He closed his eyes momentarily and responded without hesitation. "Carmen and I have grown apart. I don't want to be with her. I want to be with you. I'm in love with you, not Carmen."

Stunned by his sudden confession, Sophia's face turned bright red. She had intentionally ignored her self-imposed rules when she allowed herself to be seduced by a married man—**almost** married man. Considering the secret she was harboring, she couldn't afford to hide anything else about her life right now. She had been stupid and careless to allow their intimacy to happen, even if she did believe at the time it was somehow meant to be. What had she been thinking?

"No. No, I can't do this. I can't ruin someone else's life like this. When you and Carmen aren't engaged anymore, you call me then. But for now, we shouldn't be alone together."

Sophia stood without warning and briskly moved toward the side exit door a few feet away from their table. She didn't look back as she left, but she knew Adam was still sitting there, frozen in place with his mouth still open and wondering what the hell just happened.

* * * * * *

Val grabbed her purse and summoned her driver in preparation for her short trip to the bank. Her plan was to withdraw several thousand dollars in cash from the Taylors' joint account and deliver the entire amount across town to a separate bank where she had rented a private safety deposit box. For now, the cash she collected would be stashed there. She didn't have time to think of an elaborate way to mask the money trail if a deposit was to be made directly into her secret account.

As she approached the front door, the house phone rang. Pausing for a second, she started to ignore it. *Maybe it's Brent,* she thought and decided to take a chance and answer the call.

The caller ID confirmed it was her son calling. "Hello, dear," she answered pleasantly.

"Hello? Who is this? Where's the man I talked to before?" a strange voice replied.

"I'm sorry? Who are you? Where's Brent?"

"I don't know any Brent. This is my phone, and I found it fair and square after that guy dropped it. Let me speak to the guy who said I was supposed to get a reward," Jimmy demanded.

"Sir, I don't know to whom you're referring, but you are illegally using my son's phone. I demand that you give it back immediately," Val snapped.

"Well, it's for sale, if you want to make a deal," Jimmy chuckled.

"Tell me where to find you, and I'll give you $100 for the phone."

Jimmy was silent as he thought over the offer. "I can't replace this phone for less than $1,000, you know. These gadgets are real expensive."

Val was livid. "Fine. But where are you? Where can I pick up the phone?"

"I'll be at Bay Park in an hour, that's close to here," Jimmy replied.

"Where is that? On Staten Island?"

"Lady, I'm in Georgetown. Where the hell are you?"

Val wasn't thinking clearly. "Oh, yes. I forgot. I can't be there in an hour, but keep this phone close by.   I'll have someone there contact you."

"Lady, this phone is dying, and I don't have any way to charge it up. You wait too long, and I guess it's 'bye bye phone.'"

Thinking quickly, Val gave him explicit directions. "Turn off the phone. Power it down. Turn it back on in exactly two hours. You'll get a call then with further instructions."

"Sure, Lady. But I think all this extra trouble is worth a couple a' hundred more," Jimmy teased.

"I'll make sure you get everything that's coming to you," Val smiled and hung up.

Before she left the house for the bank, she placed a call to Sid Taylor's Washington office in the Hart Senate Building. Val spoke with one of Sid's personal aides who was sympathetic to the Taylors' situation and gladly volunteered to make the exchange on behalf of their son. As far as the aide knew, Brent had dropped his cell phone somewhere, and the nice man who found it wanted to return it. A $1,200 cash reward had been promised to the Good Samaritan.

Sid's aide jumped at the chance to do a good deed for Mrs. Taylor. He volunteered to handle the exchange personally. He promised he'd be back in touch once he had recovered the phone and rewarded the kind man.

Finally, Val was free to do her banking. Opening the front door, she spotted the limo driver with his eyes closed as he leaned against the parked vehicle.

"You're not paid to sleep, you lazy bastard," she screamed for all to hear as she clomped down the steps of the residence.

The startled man jumped and quickly sprinted to open the rear car door for the Senator's perturbed wife.

CHAPTER 16

He had been dreaming about the day he was introduced to heroin. His father had first shown him the substance while they toured a police department in upstate New York. He couldn't remember which city, but he remembered everything he'd been told about the drug.

"See that, Brent? Drugs like that will ruin your life. It doesn't take much to do it, either," Sid Taylor had said more for the benefit of the news cameras than for his son.

The Senator had been invited into the facility to present an award to the team of police officers who had broken up a state-wide drug ring. Photo ops were taken advantage of, and the Senator and his twelve-year old son stood front and center of packages of heroin, cocaine, and a heap of bottled opioids.

One of the heroin packages had split open and the innocent boy timidly reached toward the spilled powder with a pointed finger. Instinctively slapping his son's hand away, Sid Taylor looked embarrassed as the media's cameras snapped the moment into history. Laughing nervously, Sid merely bent down to his son's level and reiterated his message. "Don't touch that, Brent. That's the devil's powder."

He had never forgotten how that single moment had so obviously affected him. He was, of course, embarrassed that his father reprimanded him so publically that the image appeared in newspapers across the state. Strike One. Plus, he wasn't going to taste it or anything, but his father obviously didn't trust him or think him smart enough to follow simple instructions. Strike Two. But the worst of all was the anger at his father that started growing from that day forward. Strike Three. If there could be a Strike Four, it would certainly be that no matter what Sid advised his son to do, Brent was compelled to do the opposite. Thus, his addiction to heroin was born that very day, even though he wouldn't become an actual user until he reached his late teens.

Opening his eyes, Brent saw the stark white ceiling above and was vividly reminded of his predicament. He turned his head and scanned the room. He was alone.

Several hours before, the Doctor had made a quick appearance and injected Brent with something that made him content and drowsy again. He again dreamed of his father. But now, whatever he had been given was wearing off. He felt goose bumps, realizing that the blanket he had been given was now thrown carelessly across a straight back chair next to the small sink vanity on the right side of the room.

His legs were twitchy, something he had experienced before but had never become a persistent issue.   A heroin boost always calmed his restless legs down. Mostly, he needed to use the bathroom and get a drink of something. His mouth was dry, and when he tried to speak, his voice was raspy. "Hey!" He tried to get someone's attention.   "Hey! Hello?"

The door lock clicked loudly, and the Doctor entered the room. He stopped at the side of the gurney and looked down into Brent's eyes.

"I need to use the bathroom, and I gotta have something to drink. Would you let me do that, please?"

The Doctor turned, went to the sink, and reached below the cabinet to retrieve a small paper cup and a silver bedpan.

"No, man. No. I can't use one of those things. Please let me up," Brent begged.

The Doctor ignored his pleas, filled up the cup with water, and returned to Brent's side. He held the cup above Brent's head and nodded. Confused, Brent wasn't certain what the non-verbal directions implied. He tried to lift his head, but the Doctor used his free hand to push Brent's forehead back down. Finally, Brent opened his mouth. The Doctor dropped sparse amounts of water in the young man's mouth until he was sure how much Brent could handle without getting choked. When the cup was emptied, the Doctor wadded up the cup and threw it in the sink's basin.

When the Doctor turned back toward Brent, he was holding a pair of scissors in his gloved hand.

"Are you gonna cut these straps off? Please?"

The Doctor didn't answer but started cutting the fabric of Brent's underwear.

"Oh, no. Don't do that! Please!" Brent begged.

The Doctor jerked the ripped underwear out from under the scared man, then quickly slid the bedpan in the narrow space between Brent's buttocks and the gurney. There was so little slack in the constraints that the fit was tight, but it would do.

The Doctor stepped back, surveying his work. He crossed his arms and waited.

Brent was sobbing. "Please, man. I can't do it like this. At least let me try to do it without you staring at me."

Nodding, the Doctor turned to walk out of the room. When the door was shut and Brent was again alone, he felt his bladder release.

However, he wasn't aware of the hidden cameras planted inconspicuously around the room. Brent was never really alone.

* * * * * *

Caroline sipped her coffee while Slick gave her a rundown of the preliminary research he had gathered on Sid Taylor.

"This man's a real piece of work," he started. Slick turned a page in his little black book until he reached the entries he searched for. "Here we go. Sid Taylor was born in 1957 and was an only child.

"His mother, Grace, was born in Boston in '33 to middle class parents. The day after she turned 18, she joined the USO troops heading for Korea. She met Sid's future father there at an army field camp. She married Warren Harding Taylor—I shit you not—two months later when she came up pregnant. She miscarried before they ever left Korea. They stuck together, though. W.H. brought her back to the states in 1951.

"They settled in Brooklyn Heights, but he couldn't find a good paying job. He decided to go to law school, and they both worked odd jobs to pay his way through."

Slick looked up at Caroline to make sure she was paying attention. She looked bored with the mundane background info.

"Now here's where it starts to get interesting." He cleared his throat once again and flipped another page in his little black book.

"Sid's father graduated from Brooklyn Law School in 1953, along with a bunch of very influential people. Some were in his class, some in the class ahead of him, but they were all there at the same time. We're talking state supreme court justices, appellate judges, congressmen, and the high-powered, high-ranking lawyers who take on and win the unwinnable cases. You know the kind of people I mean. Powerful. Rich. Even some famous people have graduated from that school in recent years. It's a hotbed for breeding high-profiled people."

Caroline waited. "And? So what are you inferring, Slick?" She impatiently looked at her watch, wondering if Slick would ever get to the meat of his findings.

"Let me be a little more specific. The name of a certain member of his graduating class stuck out prominently on the list." He looked at her with a sly smile.

"And that person would be …?" Caroline urged, drumming her fingernails on the desktop.

He could hardly contain his excitement. "Vincenzo DeLuca."

* * * * * *

Jimmy waited two hours and turned on the cell phone, exactly like the woman had told him to do. He was already thinking about what a $1,200 windfall could buy him: a nice meal, a warm bed, and maybe a new sweat suit. It got real cold around D.C. in the winter, and it wouldn't be long before he'd need to switch his wardrobe.

He scrounged through two different bags in the shopping cart filled with all his earthly belongings. Locating the wadded up jacket he had worn the night he found the phone, he pulled it out and shook it free of dust. *I oughta at least look nice when I get that money.* He slipped on the old blazer, a reject from the student trash bins at Georgetown University.

He pushed his cart adjacent to a sidewalk bench and took a seat. He reached into the loaded cart and retrieved the phone, now powered on. As it rang in his hand, he almost dropped it, startled at the vibration it sent through his fingers.

"Yeah?"

"Hello, sir. I'm a representative of Senator Sid Taylor's office, and I have been asked to arrange a meeting with you to pick up the Senator's son's phone and offer you a handsome reward," the eager aid explained.

"Who are you again? You people are confusing me. First I talk with a man, then a woman, and now somebody else. Did you say you're from a Senator's office?" Jimmy wanted to know.

"Yes, sir. Senator Sid Taylor's office. I'm prepared to meet you within the hour to collect the phone and provide you with a substantial cash reward," the aide clarified.

"Forget it," Jimmy snorted into the phone. He powered down the phone and stuck it in his jacket pocket.

These people are so anxious to get this phone back, there's got to be something on it they're trying to hide. And somebody's a Senator? Think I'll keep it for a little while longer. Maybe they'll up the reward if I keep 'em hanging for a while longer.

Satisfied that he made a smart move, Jimmy pushed his squeaky cart down the street and around the corner. The hot meal and warm bed would have to wait a while.

CHAPTER 17

It seemed like hours since anyone had entered the white room.

Brent lay naked on the hard gurney, wondering if he would be tortured for some ungodly reason or if death would sneak up on him through starvation and neglect. Regardless, he believed that he would never leave the room alive. In between his irrational thoughts about death and escape, he prayed to the God he had neglected for so long.

He needed more H. He had to have some soon, or he would start chilling again and maybe lose control of his bowels. He had been allowed to use the bedpan once, but since then many hours had passed. He *thought* it was hours; surely it couldn't be days. Between the drug-induced sleep and no clock to gauge his captivity period, he had lost track of time.

Brent tried to get attention the only way he knew. "Hey! Hey! Somebody!" he bellowed in his still raspy voice.

This time, it took several minutes before he heard the familiar click of the door lock. The Doctor stepped into the room, wearing the same clothing and mask as before. He held a small dry erase board and marker in his gloved hands.

"Why don't you talk to me?" Brent said when he noticed the note board. "Just talk to me, man," Brent pleaded.

The Doctor stood close to the gurney, the tray of torture instruments still in Brent's direct line of vision. Glancing back and forth between the tray and the man, Brent started to hyperventilate.

The Doctor shook his head, as if to indicate he wasn't ready to use the scalpels yet.

"I need some more horse. Please. I'm getting jumpy. And I'm still hungry and thirsty. Will you at least feed me or put me back to sleep? If you're looking for money or information, I'll give you anything."

Looking into Brent's eyes, the Doctor merely shook his head again.

"Please, man! I'm dying here, I feel it," Brent cried.

Once again the Doctor shook his head, but began to write on the board with his left hand. When his message was complete, he held the board in front of him where Brent could read it.

NO MORE DRUGS

"No, man! You can't be serious! You can't do that to me!" Brent screamed, the veins on his temple pulsating with each word.

Ignoring the outburst, the Doctor turned and exited the room, leaving a desperate and sobbing Brent alone to face his personal demons.

* * *   * * *

Slick leaned back in his chair, waiting for Caroline's reaction to his first "ta-da" revelation gleaned from his intensive research. She merely stared at him as if to say, "And?"

"This is big, Caroline. The fact that DeLuca—The Viper, as he was later called—and Sid Taylor's father were law school buddies opens a big hole in the Senator's claim that he's never been affiliated with organized crime."

Caroline studied Slick's eager face. "Have you found that connection yet? A **valid** one involving Sid and not his father?" she asked.

"I think I might have. But you may not like what I have to tell you."

"Get on with it then," she directed as she settled back in her chair.

Slick silently reread the last notes he'd shared, then started summarizing the fresh information.

"Okay, where was I? DeLuca and W.H. Taylor became big buddies during and after law school. After they graduated, Vincenzo invited W. H. to join the DeLuca family business to become what the old crime families called their consigliere. Seems W. H. had been the valedictorian of the 1953 graduating class, which made Vincenzo feel a little less than adequate to fill that particular job for the family. Anyway, seems that Vincenzo was more inclined to participate more *actively* in the family business, if you know what I mean." Slick flipped to the next page in his notepad.

He took a sip of coffee and continued. "W. H. enjoyed his new job, was well respected, and got used to the big money. After several years, around the time Sid was in diapers, W. H. unexpectedly took an extended leave of absence. His wife, Gracie, had grown weary of her husband's constant and extended business absences from home. She demanded that W. H. get reacquainted with her and their son without business interference, and she insisted that the family take a month-long European cruise. He complied, hoping to be able to save his marriage as well as his job."

Caroline shifted in her seat. "This is all very interesting, Slick, but I don't see where you're going with this."

"Just gimme a minute. I'm getting there." He spit out his gum in a tissue as if to prepare for a special speech. "As I was saying, W. H., Gracie and young Sid took off on this cruise out of New York, heading for Italy. Guess who was also on the ship? The beautiful nineteen-year-old, Lucinda Bellini. She had immigrated to the U.S. the previous year and was returning to visit family in the old country.

"Unbeknownst to the Taylors, Vincenzo DeLuca had also booked passage on the same ship, expecting to surprise his buddy W. H. with enticing opportunities for entertainment and camaraderie during the long and boring journey across the sea. However, that particular surprise didn't go over so well with Gracie. W. H., feeling pressure to follow Gracie's wishes, avoided his friend as much as possible, causing Vincenzo to seek other companionship. That's when he met the unaccompanied Lucinda on the ship's deck and the rest, as they say, is history."

"What a beautiful romance." Caroline clapped unenthusiastically. "Slick, I've got a lot on my calendar today, so could you move this along? I know there's a point to this story somewhere," she urged.

"Right. Well, when the boat arrived in Italy, Lucinda invited Vincenzo to the Bellini manor, which was a big estate in the middle of the Sicilian wine country. Joining them for a few days were the Taylors. One big happy family, you might say. But, here's the kicker. The Bellini family was heavy into organized crime back then. They made the New York DeLuca family look like little league. It's not clear if Lucinda was fully aware of how the family made their fortune, but my guess is she was tuned in. So, when the romance sprang between Vincenzo and Lucinda, so did the beginning of an expanded and more powerful DeLuca family presence in New York. Once they married a year later, it was a done deal.

"Now, enter W. H. Taylor again. His role as consigliere for the DeLucas now included a broader band of responsibility. The Bellinis were interacting with him, too, giving him orders discreetly from the background.   W. H. had become a powerful man—extremely powerful man—almost overnight. But so did Vincenzo.

"The DeLucas prospered in a variety of businesses, some unsavory, and their fortunes grew.   It was a good arrangement, and the Bellinis lended support and strength in whatever forms were necessary for the New York family partnership to thrive. And it did. The Taylors continued to reap big benefits for years.

"Vincenzo and W.H. maintained their working relationship until 1988 when W. H. decided to retire. He had lung issues from all those years of smoking, and his ticker wasn't as strong as it was supposed to be for his age. Gracie convinced him that it was time for him to enjoy what years they had left together.

"Now this is interesting, too. Young Sid Taylor met his future bride at the DeLuca home where she'd been staying during the summer of 1985. Val Bellini was barely twenty years old when she met Sid, who was eight years her senior. He had already graduated from law school, same alma mater as dear old dad, and was looking to settle down. He pursued her, and they were soon engaged. They married in 1990."

Caroline yawned. "Slick, you're boring me to tears. I'm going to fall asleep in my chair if you don't hurry up and get to the point," she chided.

"Fine.   Bottom line.   When Sid Taylor visited Val at the DeLuca estate back then, Vincenzo—The Viper—was the official head of the DeLuca crime family. Full throttle. I found

Sid's name on some old DeLuca business documents that appear a little shady. He signed off as the Registered Agent for some shell companies that have already been proven to be a part of the old DeLuca holdings. I believe Lucinda and Val both have knowledge of criminal activities, illegal business dealings, and so many other bad things that would make your head spin. And to top it off, I have a lead on some current DeLuca Enterprises business dealings that involve criminal actions that may or may not have been conducted or approved by any or all of the surviving Giordano family members—and maybe even Val and Sid." He snapped his black notebook shut.

Caroline's eyes widened as big as saucers. "You definitely have my attention now. Good grief, Slick. You nearly put me to sleep with all this interwoven family history, and then you pulled off a slam dunk! You just accused my best friend, her mother, her cousin, her children and a U.S. Senator of alleged criminal misconduct! Can you back any of this up with documentation?" she asked anxiously.

"Just gimme a little more time, Caroline. I don't think it'll take me very long from here." He started to rise from his chair, but sat back down unexpectedly. "Could I ask you something that you might find a little off subject?"

She nodded her agreement. "Sure."

"Do you believe in psychic premonitions?"

CHAPTER 18

The loud disco music was reverberating throughout the small room. The lights had been turned off, and darkness surrounded him. He whimpered, he cried, he prayed aloud, he cursed, and he shivered, all in vain. There was no one to hear him. Even if someone had been in close proximity, his raspy whispers would never be heard over the blare of the incessant song—the same one that had played over and over without stopping for hours.

When he thought he couldn't take it anymore, he screamed the guttural sound of a wounded animal trapped in a snare. He was so weak he hardly had the strength to move now, but screaming didn't take much effort. It was the only form of communication he had left. Maybe God would hear him and have mercy. Maybe he would die right then and there.

But he didn't. There was no mercy, unless you could count the lack of physical torture that he knew he would eventually endure.

When the overhead light snapped on, the music abruptly stopped. Turning his head to give full attention to his captor, he realized in horror that the Doctor was not visiting him. The Dominator sauntered into the room, sticking out his chest to display his muscular build and his control.

Brent lost control of his bladder as he continued to whimper. "Oh, no. Oh, God no," he sniveled.

But the Dominator didn't move from the center of the room. He peered at Brent curiously with his solid red eyes. He laughed, and spoke muffled words from behind the leather head piece. "I'll give you what you want, Brentie boy, if you give me what I want first." In his hand he held a hypodermic needle with a yellow-tinged juice oozing from the tip of the sharp point. He gently squeezed the plunger of the syringe causing a drop of the precious drug to ooze from the needle point. "Don't make me waste this."

Closing his eyes tightly, tears rolled down the side of his face into his ears. Brent pitifully cried. "I ... I ...want it," he stuttered between sobs.

"That's a good boy. I'm going to lay this syringe on the sink. Then I'm going to release you from the table, but don't try to move too fast. Sit up slowly. You may not be able to stand on your own for a little while."

Brent nodded, choking back terror and trying to think only of the euphoria he would once again feel after he was given a conciliatory liquid dosage of "devil's powder."

He had personally never injected himself with liquid heroin before, always snorting the powder form instead; but, he knew how quickly such a serum would send him off into ecstasy. He believed the liquid version of H was what the Doctor had given him the day before. If it was, he liked the injections better. They worked faster. If he ever got out of that room, he'd never snort again. If he had to, he'd smoke it. But, no more snorting.

As he tried to sit, his head spun. He couldn't use his arms to brace himself because he was still shackled. The Dominator helped him sit upright.

"Now slowly swing your feet over to the side of the table."

Brent did as he was instructed and swiveled himself to the side of the gurney.

"Excellent, Brentie. Now, I'm going to move that chair over there by the sink to a spot in the middle of the room. You stay put. You don't want to hurt yourself," the Dominator said with fake concern.

The blanket that had been used to cover Brent was still heaped on the chair. The Dominator spread it across the floor in the center of the room, reminiscent of a picnic tablecloth. Then he moved the straight backed chair to the center of the blanket, facing the door. Once satisfied with the arrangement, the Dominator returned to Brent's side and took him by the arm.

"Easy does it, Brentie. Let's get you into that chair." Brent shuffled on his weak legs but managed to make it to the chair. He sat down, relieved to be off of his rubbery legs.

The Dominator stood in front of him, unzipping the fly of his leather suit. "Now before I tell you what to do to me, let me see what you've got. I expect you to get hard within the next minute. Show me." The Dominator moved backwards a step.

The nude and flaccid Brent didn't move a muscle.

"If you don't get hard within sixty seconds, you don't get your medicine. You'd better start thinking of something that'll get you going, or I'll strap you back on that table and turn the music up so loud your eardrums will burst."

A tear ran down Brent's face. He flinched when he thought the Dominator was about to step toward him. Immediately, his shackled right hand reached for his member. With eyes closed and jaws clenched, Brent became rigid in less than thirty seconds. He was thinking of the first time he snorted his beloved heroin.

"That's more like it, little man. Nice." With leather clad gloves, the Dominator reached over and rubbed Brent's head.

Brent looked up into the red eyes of his captor, and immediately thought of the devil. "Can I have my medicine now?" he asked meekly.

Laughing, the Dominator shook his head. "You haven't worked hard enough for it yet." He reached inside his zipper and freed his penis. "This needs some attention," he commanded as he straddled Brent's chair. Immediately, Brent opened his mouth and accepted the offering.

When the Dominator was about to reach a climax, he pulled away. "Stop, now!" he shouted. Brent flinched again.

"Get up and stand behind the chair. NOW!"

Brent stood slowly, using the back of the chair as support as he cautiously shuffled into position.

"Now bend across the top of the chair back. Bend down as far as you can get," ordered the Dominator.

Again, Brent did as he was told. He watched the Dominator go to the sink, hopeful that he was retrieving the syringe. That was not the case. He reached under the sink and pulled out the cat o' nine tails. Slapping the stiff leather fringe across his thigh, he walked slowly toward his victim.

"Let's see how much pain you can tolerate," the leather-clad man barked as he thrashed Brent's buttocks with the whip. After three lashes, he stopped.

"How was that?" he laughed.

Brent openly cried. "Please stop. Please. I beg you, please stop!"

"Once I'm finished, I'll stop. Until then, you do as you're told."

Leaning across the chair, Brent was choking on spit and snot. His eyes were bloodshot and swollen from his constant crying. His buttocks felt as if they had been seared with hot coals. Brent was ready to die.

He turned his head enough to glimpse the syringe laying on the sink's vanity. He licked his lips involuntarily and thought of the euphoria he would feel when the substance coursed through his veins. Surely he could hold on for a little while longer.

When he felt the Dominator push his rigid member against his skin, he knew what would happen next. He lowered his head and braced for what was sure to be excruciating pain.

But he found the experience surprisingly easy to endure. In fact, he found it pleasurable, as his facial expression reflected.

When it was over, the Dominator directed Brent to get back on the gurney to be strapped in. Brent complied like a trained puppy.

Once the young man was securely on the gurney, the Dominator quickly left the room.

"Wait! Wait! My medicine!" Brent screamed. His eyes were wild with terror.

When the Doctor entered the room, he held a peeled banana, a juice box, and a tissue. When Brent calmed down, he was fed the banana and allowed to sip the mixed berry flavored liquid. The Doctor wiped Brent's mouth with the tissue, nodding his approval.

Only then did Brent get his medicine: heroin laced with a healthy amount of fentanyl.

* * * * * *

"Did you get all that on film?" the Dominator asked the Doctor when they were once again in private.

"Every second, including the kid's quick erection. Do you know what the boss wants us to do with the video?" the Doctor inquired.

Without hesitation, the Dominator answered. "Said before doing anything, make sure your IP address couldn't be traced. Route it through some foreign cities or something. When you're positive it's masked, send it to the cell phones and emails of his parents, the father's Washington Senate office, and get it out on social media. Make sure it hits the desks at major newspapers in Washington, Virginia, Maryland, New Jersey and New York. Hell, send it to the Taylor kid's cell phone number, too."

"Got it. The kid should be sleeping for quite a while. When he wakes up, he's going to be hooked like never before. This kid's on Cloud Nine right now. The fentanyl additive is tricky, though. We have to be careful not to let him OD."

"Yeah, the fentanyl was a nice touch. Thanks for getting it," the Dominator commented as pulled the leather headpiece from his head. "God, that thing's hot, but I kinda like it."

The Dominator left the control room, eager to personally describe every detail of the past hour to the boss. He wanted to gloat about how easy the conquest had been.

CHAPTER 19

When the aide called Sid at his home office, the senator was shocked by what he was told.

"The gentleman who found your son's phone hung up on me before I could arrange to deliver him the cash and get the phone back. How would you like me to proceed, sir?"

Sid didn't have any idea what the aide was talking about and told him as much. "I didn't know about this. Who told you to contact a man about my son's phone?"

The aide hesitated. "Mrs. Taylor called today and asked me to reward a local gentleman who had found your son's phone. I took money from the office petty cash and called your son's number to arrange for the exchange."

Sid was livid. He had planned to handle the matter himself, and he certainly hadn't wanted to involve his D.C. office staff in his son's irresponsible life issues.

"Well, thank you for trying," Sid replied politely as he rushed to end the call.

"You're welcome, sir. Would you like me to try again while I still have the $1,200 signed out?"

"No need. I'll handle it from here. If my wife calls you back, just refer her to me. And, go ahead and put the money back in petty cash," the Senator directed.

When the call was completed, Sid stomped around his desk and darted from his private office into the home's main hallway. "Val!" he screamed as he wandered aimlessly through the sizeable house. "Val! Get in here! Where the hell are you?"

A member of the household staff heard Sid's bellows as he entered the wood paneled library. The room doubled as a music room, and the startled maid was dusting the grand piano that had been in the Bellini family since the 1950s. In a nervous voice, the young woman informed Sid that Mrs. Taylor had called for the driver to take her shopping several hours before.

The furious man stomped his foot as he spat out "Damn her! That witch!"

Clearly flustered, the maid stood frozen, wondering if she had inadvertently revealed something she shouldn't have. On more than a few occasions, she had overheard Mrs. Taylor scream at the senior household staff for insignificant actions that …to a more understanding employer… would have been considered unworthy of mention. More often than not, Mrs. Taylor's unpredictable rants were totally unjustified.

In fear of losing her job when Mrs. Taylor returned, the maid dropped her head and silently prayed. She asked for mercy from the woman whose husband (and most of the staff) so aptly referred to as a 'witch.'

* * ***

Meanwhile, an optimistic Jimmy roamed the streets of Georgetown, whistling a happy tune and smiling at everyone he passed. He had less than $10 in his pocket which had to last him until some generous soul took pity on him and handed out some loose change or maybe a dollar bill.

He realized he might have to use all his meager funds to make a small investment. Otherwise, the prized phone would be of no use to him. He desperately needed a charger for the near-dead device.

Weighing his limited options, he concluded he didn't have enough money for the kind of charger this fancy cell phone would require. Instead, maybe he could try his luck at the bar where he usually got the best 'donations': Disc♂Dudes. The bartender there had been nice to him before, and maybe he had a charger that would work on the fancy phone.

It would be a win-win for Jimmy if he was able to get a drink while he waited for the cell phone to charge up.   If he had to spend his last few dollars on anything, he'd prefer to buy a stiff drink to help him stay positive through the rest of the day.

* * * * *

When Jimmy knocked on the locked front door of Disc♂Dudes, he realized he had arrived a couple of hours before the lounge officially opened for the day. "Hey, anybody there?" he shouted and knocked harder, hoping the bartender was already inside getting the bar set up. "Hey!" he kept yelling. Passersby were glaring at him as he persistently banged on the unanswered door.

Eventually the door cracked open, revealing the bartender peeking out under the chain lock which prevented it from fully opening. "What is it, Jimmy? You know we're not open yet."

"Hey, I gotta get a phone charged up.   It's kinda an emergency. Thought maybe you could help me out," Jimmy said, showing his dark yellow teeth as he grinned hopefully.

"Whose phone is it, Jimmy?" the suspicious bartender asked.

Without hesitation, Jimmy provided his modified version of the true story. "I found it near the alley. It was already low on power, but it was still working. Somebody called the phone and said they'd give me a reward if I'd give it back. Problem is, they're supposed to call me and tell me where to meet them, but the phone's dying." He pulled the phone from his pocket and looked down at its black screen. "Oh, no! It's already dead! I can't return it if I can't answer it!"

Seeing the phone in Jimmy's hand, the bartender considered the request. Believing the story, he unchained the door and opened it wide. "Come on in, Jimmy. My charger works with that phone. But you gotta sit your ass down and don't bother me while it's charging. I got work to do."

Relieved, Jimmy answered. "Hey, no problem. You won't hear a peep outta me. Especially if you would maybe give me a little something to keep me occupied, like a drink on the house?" Jimmy smiled coyly and winked.

"You can have one beer—on the house—but after that one's gone, no more. Understand?" the bartender firmly told him.

"Got it. You're a good man, hoss." Jimmy answered, causing the bartender to raise his eyebrows in response.   "Sorry, man. I just don't know what to call you," Jimmy explained.

"Just call me 'Bartender.' I try not to share *everything* with the customers," he replied as he slid a cold mug of beer toward the grateful homeless man.

"Okay, Bartender. Whatever you say.   Cheers!" Jimmy toasted as he lapped up the rising foam cresting around the mug's rim.

* * * * * *

After Rick abruptly ended their early morning call, Carmen thought briefly of trying to entice Teddy into her web. However, her research on the DeLuca Enterprises executive officers led her to believe that Teddy seemed the least likely candidate who would take the bait. He seemed too wishy-washy and appeared to have underlying feelings for Sophia which, if true, would complicate the entire situation even further. Thus, Carmen decided to contact Rick once more. This time, she would lure him to meet with her on the pretense of revealing information she had obtained which could negatively impact DeLuca Enterprises.

Hesitantly, Rick agreed to secretly meet Carmen that afternoon in a small chain restaurant located on the outskirts of Hicksville. The chosen location was far enough away from their respective homes and businesses that there was little concern of discovery by family members or known associates.

Carmen waited down the street until she saw Rick's car pass and pull into the restaurant's parking lot. She allowed him enough time to find a table and order coffee before she made her grand entrance. She wore her sexiest business attire and carried a Gucci briefcase, trying to display her feminism while projecting a hint of seriousness.

When Carmen entered the restaurant, Rick stood. Clearly pleased with what he saw, Rick smiled broadly and extended his hand when she neared his table. Like the gentleman he was, he pulled the chair out for her and gently pushed it forward until she was firmly seated.

He sat next to her instead of across from her, which gave the impression of something more intimate than a routine business lunch. *Seeing how alluring she is, I wonder why I dismissed her so easily when she called the first time,* Rick wondered.

Carmen smiled shyly, as she surmised what Rick was thinking. Instinctively, she leaned forward just enough to reveal her cleavage—a premeditated move she had carefully planned when she chose that particular silk blouse to wear to meet Rick.

"So, shall we begin?" she asked the obviously intrigued Rick.

"Why don't we get you some coffee or something else to drink first? What would you like?"

"This will be fine," she stated as she reached for the glass of iced water that had already been waiting for her on the table.

"All right. Can I interest you in some food?" Rick asked, apparently trying to extend the brief meeting time they had scheduled.

"No, thank you. I think you'll want to hear what I'm about to tell you, so I'll get to the point." She took another sip of water and set the glass down on the table before looking into Rick's admiring eyes.

* * * * * *

The Bartender had fallen back on his word. He had repeatedly filled Jimmy's beer mug with complimentary brew during the two hours he allowed the cell phone to charge. They didn't speak; he just kept refilling the poor man's mug. Jimmy did his best to stay quiet in hopes the beer would keep coming.

By now, Jimmy had consumed enough beer to move away from the bar to a more comfortable booth where his relaxed body could semi-recline. The Bartender glanced at Jimmy occasionally, watching him close his eyes and then jar himself awake to take another swig of beer.   Finally, Jimmy leaned his head against the wall and snored lightly with his mouth open. The Bartender laughed to himself at the sad spectacle.

When the phone was fully charged, the Bartender disconnected the cord and powered up the phone. Immediately displayed on the bright screen was a message and attachment from an unknown source. With no pass code required to open the phone, the Bartender clicked on the message and opened the attached file.

His eyes widened as he muttered, "Oh, my GOD! That's Mr. T!" Heart pounding and thoughts bouncing erratically, the Bartender nervously forwarded the scandalous movie to his own cell phone, saving it as "Mr. T." Then he impulsively deleted the movie from Jimmy's phone. He wasn't certain why he did it, but he didn't want the movie on the streets for just anyone to see. He didn't want to delete it, either.

"Jimmy!" he bellowed, rousing the napping man in the booth.

"Yeah!" a startled Jimmy replied.

"Phone's ready."

Jimmy moved slowly out of the booth, stretching as if he had just awakened from the best sleep he'd had in days.

"Thanks, Bartender," Jimmy said as he reached across the bar for the phone. "And thanks for the sustenance," he chuckled.

"Hope that holds you for a while," the Bartender said as he followed Jimmy to the locked door to let him out.

Jimmy waved and left the entry. As he walked away, the Bartender could hear the phone ringing in Jimmy's hand.

CHAPTER 20

No one had disturbed Brent for several hours, and it was past time for more medicine. He had been forced to repeatedly urinate without the bedpan, and now he needed to have a bowel movement. He could tell it was going to be runny—all he'd had to eat was a banana, but he'd had plenty of juice to drink during his captivity.

It was bad enough having to lie in piss, but he had struggled to control his diarrhea for as long as he could. The stomach cramps were getting bad, and he didn't know how much longer he could hold it in.

"HELP! Somebody help me!" he yelled at the metal door. "PLEASE HELP!"

When the metal door opened, Brent was relieved to see the Doctor enter. "Thank God, it's you. I gotta take a shit real bad." Brent exclaimed.

Without breaking his stride, the Doctor retrieved the bedpan. Brent raised his hips as far up as he could to allow the bedpan to slide under him.

"Thank you, man. I was getting desperate," he said as his bowels released, no longer embarrassed to use the bathroom in front of the Doctor.

When he finished, the Doctor removed the bedpan and turned to exit the room.

"Hey! Hey! What about my shot? Can I have my shot now?"

The Doctor shook his head as he walked to the door.

"Can't you at least wipe this shit off my ass, man?" Brent whimpered.

In keeping with his habit of not talking, the Doctor ignored the captive and left the room to empty the bedpan.

"Somebody help me, please," Brent cried hysterically as he was left alone with his suffering.

* * * * * *

Jimmy answered the phone on the first ring, now more inclined to talk to the people who would be paying him handsomely for the phone he found. This time, it was going to cost a lot more than $1,200.

"Who is this," Sid asked.

"It's Jimmy. I'm tired of playing games with all you different people. I just want to talk to one person from now on."

"You can talk to me from here forward. I'm your only contact. You talked to me first anyway, remember?" Sid reminded him.

"Yeah, I remember. Now listen, I understand this phone is valuable, and it's worth more than $1,200. I was thinking more like $2,000 for this 'particular model.' Does that sound reasonable to you, mister?" Jimmy fished.

"No, it does not. But considering how much trouble it's been to get it back, I'll make an exception. I'm willing to pay you $2,000 but not a cent more. No more discussion. No more deals."

"Sounds okay to me, mister. And I want it in small bills. No 50's or 100's. Now where can I get the money?" Jimmy smiled contently as he made his demands.

"Small bills, it is. Where can my representative find you?" Sid asked.

"I thought this was between you and me?" Jimmy questioned.

"Today, I can't get there myself, but I have a reliable person who can do this for me. Now where and when?" Sid asked impatiently.

"Don't lose your cool, mister. We got a deal, remember? I'll be standing on the corner of 34th and Prospect in two hours. Your person will know me by my shopping cart that has an American flag attached to the front."

Sid grimaced as he pictured what the exchange would look like to a passerby. "Got it. Don't be late. My man will be driving a black SUV. He'll pull over, and you go up to the passenger side window. You can make the exchange then."

"Small bills, remember?" Jimmy reminded him.

"For Christ's sake, yes. I remember," Sid said as he hung up without another word.

Immediately, Sid called his contact in Washington to explain what he needed done.   When everything was agreed upon, Sid hung up and shook his head.

Damn imbecile. I can't believe that kid is mine.

* * * * * *

When Val finally returned home, she was met at the door by a fuming Sid.

"What's got your dander up," she nonchalantly remarked as she passed him at the foyer.

"You have, Val. As usual. What the hell were you thinking calling my D.C. office about Brent's phone? You know damned good and well that we don't get my office staff mixed up in our personal business, especially when it comes to Brent's affairs."

Sid was angrier than she had seen him lately. "I didn't think it was anything to worry about. Brent simply dropped his phone somewhere, I presumed. Calling one of your errand boys in Washington was the quickest and easiest way to get it back to him." She put her shopping bags down on the foyer table, dismissing Sid's concerns.

"Asking an official aide to take $1,200 out of my office petty cash fund for a personal errand is not something that can be easily explained away. You were out of line, Val." Sid's face was red with fury.

"Well, I'm sorry. I wasn't thinking," she said softly as she unloaded the day's purchases from the heavy shopping bags.

"Of course you weren't thinking. You never do. I've told you a million times, Val. Do NOT consider my Washington office staff as your personal shoppers, messengers, or errand runners. That is NOT part of the deal!"

"Sid, what else do you want me to say? I told you I'm sorry. It won't happen again."

"Damn right, it won't. I'm informing my staff not to take calls from you unless you are asking to speak to me. Do you understand, Val?"

"Yes, dear," she murmured, acting as though the words didn't bite her. She turned to walk away when both her cell phone and Sid's chirped loudly to announce an incoming message.

Finding the simultaneous message alert to be strangely coincidental, they both stopped and retrieved their cell phones. Before Val could view the message, Sid's red face turned stark white. "Jesus Christ," he mumbled with eyes wide and mouth open.

Puzzled, Val managed to open her phone to the message she had received. She audibly gasped as the explicit images displayed clearly on her phone screen. "Oh, my God!" she exclaimed and dropped her phone on the floor.

"What now, Sid? What are we going to do now?" Val moaned as she slowly eased herself into the chair near the stairway.

"Let's go see if there's anything on television about this," Sid said cautiously, praying that the worst had not yet happened. *This is going to cause a media shit storm if it gets out,* he thought.

Her thoughts followed a different path.

* * * * * *

Rick had listened to Carmen's summary of concerns for a few minutes, then called the waitress over and ordered a beer. If the establishment had sold hard liquor, he would have ordered a double of their strongest whiskey.

"Are you absolutely certain, Carmen?" he asked, bewildered that he had not already been made aware of what she had told him.

"Positive," she said. "His name is Raymond Silvio. He does work for several high-profile attorneys around the area, but he's also been working for years for your Aunt Caroline. He's looking into DeLuca Enterprises right now, and I can only suspect it's at her direction."

"But why? And I don't get how you would know about this." Rick was perplexed at the entire revelation.

In an attempt to convincingly modify her background story, Carmen stuck as closely to the truth as she could without blatantly lying. "As I said before, our import/export business—the fine art segment—is trying to work out a business arrangement with DeLuca Enterprises. When we consider potential new partners, we try to do as much research as possible before we commit to a contractual arrangement. It's routine. But when I went to the courthouse to ask for some papers on your business history, the files I wanted to review were checked out. The person looking through those files was sitting at a table on the other side of the room. The clerk told me Mr. Silvio would be finished with them shortly if I wanted to wait. I said I would come back later, but before I left I got a good look at the man. Mr. Silvio has a web page, which I checked as soon as I got back to my office. I recognized him by his picture. After a little more snooping, I found out the rest." She drank more water as Rick downed his beer.

"So how do you know Aunt Caroline sent him?"

Carmen smiled. "I don't, not for certain. But logically, she's family. Mr. Silvio does a lot of work for her—she's his primary customer. I just thought you ought to know. It might mean something and then again, it may be nothing at all. Could be just a check to ensure all the DeLuca Enterprises filings are up to date. Who knows? But I still think it's something you should check out discreetly, especially if you weren't aware of his probing into your companies' files. One never knows what others' motives might be. This could be something you could head off, provided of course there *is* something that needs to be addressed." Carmen sighed and smiled sweetly.

"You're absolutely right, and I can't begin to tell you how much your candor means to me. Of course, there's nothing to be concerned about—we're above board, and have been for many years. Sophia can attest to that. Still it does sound peculiar that Aunt Caroline might be covertly checking on something that she could approach any of us directly to find out."

Carmen nodded her head. "Well, that's all I have for now. I suppose I should be taking off," she said as she gathered her briefcase and started to rise from the table.

"Maybe we could get a drink sometime?" Rick asked slyly.

Without batting an eye, Carmen reached over and patted Rick on the shoulder, giving it a little squeeze before removing her hand. "I'd really like that, Rick. I'd like that very much," she responded.

She turned, giving him full view of her tight-fitting skirt and stiletto heels as she gracefully moved to the exit. Before she opened the door, she looked back over her shoulder at the gawking Rick. She flipped her long hair and winked provocatively as she excitedly left the building.

CHAPTER 21

Thomas had followed the instructions carefully and asked Maureen for time off while Lucinda and Juliana were still traveling. He was counting on Maureen to be so flustered from the scandalous events that she would approve his impromptu leave without thinking twice.

He realized his sudden absence from the DeLuca mansion might prompt speculation about his involvement in Sophia's assault, but he was prepared to explain himself when he returned.

He had been ordered to leave immediately for a two-week, all expenses paid vacation. He was supposed to be visiting family in Colorado, but in reality he had been sent to Boston. He didn't know a soul in Massachusetts. That had been the plan all along.

After a couple of days, Boston sightseeing was no longer appealing. He had explored every spot he'd ever thought about visiting there—even the Cheers bar, which disappointed him greatly. He should have insisted on a different city to be pent up in. After all, historical monuments and ships just didn't do it for him. He'd seen enough of that in New York.

All that currently held his interest was television, and that was boring, too. How many reruns of *Bonanza* and *CSI New York* could one man take?

He was thinking about contacting his benefactor to insist on a change of locale. Money wasn't an object, or so he'd been told. His bank account balance had been augmented with a hefty $50,000 deposit. All he had to do was get out of town and stick to the story when he returned to New York.

He always wanted to go to Florida. *Why didn't I ask to be sent to Miami in the first place? I think I'll call her. What can she say but 'no?'*

* * * * * *

Brent was in agony. His withdrawal symptoms were getting worse, and the pain he was feeling was overwhelming. He was cold, nauseous, and cramping. His legs and arms were visibly shaking, controlled only as much as the straps across his body would allow. As he had on several occasions while being held captive, he thought he was about to die. He wished he would.

When the metal door opened once again, Brent hardly noticed. He was less alert to his surroundings now. The Doctor slowly approached the gurney and looked with concern at the suffering young man. Sympathy for Brent showed in his eyes above his always present surgical mask.

To gauge Brent's responsiveness, the Doctor reached for a scalpel on the nearby tray. He held it up above Brent's face. Brent didn't bat an eye. Instead of a fresh wave of terror on his face, Brent's expression remained unchanged from the unfocused stare he had maintained since the Doctor entered the room.

Laying the scalpel back down on the tray, the Doctor turned and stepped in front of the mirror over the sink. He signaled for more medicine through the two-way mirror over the small vanity. Seconds later, the door cracked open and a hand was extended through the open slot. Handing off a fresh hypodermic needle to the doctor, the hand withdrew and the door was shut again.

"Here you go, son," the Doctor said in a low voice, uttering his first audible words to Brent. He injected Brent with the same heroin/fentanyl mixture as he had before.

He watched Brent's body react to the soothing drug, and patted him on the shoulder. The Doctor gently placed the blanket over the young man's nude, restrained body. Before he exited, he made one more statement in a soft comforting voice. He hoped Brent understood him when he told him, "It won't be long now, son. You'll be out of here soon."

* * * * * *

Sid was inconsolable. Val paced in front of him as he sat on his leather couch in front of the television in the room he used as a home office.

Head in hands, he moaned and breathed rapidly. "How could he do this to me? How could he let something so grotesque be filmed when he knew it could be leaked to the press?"

Val looked at her husband with disdain. "Do this to YOU? What about me? I'll be the laughing stock of all my friends. We're going to be freaks of society now! I won't be able to show my face in public for months! You aren't the only one who will suffer because of his indiscretions!"

Sid sneered at his haughty wife. "If you hadn't babied him all these years, encouraging him to be 'himself' when I tried to get him into sports and manly activities, maybe he'd have become the man I wanted him to be! You're the one to blame. 'Sensitive child,' my ass!"

"Shut the fuck up, Sid! I only wanted him to be happy. YOU are the one who never even tried to understand him!" Val was crying now. Feeling defeated, she sat on the couch next to her husband who immediately stood up and took her place pacing the floor.

They simultaneously glanced up at the local news and saw the channel was replaying the images of their only son and his sex partner. Thankfully, the intimate parts of the encounter had been censored, but it was unmistakable what was happening between the young man and the man dressed as a sexual dominator. What made it worse was the shot where Brent looked directly at the camera and licked his lips. He appeared to be a voluntary participant, and was obviously enjoying himself.

Suddenly, as if to erase the film from his mind, Sid changed the channel to the national news network. What the distressed parents saw was more of the same, but this time the video was labeled as *Breaking National News*.

"Oh, God! It's gone national!" Sid exclaimed. Val hung her head and continued to weep.

Sid raised his chin and yelled at the ceiling, arms held straight out and palms opened upward. "Jesus! Could this be any more humiliating?" He paced a few more steps and stopped in front of Val.

"You realize I may lose the reelection because of this, don't you? YOUR son has just ruined our lives!"

Val looked stunned. "No, why should **this** cause you to lose? You've already fucked everything up yourself, going on about legalizing marijuana and passing out drunk at your own fundraiser. You can't blame **your** career-ending mistakes on Brent!"

For the first time in his life, Sid wanted to strike Val. He had never raised a hand to her or Brent and never wanted to. But right now, she was pushing every button he had. He restrained himself and instead, left the room hastily.

If I get arrested for domestic abuse, my reelection is doomed for sure.

* * * * * *

Carmen called Adam as soon as she left the restaurant meeting with Rick.

"I think I hooked Rick," she said gleefully.

Adam remained silent for too long. "Adam, are you there?" she asked.

"Yeah. Carmen. I don't know about this. We may be going about it all wrong. Come back to the office, and let's discuss an alternate approach. There's got to be another way."

"What's changed, Adam? You can't be serious," a surprised Carmen responded.

"Let's talk about it when you get here," he suggested, not wanting to reveal his thoughts on an unsecured cell phone line. He hung up, not allowing her to say anything more until they could talk privately one-on-one.

It took about an hour for Carmen to drive the distance between the restaurant and the Import/Export office. Carmen made a beeline to Adam's office to find him staring out the window, apparently daydreaming.

"What's happened, Adam? Is our cover blown?" Carmen immediately asked.

"No, nothing like that, Carmen. Sit down," he commanded his partner as he turned from the window.

"This better be good, Adam. If you think we have to change our tactics, something big better be driving that decision," she warned.

"It's big as far as I'm concerned," he said. "You won't like it, I'm afraid."

She stared at Adam, waiting for an explanation. He took his time trying to find the right words to express his feelings.

"I don't believe Sophia Giordano is guilty of anything. I've gotten to know her, and frankly …. "

"Oh shit! No, Adam! You can't be serious about this! Don't tell me you've fallen for her! That will ruin everything!" Carmen exclaimed.

"Wait…Carmen. It's not like that. She's not like that."

"Please tell me you haven't …oh, no! You have! I can tell by the look on your face! You've actually taken her to bed! Oh Adam! How could you? You know the first rule is never get intimately involved with a target!" Carmen stood up and walked to where Adam stood by his desk.   "We're compromised!"

"No, we're not. All we have to do is call off our engagement. No one will be the wiser. Anyway, if you've 'hooked' Rick like you said on the phone, I can only imagine what your next step would have been."

"I wouldn't have gone that far and you know it. It would have just been a tease until I got the answers I needed. But you! You crossed the line." Carmen looked like a pouting child who had been forced give up her favorite toy.

"Just work with me on this, Carmen. No one has to know, and I can deal with Sophia. I promise if I discover anything at all that makes me change my mind about her, you'll be the first to know. I promise. You can still work on Rick, too. But we have to come up with a convincing story about our mutual decision to break our engagement. If we're going to keep moving forward on this, we have to be in sync."

Reluctantly, Carmen nodded. "All right, Adam. But don't get crazy on me. You've got to swear you'll keep me updated—even on your intimacies with Sophia—or this whole project will backfire. Deal?"

Adam grinned broadly, relieved that his confession had gone over positively. "Deal," he happily responded.

* * *   * * *

Sid's contact in Washington had retrieved Brent's phone from Jimmy without complications. Jimmy was happy with the big wad of twenties and was last seen heading toward the closest bar.

As instructed, Sid's contact headed straight to a FedEx office to overnight the recovered cell phone, forwarding it straight to Sid's home address in New York.

The Bartender had sold the Mr. T. sex video to the national news network based out of New York. He was expecting a $25,000 check to be overnighted to his apartment address, and twenty-four hours later he planned to be drinking Mojitos in Jamaica.

All was well in Georgetown.

New York, however, was a different story.

* * *   * * *

After a few thousand dollars were wired to his man in D.C., Sid felt relieved that the phone issue was behind him. He only hoped that his contact's boss didn't ask for any return favors in the near future. His career path was shaky enough as it was.

Over the years, the senator had attempted to minimize his communications with the Bellini crime family, only reaching out to them when it was a bona fide emergency. This cell phone issue was such an emergency, or so he thought. But, whatever was on that phone couldn't be any worse than the disgusting video that was leaked to the public. He couldn't take the risk, though, and acted as promptly as he could to recover the phone.

Sid kept telling himself that he had to reach out to the 'family' for Val's sake; but, he knew deep down he primarily wanted to hide his son's lifestyle from his constituency. Too much effort and money had already been spent over the years trying to do just that. Until now, the secret had stayed buried.

Sid had always maintained a neutral political stance when it came to issues like drugs and gay rights. He avoided the subjects when he could, and tried instead to change the hot topics to equal rights or something more along those lines. Apparently, his strategy had been successful as evidenced by the long tenure in office he had enjoyed to date.

Sid had sufficient charisma to outshine anyone foolish enough to run against him in the past. Now that he was aging—not to mention faltering too often and drinking too heavily—it wouldn't be unrealistic to see someone more vital and progressive trying to unseat him from his Senatorial throne. He'd do some damage control and shake a few more hands. Reelection was old hat to him, a seasoned veteran of the campaign trail. He knew how to sway the fence riders and motivate the voters. But, all that would have to wait.

Now he needed to find Brent and ensure nothing else so disturbing surfaced in the media while his reelection was ongoing. Once he officially retained his Senate seat, Brent could do whatever the hell he wanted afterwards. Sid planned to retire at the end of his next term, taking full advantage of the government pension and all the lucrative investments he had been privy to through insider information. Illegal? Yes. Was he worried about it? No.

He chuckled to himself, thinking about how he wasn't the only one who had dipped into the forbidden insider investment pot. If he ever went down for that particular sin, he'd be taking so many other elected officials with him that they could run the country from prison! *Nope. Never gonna happen,* he thought confidently.

Twin Sins

CHAPTER 22

Caroline's office door opened, and she was shocked to see Rick Giordano standing in the doorway.

"Aunt Caroline, am I interrupting anything?" he asked timidly.

"No, Rick! How good to see you!" she said happily as she rose from her desk and went straight to him. A quick hug and a kiss on the cheek displayed her delight at the pleasant surprise.

"Please come in. Tell me, how is Sophia doing?"

Rick responded by shrugging his broad shoulders. "You know how she is. She's acting like it never happened. She's all business and won't accept any pity. She's too strong for her own good, I think. She always has been, though. Shouldn't surprise any of us."

"Good, I suppose. The last thing she should do is give in to self-pity. I think she's taking the right approach, considering who we're talking about. You Giordanos are made of tough stuff," she answered and smiled.

"True enough." Rick paused before he started the conversation he had rehearsed on the drive to the law office. "Aunt Caroline, have you hired a private investigator?" he asked bluntly.

"I employ private investigators routinely, Rick. Why are you asking?"

"One of our clerks was at the Courthouse checking on some filings for me," he lied. "I understand Raymond Silvio had the DeLuca Enterprises files checked out at the time. I was wondering if you sent him. You know, of course, if you have questions about our business, our doors are always open to you," he said without flinching.

"Rick, I did ask Mr. Silvio to check on someone for me, but it had nothing to do with DeLuca. If you must know, after I heard about the attack, I retained Mr. Silvio immediately—called him from Italy, in fact. I'm telling you this in confidence because I believe you misunderstand my motives."

Rick nodded. "Please, Aunt Caroline. I'd like to understand what's going on. Whatever you tell me won't go any further than this room."

Caroline smiled reassuringly. "I called Slick—that's his nickname—as soon as I heard that Sid Taylor might have attacked Sophia. His assignment was to find out whatever he could about Sid, unearth any skeletons he might have been trying to hide, and report back to me confidentially.

"Slick told me he found a Taylor connection to DeLuca businesses some years ago, back when the company was under the control of Vincenzo DeLuca and when Sid's father worked for him.

"I realize Juliana and Sophia have legitimized the businesses since then, so there shouldn't be anything to be concerned about. Slick was just doing what I told him, and that's where the information led him. He's a good investigator. He's thorough, but he's loyal and keeps anything he uncovers strictly to himself. Very trustworthy man. Please don't be concerned, Rick. I'd never do anything to hurt the Giordanos or DeLucas. You know how I feel about all of you."

Rick felt relieved. "Of course, Aunt Caroline. It just concerned me that someone might have hired a private investigator to look at our company's business. I wanted to be sure it was you and not someone with some other nefarious motive. I feel better about it now."

"Good. And for the record, I still don't understand why Sid would have attacked Sophia the way he did. Unless it was lack of self-control under the influence of alcohol, I can't figure it out. But, Slick is still looking into the Senator's background, and we may still find something." She paused for a moment and watched Rick nod in response.

"By the way, Rick. Have you seen the news about the Senator's son, Brent?"

"No, I haven't been watching television today. I haven't turned on the car radio, either. What's going on with Brent?" he asked.

Caroline shook her head, and sighed. "The Senator has a real public relations problem right now, and it's all over the news. National news has picked it up, too."

Rick looked puzzled. "What's Brent done now?"

Caroline leaned back in her chair and told Rick what had been blasted repeatedly on the local and national media.

"Oh, my God. Brent's gay? I always thought so, but I never knew for sure." Rick was doubly stunned.

"I'm afraid Val and Sid will have a tough time getting through this. I pity both of them, but we can't let this horrible mess overshadow our own concerns about Sid. We'll still get to the bottom of Sophia's attack, but it may be harder to get Sid's full attention now that this particular news has broken," Caroline reminded him.

"Absolutely, Aunt Caroline. I still plan to find out exactly what happened that night. Someone's got to pay for what Sophia's had to go through."

* * * * * *

Back at DeLuca Enterprises, Rick hurried into Sophia's office. Teddy was there with her, discussing the legal intricacies of amending the corporate bylaws of DeLuca Enterprises.

"Hey, I'm glad you're both here. Have you seen the news?" Rick asked as he went straight for the remote, turning on the 60" television mounted in Sophia's office. Both Sophia and Teddy turned their attention to the images televised on the national news network.

"Oh, no! Is that Brent? Is that Brent Taylor?" Sophia exclaimed.

"Yep. Looks like Sid's got a lot of damage control to do. He's in the middle of a PR nightmare right about now." Rick commented.

Teddy said nothing, staring at the screen in amazement as his eyes were glued to the censored images. He merely shook his head as if watching a train wreck.

Sophia muttered, "This will ruin what's left of Sid's career in the Senate." Her eyes, too, were still glued to the disaster on screen.

Finally Teddy spoke up. "Serves the bastard right. He doesn't deserve to be a Senator. I don't care what his son does, this is still about Sid, as far as I'm concerned. He should withdraw from the Senate race. If I had anything to say about it, he would hand his Senate seat over to Sophia. She deserves to take everything away from him the same way he took her innocence away from her."

Both Sophia and Rick gawked at Teddy. Neither said a word for a few seconds, letting what Teddy said sink in.

Rick broke the spell. "You know, Teddy. You've hit on something there. Sophia should take his Senate seat.

Sophia is smarter than Sid ever hoped to be. She sure as hell knows how to run a business. She could absolutely handle being a Senator. How about it, Sophia? Want to force Sid out?"

"What? You're both crazy. Why on earth would you ever think that would happen? We couldn't force him to withdraw, no matter how much dirt we have on him. Give me a break, guys. You're dreaming," Sophia laughed.

Teddy looked at Rick and nodded. "This should be our mission of revenge. Get Sophia on the ballot for the election. She can run as an Independent, if it's not too late."

"Wait just a minute. I'm in the room, you know. Don't talk about me and what I should do without including me in the conversation. For goodness sakes, guys. What if I don't want to be a Senator? Besides, there's a minimum age requirement, and I haven't reached it," Sophia declared.

Both Teddy and Rick looked deflated. "She's right, Rick," Teddy answered, recalling his civics lessons. "A person has to be at least 35 to be a Senator. But if there was an open seat in the House of Representatives, she'd qualify. The minimum age is only 25 to hold that office."

"I don't plan to run for Representative, either. Stop this nonsense." Sophia was acting angry.

"Would you consider running for Representative when the next New York seat comes open? We could force Sid to endorse you, considering the pressure we could put on him by then," Rick pleaded.

Sophia watched Rick and Teddy with interest. "Why? Why is it important that I enter politics?"

"Don't you see? With political influence, we can own the world! DeLuca Enterprises will prosper, and the family will be respected. It couldn't do anything but help," Rick explained.

"Then why don't you do it, Rick?" Sophia queried.

"You're prettier and smarter," he laughed. "Besides, you could get the respect you deserve by doing the job well. It's a great solution to all your feminist concerns about not being taken seriously. You will be an example to all women everywhere. It's quite an accomplishment for you, and for all the women out there who need a voice to speak on their behalf. Consider it, Sophia."

Teddy agreed. "Do it. You deserve it. We'll handle all the election details, and you just ride the wave to Washington where you'll make your impact."

Sophia studied both their anxious faces. "I'll think about it. Now get back to work, guys. We've got a business to run right here," she commanded and shooed them both from her office.

* * * * * *

Rick and Teddy sauntered into the break room to get a cup of coffee, but Teddy took his cup to a small table in the corner instead of returning to his office.

"Let's talk, Rick. Take a seat, would ya?" he asked.

Rick sat down across from Teddy, taking a sip of the strong brew before locking eyes with his business associate.

"There's still time for Sophia to enter this year's Congressional race as an Independent candidate. The

Primary will be coming up soon, so we'd have to hustle. I can do the legwork, but we both know she'd be an effective member of Congress. Not only would it help her self-esteem, she'd be doing the country a great service, too. She's brilliant, you know. She has an eye for efficiency, and she knows how to envision an effective result without sacrificing quality. She thinks ahead about cause and effect. She's the whole package."

Rick smiled coyly. "You're right about all of that, but you're wrong about Sophia being a good candidate this year. Not now. She's not hungry enough. She's wounded, and she needs to heal."

"That's just the point, Rick. This challenge will heal her more quickly than anything. You know how she is. Sometimes, I think I can sense her feelings. Even yours, old buddy. I guess we've been around each other way too much," Teddy said, smiling across the small Formica-topped table at his best friend.

Rick scooted back his chair and picked up his coffee mug to return to his office. "Let me think about it a little more." Rick tapped Teddy on the shoulder as he left him sitting alone with his thoughts.

"Just talk to her, man," Teddy yelled over his shoulder as Rick disappeared around the corner.

CHAPTER 23

Building a reliable bomb was serious business. It took skill and patience, traits that were foreign to Big Al. However, he had made enough trustworthy contacts within the organized crime family over the years that it wasn't difficult to reach the right guy—commonly known within family circles as the best in the business and appropriately nicknamed "Boomer."

Big Al drove around the corner of the Staten Island warehouse toward Boomer's small workshop. He saw Boomer taking a smoke break in the adjoining alley, less than 50 feet from the entrance of the shop.

"That looks dangerous, my friend," Big Al noted as he exited his vehicle and approached the tall, skinny man.

"I didn't get to be 58 years old by taking unnecessary risks," Boomer chortled. "Ain't nothing close enough around here that's gonna blow because of a damn cigarette."

Big Al smiled broadly, knowing what Boomer said had to be true. During the 1980s, Boomer had spent five years as a demolitions expert in the army, losing three fingers on his left hand to prove it. The explosion that maimed him had nothing to do with his own skill set; rather, he was teaching a cherry enlistee, and the kid wanted to see what he could do on his own. Unfortunately, the kid went home in a box, but the army gave Boomer an immediate medical discharge and permanent disability benefits. Since then, Boomer had been doing odd jobs for the Bellini family, and made good money when he was called upon. To date, all his 'products' had been stellar quality and worked like a charm.

"You finished my job yet, Boomer?"

Throwing down the cigarette butt, Boomer used the ball of his boot-clad foot to grind the tobacco stub into the gravel.   He grinned at Big Al and answered, "It was ready yesterday. Come on in. I'll show you how it works and how to handle it."

Big Al obediently followed Boomer through the door into the small workshop. "I gotta ask, Boomer. You got this one set up so I can set it off by phone?"

Boomer laughed out loud. "I even got the speed dial set up so you don't have to remember anything except the number 7. Seven go to heaven, that's my motto."

Big Al laughed with Boomer. "There's gonna be at least one on that glory train; but if it takes out a few more, what the hell, eh?"

"You're my kind of sick bastard, Big Al.   The more the merrier," Boomer evilly answered as he uncovered his latest masterpiece to present to Big Al.

* * * * * *

Slick Silvio wanted to talk to his mother again, but he didn't have time to visit her.   Instead, he sent her what he considered to be a telepathic message. "Moms, if you hear me, gimme a sign," he said as he drove toward his office in Syosset. "Come on, Moms. Let me know you're listening," he pleaded with the road ahead.

"I'm right here, Raymond," she said from the passenger seat.

Clearly startled, Slick slammed on the brakes. Fortunately, no one was behind him or the resultant rear-end collision would have been totally his fault.

"Geez, Moms. You scared me. Don't do that to me!" he yelled.

His mother's spirit cackled at the expression on Slick's face. "HA! You're as white as I am right now. What's a'matter? You seen a ghost?"

"Moms, that ain't funny, and you know it. Geez. I'm just trying to get a little help here, you know? I need to talk to you, and you're trying to scare me to death!" he complained.

"Now, now, Raymond. You always did overreact. Calm down, son. But, I wanna know why you didn't come visit me instead of makin' me come to you? You know this kind of travel is hard on this old soul." She pouted as she waited for an answer.

"I didn't have time to go all the way over to the cemetery, Moms. This just didn't seem like it could wait, you know?"

"Well, I'm already here now, but next time you gotta come to me," she scolded.

"Okay, Moms. I promise," the devoted son said to his dead mother.

* * * * * *

When Sophia went in the break room to make a cup of tea, Teddy followed her. He stood a few feet behind her while she searched for her favorite cup and saucer in the cabinet. When she noticed him there, she asked politely, "Can I make you a cup of tea, Teddy?"

Teddy sat down in the same seat he had occupied when he had spoken with Rick earlier. "No, I'm good, but I have a serious question for you," he replied.

"You don't have to say anything else. Yes, I'll marry you," she giggled.

"Sophia, cut the crap." The two of them laughed together as Teddy continued. "Has Rick talked to you?"

"Yes. He was quite persuasive. I'm not sure he was totally on board when he first came into my office, but I believe he convinced himself 100 percent during our discussion. He certainly convinced me."

Teddy looked stunned. "Does that mean you'll consider running this November for a seat in the House of Representatives?"

"That's exactly what I mean. But, you promised to spearhead all the paperwork and campaign matters. Rick and I thought perhaps Aunt Caroline could take over some of your DeLuca legal workload as a favor to her favorite Godchild." Sophia dipped a teabag in her microwaved hot water. "Besides, I think you are right. A challenge like this is what I need to get myself back together. You know me too well, Teddy Brantley," she smiled.

"Sometimes I think I know you as well as I know myself," he said as he stood to embrace her. "Congratulations, Congresswoman Giordano."

"I haven't won yet, Teddy. You might want to save that for later."

Teddy shrugged his shoulders. "Doesn't matter when I congratulate you—now or later. You'll win. We'll make damned sure of that."

* * * * *

Slick Silvio sat in his parked car outside his office/deli building, trying not to look conspicuous as he talked openly with his mother's spirit. He held a cell phone up to his ear so that any passersby would assume he was on a call and not talking to himself.

"Raymond, take that silly thing away from your ear. I'm right here. Don't act like you're talking to me on the phone!" his mother scolded.

"Moms, this is not for your benefit. How do you think it'd look for my business if people saw me talking to myself in a parked car? Huh? They'd think I was loony tunes!"

His mother smiled. "Well, son, you are a little loony tunes, you know. You're talking to an empty passenger seat! Nobody can see me but you. You do look pretty stupid ranting and raving at the empty seat next to you!" She burst out laughing as Slick became more peeved by the minute.

"Moms, just listen, okay? While I was checking out Senator Taylor, I found out he's having a campaign rally at Port Jeff on Saturday. I think I need to go to it just in case my vision has something to do with that rally. But I gotta tell you, I don't know how to approach him. How do I warn someone about **something**—but I'm not sure what 'cause I can't put my finger on it yet— but I **think** it might happen, but it's all based on my intuition?"

"That's a tough one, I'll grant you that. But Raymond, why don't you skip trying to warn him? You're right. He won't believe you, and he'll just chalk you up as a crazy person. I suppose I'd just go and look around the rally. If it seemed familiar—like what you saw in your vision—then I'd probably try to figure out whatever's about to happen. If I could stop it myself, I'd try. If I couldn't, then I'd try to figure out a diversion—a way to get emergency people there — like maybe start a fire or something. You can figure it out from here. I'm tired. I'm going back to Forest Lawn," she announced as her image slowly faded away.

"Thanks a lot, Moms. Thanks a friggin' lot." Slick muttered as he shook his head in dismay.

He opened the car door, but groaned loudly as he stood upright on the hard concrete surface of the parking lot.

I gotta get some more Percocet from Leo. I wish I hadn't taken my last one before I called on Moms. I'm beginning to think Moms is just a big pain in the rear, he chuckled as he gingerly made his way to his office via the steep wooden steps erected on the side of the old building.

CHAPTER 24

By the time Saturday morning arrived, Brent Taylor had no idea where he was, and wasn't sure who he was. Still strapped to the gurney, heroin/fentanyl injections had been routinely administered to him by the Doctor.

Brent had also been given parenteral nutritional support through a large intravenous catheter inserted in his arm. Finding the right vein had been difficult for the Doctor, but finally the needle was secure and properly taped in place.

Thus, during the past several days, the drugged young man had been injected with a standard premixed 'food' solution which contained enough essential nutrients to get him through his captivity period. The carefully balanced intravenous solution kept Brent from starving while he was unable to ingest solid foods.

After the Doctor checked on Brent at 6:00 a.m., he met with the Dominator one last time before 'officially' discharging his patient.

"Get a message to the kid's mother. Tell her he'll be in a cab outside the New York Presbyterian Emergency Room entrance at 10:00 a.m. Tell her he is free to go. No need for further discussion with the mother," the Dominator told him.

"Take him somewhere away from here to flag a taxi. Get him in the back seat, and give the cabbie a hundred dollar bill to take him to the meeting spot. Let the driver know that the kid's mother will be getting him, so he should wait outside the ER entrance till she arrives. Oh, and make sure the cabby knows to forget he ever saw you. Might have to slip him an extra hundred for the memory lapse."

The Doctor nodded during the Dominator's spiel of instructions. "Understood."

The two shook hands, and the Dominator left the premises.

The Doctor, however, had several hours' work ahead of him. First, he would have to remove the feeding catheter, then clean and bandage the wound accordingly. He wanted to make sure Brent wouldn't get an infection. The Doctor had taken extra care to ensure all instruments—even the torturous ones he flashed but never used—were sterile. No hypodermic needles were used more than once. He prided himself on taking the right precautions when it came to cleanliness.

He did feel bad about how he was made to treat Brent. The young man wasn't evil, just misdirected. In the Doctor's opinion, Brent had chosen several wrong paths in his short life; but considering his family, who wouldn't have done the same thing?

And we've pumped him full of drugs and plan to give him right back to his parents. I'm not sure who I feel sorrier for in this case.

* * * * * *

Early Saturday morning, Big Al went by the Senator's campaign office to pick up his paperwork and event badge for official entry to the afternoon fish fry. He whistled as he entered the office and spotted Lorie, his friendly campaign co-worker.

"Hi, Mr. Johnson! So glad you are going to be with us today! By the way, I told my office manager about your scouting the rally area for security concerns, and she was very impressed. To think, we have our very own security specialist helping us out! What a blessing you are to all of us, especially the Senator!" Lorie was overly enthusiastic.

"Hey. My pleasure, I'm sure. Now, what all do I need to be an official volunteer at this shindig?" Big Al asked through a fake smile.

"I have your package right here," she said as she reached across her desk to a pile of manila envelopes. "This contains your campaign badge and tee shirt—you'll have to wear them both while you're working at Port Jeff—and a map of the area we reserved for the rally, plus a schedule of the afternoon events. There's also a list of contacts and phone numbers. Your name and the phone number you provided are on there, too. Don't be surprised if you get a call from another volunteer with a silly security question," Lorie giggled. "Now, let's get you on your way!"

Big Al— also known as Gus Johnson— headed straight for the door before Lorie had a chance to say anymore. He was out the door while she was still waving goodbye.

* * * * * *

Val was primping at the vanity in her dressing area, making herself presentable for Sid's campaign rally set for early afternoon in Port Jefferson.

As she carefully applied her mascara, her cell phone rang. She didn't recognize the number, but she was afraid to ignore the call. She hadn't heard anything from or about Brent in days.

The number was identified only as 'Blocked.'

"Yes?" she said hesitantly into the phone.

"Your son will be in front of the New York Presbyterian Hospital's Emergency Room entrance at 10 o'clock. He'll be alone in a taxi. Don't look at or talk to the driver; just get your son and leave. The fare has been paid." The call disconnected.

It was already 9:00 a.m. She was supposed to meet Sid in two hours at the campaign office where they would be driven together to the event. *Plans change,* she thought. *Brent's more important.*

Never questioning the source of the phone call, Val calmly finished her beauty routine and called for the driver to have the limo ready in five minutes.

* * * * * *

A few steps from the entrance of his campaign office, Sid passed a tall, somewhat older man who had just left Camp Taylor and was headed toward the parking lot.

Hearing the tinkling sound of the door-mounted cow bells, Lorie smiled broadly when she saw Sid Taylor enter. "Senator! Good morning," Lorie enthusiastically greeted him. Sid waved at Lorie, but was already being rushed by a swarm of volunteers. As was protocol in such a situation, Sid shook hands, gave hugs, and patted backs of the campaign crew. When he was able to break free, he made his way toward Lorie.

"We're so glad you came by here first, Senator. We hoped we'd have a chance for a group photo with you and all our volunteer staff. Oh…except Gus. You probably saw him on your way in. He's part of our volunteer security group. He left to do a final check of the rally location. I hope we get a picture with him later since he will miss this one," she remarked.

"I'm sure we will, Lorie. Let's see…how about a picture over here under the campaign sign? Or maybe we should all go outside in front of the building. You make the call, Lorie. I'm sure you know which shot would look better in our newsletter," Sid said pleasantly.

Flattered and elated, Lorie decided the staff should all gather around her desk for the group photo, with Sid's hands resting on her shoulders as he stood behind her chair. The other volunteers had to jockey for a good spot in the background to get their full faces in the frame.

* ** * **

When Val's driver approached New York Presbyterian Hospital, he circled around to the entrance of the ER. Along the circular curb, Val spotted a taxi with a passenger leaning his head against the back right window. She instructed the driver to pull behind the parked taxi and stay put.

Peering through the taxi's rear window as she got nearer to the vehicle, she recognized the shape of Brent's head. As she opened the rear door, Brent's slumped body almost fell onto the sidewalk. Val's quick reflexes kept him from toppling out, but she didn't have the strength to hold him upright for long.

Raising her head above the taxi's rooftop, she caught the eye of her driver and motioned for him to come to her. He sighed and hesitated, but exited the limo as directed.

The two of them managed to get a barely conscious Brent out of the taxi and into the back of the limo. Neither said a word to the nervous cabbie, who drove away quickly when the passenger was removed and the taxi's back door was shut.

* * *   * * *

A stage/platform had been temporarily erected in the grassy area of Waterfront Park near the edge of the harbor. Specifically, it was built so that the waterfront would be to the speaker's back, giving the audience a breathtaking view of the sky meeting the ocean on the picturesque horizon. In addition to the view, the speaker, Senator Taylor, would have the audience's full attention— hopefully without distraction.

 Having the stage at the edge of the water also provided ample space on the sprawling lawn for the fish and hushpuppy cooks to continuously prepare the food for the hungry crowd. Additional stations had been set up from which volunteers would hand out popcorn, cotton candy, and hot dogs for the children who preferred those edibles over the more-adult fare of fried fish. Picnic tables were reserved, and rented folding tables and chairs were plentiful.

Red, white and blue balloons garnished every post or pole that would accommodate them. Banners and streamers were scattered throughout the entire area. The grounds resembled a carnival instead of an election strategy.

By 1:30 p.m., Senator Sid Taylor's fish fry and campaign booster rally was ready for the onslaught of the general public.

And Big Al was ready for the Senator.

* * * * * *

Brent could barely speak to his mother in the backseat of the limo. His head wobbled uncontrollably, and he was in and out of consciousness during the entire ride to the Taylors' home on Long Island. When he was able to focus, he smiled at his mother as if she were his guardian angel. With her arms wrapped around her son as best she could, Val tried to comfort him as he passed in and out of his drugged fog.

"Can't you drive any faster?" she screeched at the driver whose eyes darted back and forth to the rearview mirror to check on the passengers. At her urging, he gunned the limo and turned on his emergency flashers. He knew if he was caught for speeding, his employer would talk the policeman out of the ticket as a diplomatic emergency—or else, Val would threaten the poor guy within an inch of his life. The driver chuckled as he imagined such a scenario.

When they arrived at the Taylor mansion, the driver was quick to assist Val in getting Brent inside the house and into his bedroom. For once, Val was appreciative of the servant's assistance and expected discretion.

"Thank you," she muttered as she arranged Brent's bedcovers. "I trust you will keep this incident to yourself. I'll make sure there's a bonus in your paycheck for your loyalty," she continued, never looking at the driver who stood at the foot of the bed. She waved her hand as if to dismiss him.

"Yes, ma'am. Thank you, ma'am," he said as he grinned and silently disappeared from Brent's room.

CHAPTER 25

"I was planning on going to the rally on my own, Slick. You didn't have to pick me up and escort me," Caroline teased.

Slick had shown up unexpectedly that morning at Caroline's home in Syosset—the same one that Perry Norton, Esquire, had owned and inhabited before his marriage to Lucinda DeLuca in 1999.

Caroline had been a resident there following a sequence of unfortunate events that caused her to seek shelter with her attorney-employer, Perry. After successfully pretending to be Perry's wife for almost three years, the two were able to resolve the haunting criminal activities of the past and avenge the murder of Caroline's ex-husband.

By the time the entire puzzle was solved, Lucinda and Perry reestablished their loving relationship and were soon legitimately married. By then, Caroline had finished law school and was on the staff of Perry Norton's law firm. She had endeared herself to Perry (and he to her) through the platonic years of their sham marriage and co-existence. Thus, he eventually legally adopted the much younger woman, officially giving Caroline the Norton name and status as Perry's only heir. After he died, he bequeathed to Caroline the upscale residence that she had occupied alone since Perry relocated to the DeLuca mansion to join his new bride, Lucinda. To date, Caroline had lived in the Norton house for more than twenty years.

"How could I let you drive all that way when we were both going in the same direction?" Slick chuckled. "Besides, now that you know my secret skill, I need to make sure you don't blab it around or get paranoid or something."

Caroline punched him on the arm, "Slick, I really don't care what prompted you to show up. I'm just glad you did. I could use some company today, and you're an ideal escort."

"Now, don't go acting like I'm harmless, lady. Just 'cause I work for you on occasion doesn't mean I can't use my own time to admire you for what you are," Slick replied shyly.

"Oh? And just what am I, Slick... besides a meal ticket?" Caroline grinned and caught his eye.

"You're a beautiful woman, that's what." Slick's face suddenly reddened. "And a real good boss. I guess it's all right for you to be both," he added as he unlocked his eyes from her gaze.

"Don't get sappy on me, Mr. Silvio. Let's get going. If you keep up that kind of fake flattery, you'll force me to buy your dinner. On second thought, I know a good place to get some fried fish and all the fixings, plus the price can't be beat," she responded with a broad grin in an attempt to make Slick feel more comfortable.

* * * * * *

When Brent opened his eyes to the familiar room in his parents' house, he felt nauseous but relieved. He could remember bits and pieces of the time he spent in the white room, but so much was still a blur to him. The only thing good about his captivity had been the drug injections—the bad parts were every other memory he could vaguely conjure up. He hoped he had dreamed the hazy thoughts he recalled about the red-eyed monster clad in black leather.

He sat up slowly, taking a moment to get his bearings. His head throbbed, but he was more lucid than he had been for a while. The bedside table clock showed it was 11:45 a.m. He had no idea what day it was.

He realized he needed to relieve his bladder, but didn't know if he could make it to the bathroom without falling.

"Mom?" he yelled as his feet lightly touched the floor from the side of the bed. "Mom?" No one answered his call of distress.

"Somebody?" he yelled as loudly as his raspy throat would allow. His last utterance invoked a mental vision of a man in scrubs and a surgical mask who would surely walk in to attend him shortly. He shivered, beginning to believe he might still be an involuntary prisoner in the familiar location, but now under the complete control of his father. He despised his father.

Rather than shout again, he slowly and unsteadily stood. The bathroom door might as well be a mile away instead of the fifteen feet or so he would have to cross. He didn't know if he could make it alone. His legs were still rubbery and unreliable. But, despite his fears, he took two tiny steps toward the private bath.

"Mr. Brent! What are you doing?" a feminine voice exclaimed. A startled Brent almost fell, but managed to catch the bedpost to gain stability.

"Let me help you, sir!" the young maid said to the stumbling Brent as she gently placed her arm around his waist for support. "I can get you in the bathroom, and I'll stand outside the door. You might need some help getting back to bed," she offered graciously.

"Thank you," he mumbled as together they cautiously meandered across the bedroom.

Once Brent was safely inside the bathroom, she left him leaning on the vanity for support. She closed the door and waited. After a few minutes, she heard the doorknob turning. She was ready to help him make the same short journey across the room, but in reverse.

As she helped him sit on the side of the bed, he looked into her eyes, admiring her young, beautiful face. "I don't remember you," he said. "You're much nicer than the others."

She smiled. "I have been here for a few years, but I don't remember you ever visiting the house before."

Brent allowed her to fluff his pillow before he laid back. "I don't like it here. I try to avoid New York as much as possible. And I try to avoid my parents, too."

"That's too bad," the young maid said. When she was assured Brent was comfortable again, she turned to leave his room.

"Wait," he called after her. "You didn't tell me your name. I'm Brent."

"Yes, I know, Mr. Brent. And I am Leona. I am happy to finally meet you."

* * * * * *

"It's almost noon. Sid's going to be angry that I didn't make it to the campaign office by 11:00 a.m. He gets so upset when he can't get the photo ops he wants," Val said snidely as she got into the waiting limo. Once seated, she sat quietly for a moment while the driver buckled himself in behind the steering wheel.

"But, you know what? I don't really give a fuck. I never planned to ride with him in that horrendously decorated VIP car. Take me straight to the rally. Oh, and once we're there, stand by with the motor running for a little while. I may be coming back home immediately if the son of a bitch gives me any grief over being late," Val barked to the same driver she had only an hour before treated with unusual civility.

* * * * * *

Before he left campaign headquarters for the rally, Sid tried to call Val once more. She didn't answer her cell phone. He'd already called four times, and now he had to assume she was 'unavoidably detained.' If she showed up later at the rally, he'd be surprised. She didn't care for these kinds of things, and right now he knew she didn't care much for him, either.

Maybe Lorie would like to ride in the VIP car with me. That would probably give her a big thrill

Sid wasn't wrong. Lorie jumped at the chance to be a part of the VIP entourage. When they pulled up to the rally point, Sid's Rolex watch showed their arrival time as 1:45 p.m. on the dot.

* * * * * *

Standing near the walkway to the rally entrance, Rick and Sophia scanned the crowd they were about to join. They waited patiently for Teddy who had promised to meet them in the parking lot at 1:45 p.m. near the venue's main entrance.

The Giordano siblings were early as usual, arriving ahead of time to see Sid and his campaign worker arrive in the VIP car. Sid looked like a typical Senatorial candidate, waving and smiling broadly at the onlookers as he exited the car. The young lady who had ridden with him to the rally appeared to be a star-struck groupie. She couldn't take her eyes off Sid's every move, and imitated every move and wave he made. If the crowd didn't already know Sid's background, Lorie might have been mistaken for an adoring girlfriend or his much younger wife.

However, Val Taylor always made certain her role as Mrs. Senator Taylor was fully acknowledged by everyone. Her absence from Sid's side made the Giordanos wonder what was happening between Sid and Val.

As Sid passed them and entered the venue, Rick whispered to Sophia, "What's up with the substitute escort?"

Sophia smiled and waved at Sid before she answered through stiff lips. "Maybe she didn't want to face the public after all this stuff about Brent hit the news. I wouldn't blame her for staying home today."

Rick nodded in agreement.

"Hey, Rick! Sophia! Over here," Teddy shouted through a stream of people who were passing closely in front of the Giordanos. Sophia waved when she saw Teddy's head bobbing above a group of "Women for Taylor" attendees.

Teddy made his way through the cluster of slow walking ladies and stopped next to Sophia. He embraced her and shook Rick's hand. "Ready?" he asked as he took Sophia's arm.

"Let's do this. I hope we can get Sid alone for a few minutes. There are so many things we need to hit on—his face being one I'd especially like to hit," Rick responded.

Sophia looked at her brother and frowned. "Cool it, Rick. Plenty of time for that," she instructed as she and Teddy walked ahead of Rick and joined the celebrating crowd.

* * * * * *

Adam Woodson and Carmen Ryan had been at the rally for fifteen minutes when they stopped at a cotton candy booth. They requested one large cloud of the pink sticky twirled cotton which Adam held tightly, allowing Carmen to pick from the serving as they turned to join the wandering crowd. Before they finished their cotton candy, Rick Giordano accidentally bumped into Carmen.

"Oh, excuse m… oh, hello there!" Rick said, startled by her presence. "I'm so sorry, I'm a real klutz. I didn't mean to bump into you, of all people," he apologized.

Both Carmen and Adam laughed at his stumbling apology. "No problem, Rick. I'm not hurt, and it's actually good to see you. You remember Adam, don't you?"

"Yes, your fiancé. Lucky man," Rick smiled as he shook Adam's hand.

"Well, yes and no," Adam answered awkwardly.

"Excuse me?" Rick said.

"What I mean is, we're no longer engaged. We are great friends and excellent business partners, but we both agree those two things form the best relationships we could ever hope for. Actually, I think Carmen and I are better as friends and co-workers, and so does she. We wish the best for each other when it comes to love, but we realize we're not ideal for each other in that kind of relationship," Adam explained while Carmen eagerly nodded and smiled at Rick.

"Well, this is, um…quite a surprise," Rick said, truly stunned. "I'm sure you both know what's best, but I can't help thinking you're crazy to let Carmen go, Adam. She's something special."

Adam agreed. "You're right, Rick. I can't argue with that."

* * * * * *

"Leona? Leona, can you hear me?" Brent called out. He heard hurried footsteps on the hardwood stairs and soon a breathless Leona entered his room.

"Yes, Mr. Brent? Are you all right, sir?" she asked apprehensively.

"I'm much better, thanks. I just wondered if you knew where my mother happens to be."

"She left a while ago to join your father at his campaign rally at Port Jefferson. Can I get you something? Some soup or some water? You must be starving," said the young maid.

Brent smiled, but shook his head. "Would you please help me to my dressing area? I don't know who put these pajamas on me, but they smell terrible and they're too big. If I can get dressed in something else, I'll feel better. When I'm a little less dizzy, maybe I'll try to take a shower later."

"I'll try, sir, but if you haven't been here in a while, will your clothes in the closet still fit you?" Leona asked.

"They should. I've lost some weight recently, so I think they'll still work. I want to try, at least," Brent responded convincingly.

Brent and Leona did another 'two-man shuffle' toward the large walk-in closet situated adjacent to the suite's bathroom. Once inside, the vast amount of clothing stored there surprised Leona.

Brent pointed to a light sweater and a pair of jeans that had once been a little bit large on his younger frame. "Those should do it. And grab those leather-soled house slippers, too," he told the compliant maid. "I may need your help changing, though. Do you mind?"

Leona looked awkwardly at her employers' son. "If I have to, but don't you want me to get one of the male staff members to help?"

"No, I don't want anyone else involved," Brent answered mysteriously.

CHAPTER 26

Alone on the second floor of the Town Center building situated on the edge of Waterfront Park, Val Taylor had been watching the rally activities below her on the grounds of the commons. She had a spectacular view from the floor-to-ceiling windows of the empty public meeting room.

Val had arrived ahead of Sid, noting that the horrid VIP car was nowhere in the parking lot. She told the driver to circle around and let her out away from the rally entrance. Val walked unnoticed into the Town Center where she had been pacing in front of the wide windows ever since.

When she saw the VIP car arrive, she could tell Sid had someone at his side. She scoffed to herself when she realized the young lady was the innocent and exuberant campaign worker who assisted in the Long Island campaign office. *Couldn't he have found anyone YOUNGER! Asshole!* she thought sarcastically, pacing even faster.

With the young woman by his side, Val watched Sid shake hands, kiss babies, and hug the female attendees. He made the rounds like the seasoned pro he was, never bypassing anyone who was of voting age. She shook her head in revulsion.

She wished she had a drink. She deserved a stiff one after the day she'd already had. At least she wasn't driving, and a shot or two of bourbon would surely hit the spot.

* * * * * *

Slick walked proudly with Caroline on his arm. He hadn't had a date since his divorce. Actually, no woman had caught his interest during the past seven years he had been single. He was surprised that Caroline hadn't piqued his relationship interests before now.

Caroline looked lovely dressed in her favorite navy blue A-line dress. She wore a light, multi-colored Pashmina thrown around her shoulders to keep the chilly air at bay. Slick had worn the best suit he owned, which happened to be a ten-year old tan ensemble that looked as if it needed a good pressing. Regardless, the couple strolled along the grassy venue arm in arm, appearing to enjoy each other's company in the carnival-like atmosphere.

When Teddy, Rick, and Sophia approached them, Slick was telling Caroline more about his premonition. "It's like I've been here before, Caroline," he began.

As he stepped beside Caroline, Rick interjected, "I'm sure you have, since this is a popular spot for the locals."

"Oh, Rick! And Sophia and Teddy! I'm so happy to see you all," Caroline exclaimed as she reached for Sophia's arm. "Where's your mother?"

Sophia volunteered to answer, "She stayed back to sit with Grandmamma Lucy, but she told me to give her regards to you, Aunt Caroline."

Caroline nodded and smiled at the beaming Sophia before she turned to her escort to begin the official introductions. "Slick Silvio, I'd like to introduce you to the Giordano siblings, Rick and Sophia. And this is my Godson, Teddy Brantley," she said with pride.

"So you're the famous Slick," Rick chuckled as he extended his hand before the others. "Glad to meet you."

Teddy and Sophia looked confused at Rick's remark since they had never heard of the man. Following along, they each greeted Aunt Caroline's escort with the same enthusiasm as Rick.

"What were you saying when we so rudely interrupted? Something about being here before?" Rick wondered.

"Uh… I was just saying this place looks like a carnival I went to once out on Coney Island. Sid Taylor sure knows how to throw a bash, doesn't he?" Slick said nonchalantly.

"Yes, Slick. He's very good at it," Caroline responded. "So, if you young folks will excuse us, we're going to look for a couple of chairs. We're not as young as we used to be, and right now my feet are screaming at me."

The group said their farewells and vowed to catch up with each other later. Sid escorted Caroline to an area out of range of the stage before he expressed his concerns.

"Something's not right here, Caroline. I want you to stay back here, as far away from that stage as possible. Stay low and be alert. The minute I walked into this place, the hair on my neck stood straight up. I smelled the cornbread—the hushpuppies and grease, I mean—and I could feel some kind of cosmic disruption or something. You gotta stay safe, so don't move if you can help it," Slick ordered as he turned to go back through the crowd.

"Slick?" Caroline called after him. He turned and came back, standing in front of her chair. "Be careful," she said as she extended her hand up to him.

Slick held her fingertips in his hand. Without thinking, he leaned over and gently kissed her lips. She kissed him back.

* * * * * *

"I know that was embarrassing for you, Leona, but thank you for helping me get dressed," Brent said as he stood next to his bed in his preppy clothes. "See, I'm already better," he laughed as he took several wobbly steps toward her. He managed to stay upright without falling, which Leona thought was a major improvement over the condition in which she found him earlier that morning.

"Mr. Brent, it's all right. I'm glad I could help you. You should probably lie back down on the bed, though. I don't think your mother will approve of you being up and around when she gets back." Leona looked apprehensive at the thought.

"That's just it, Leona. I need to leave. I was wondering if I could impose on you for one more thing? Will you take me to the rally that my Dad's holding? You do drive, don't you?"

'Yes, I drive, but the house car was already used to take your mother to meet the Senator there. I take the bus to and from work. I have no car." Leona frowned, sorry that she had to disappoint the nicest Taylor family member.

"My parents used to let me use their Mercedes sports car when I was at home. I know where the keys are kept. If you could drive me out there, my parents would be overjoyed if I showed up," Brent lied.

"Oh, no, sir. No. Your parents wouldn't want someone besides you driving that car. I've heard how they love it. And you're in no condition to drive. Why don't I just call you a taxi?" Leona tried to compromise.

"No, that won't work. I really want to make a grand entrance. I haven't seen my Dad in over two years, and I want to give him the best surprise he's ever had." Brent gave her his most pitiful look. "Besides, I'll pay you extra for your efforts."

How could she refuse such a remorseful son. Less than an hour before Brent was saying he hated his father, and now he's had a change of heart. If she could help him get to his father, she would do everything in her power.

"All right. But you'll have to guide me to the rally. I don't know much about getting around in that area. And I don't know **anything** about driving a Mercedes. What if I have a wreck? Oh, my Lord! Just the thought of that makes me nervous," Leona told him.

"Don't worry about property damage. That's what insurance is for," Brent chuckled as she reluctantly helped him walk toward the stairs.

* * *　* * *

Sid was concerned that the Giordanos and their sidekick, Teddy Brantley, were in attendance as something more than campaign boosters. In fact, he had noticed that Rick Giordano kept staring at him when he made his way through the crowd. Teddy Brantley did the same. Sophia, on the other hand, acted as though she didn't want to look at Sid. When Sid turned in her direction, she turned the other way.

The campaign fundraiser at the DeLuca mansion had been a flop—both financially and in the media. If only he had controlled his drinking, the whole publicity mess would have been avoided, and so would the allegations hurled at him about attacking Sophia. Surely he'd remember something like that, even if he had been drunk out of his mind. Ever since that night, Val treated him like scum. Maybe he was a little unscrupulous, but he wasn't evil...not deep down, anyway. But no matter what, he was going to have to address those issues head on when he gave his speech. He even planned to talk about his son, disgusting as the news about Brent had been. Sid planned to make the boy look like an angel who had accidentally clipped a wing.

* * * * * *

Lorie insisted that Sid meet Gus Johnson, the volunteer security person who had so diligently worked to make the venue a safe haven for Sid and his welcomed guests. She looked around the crowd and spotted him several feet away from the stage. Lorie reached for the Senator's arm in an effort to guide him toward their special volunteer.

"You really need to thank Mr. Johnson, Senator. He has worked so hard for us this week. I believe I already told you about how he spent several hours scouting the area for any potential security issues. He wanted to be sure we'd all be safe here," she reiterated.

"Yes, I'm aware. Sorry we couldn't get a group picture with him earlier. Let's do a special one with just him," Sid suggested.

Big Al, aka Gus, caught a glimpse of the Senator and Lorie as they headed in his direction. *He can't get close to me...he'll recognize me as a part of the Bellini family. I never thought I'd have to face him again after all these years. I gotta move quick!*

Pretending he was unaware of the Senator and Lorie making their way toward him, Big Al turned and quickly walked away—walkie talkie near his face—acting as though he were about to handle some imminent security issue.

"Ah, too bad," Lorie said to Sid. "Looks like he's being called to duty."

"We'll catch him after my speech," Sid reassured her.

* * * * * *

"What time is it?" Brent asked his nervous driver.

"The car's clock says 2 o'clock. What time did you want to be there?" Leona queried.

"I noticed the flyer for the rally as we were going out through the kitchen. I think it said his speech was supposed to start at two-something, but I couldn't read it clearly."

Brent had a photographic memory, but it hadn't been helpful that day. He had quickly glanced at the rally flyer on the kitchen counter when Leona was helping him out the back door to the garage. But his eyesight was still unfocused and his head still pounded.

The specific rally details he needed to recall had been written on the letter-sized blue paper in a smaller font. His eyes just wouldn't focus well enough to take a clear picture in his mind.

As a result, he didn't know exactly when the speech would begin or how long the speech would last. He wasn't sure how much time he had left to accomplish his mission.

"I hope we make it there before he stops talking. I really wanted him to look from the stage and see me coming," Brent explained.

"Oh. Well, we're only a few miles away. I think we can make it," Leona said and smiled.

* * * * * *

Slick paced nervously through the crowd, looking at everyone and everything that reminded him of his premonition. He closed his eyes and stood stiffly at the exact spot where he was knocked down in the vision. The hairs on the back of his neck prickled. A shiver coursed through his rigid body.

When he opened his eyes, he saw Sid approach the stage with Lorie by his side. When Slick looked at his imitation Rolex, he saw it was 2:15 p.m., a mere twelve minutes before the vision indicated his watch would be broken.

Slick scanned the crowd for Caroline. He couldn't see over all the heads in the crowd from his vantage point. He moved to the edge of the stage and stepped one step higher for a better view. Finally he spotted Caroline in the chair where he had left her. Gathered around her were Sophia and Rick, and Teddy Brantley stood behind her with his hand on her shoulder. *Good. Everybody she cares about is with her and a safe distance away. Now if they'll just stay there for a few more minutes …*

* * * * * *

Cheers and applause erupted throughout the gathering when Sid and Lorie approached the microphone at center stage. Sid held up both hands, palms forward, to acknowledge the applause and shush the crowd.

Lorie spoke first. "Welcome everyone! What a wonderful day for a fish fry and to show our appreciation to the man who made it all possible... Senator Sid Taylor!" she exclaimed as the clapping and cheering continued. Sid saluted the crowd as he took the microphone from his campaign groupie.

"Thank you, Lorie! Thank you all! And let's all recognize Lorie for the outstanding job she's done getting everything organized and planned for this big celebration! Let's give her and all our great volunteers a special round of applause for their excellent work and dedication! Look around at the volunteers here wearing our campaign tee shirts—they're the oil that keeps this old Taylor machine running! Give 'em all a hand, folks!" Sid shouted as he graciously half-bowed to Lorie and to those volunteers he could see nearby.

As he scanned the happy participants, Sid spotted Big Al standing at the edge of the crowd. For a second, Sid Taylor's face clouded over, and he almost lost his flashy smile. Recovering quickly, Sid smiled broadly once again, but his mind was working fast. *Where have I seen that man before? His face looks familiar, but I can't place him. He must be the security guy I passed when I got to the campaign office, but I only saw him from behind ...that face, though. Who is he, really?*

Shaking off his concerns, Sid quieted the crowd again as he began his well-rehearsed speech.

"Thank you, good folks of Long Island. Thank you, welcoming citizens of Port Jefferson. I come to you today as a humble man, one you may not recognize from years before.

"To say that my own family has recently suffered would be a great understatement. More often than not, public figures and elected officials are expected to be held to higher standards than ordinary citizens. But that is a superficial way of thinking—we are not immune to life. Bad luck and bad decisions happen to everyone, affect everybody, even those of us you trust to routinely make sound and decent decisions on your behalf, the kinds of decisions that impact your lives every single day as residents of our great state.

"I'm here today to speak from the heart, something most campaigners don't often do. I'm here today to admit to you that I have a problem with alcohol, and have had this problem for longer than I have held my Senate seat.

"You all saw the humiliating media coverage of my drunken episode at a recent fundraiser event in Southampton. That was inexcusable. All the years that I have been a highly functioning alcoholic, I have tried to maintain good behavior, especially in public. I never intended to embarrass the good citizens of New York, and especially not my family. What I do want to emphasize is that I've never jeopardized the good citizens of this state by making any decisions while under the influence of alcohol or any drug. And the "out of context" clip that you heard on the media about legalizing marijuana? Well, that was just a single statement, not the entire conversation. I ask you to consider what so often happens to politicians during election campaigns. Occasionally videos of an entire conversation become spliced together to make a final version that is an inaccurate or misleading slant on the actual topic. That is what happened to me. I am guilty for overindulging in alcohol that night. But that is all. I was embarrassingly, inexcusably drunk, and I admit it.

"Perhaps you recently saw in the media a distasteful video of my son, Brent. First, let me say that I love my son. I am a father, and I love him without conditions. He may have made choices that I don't condone or comprehend, but he is MY son. Secondly, I want to help him, not condemn him. I want him to have the best life has to offer and not be rejected or cast aside because his life choices aren't the same as ours. I ask you, as fellow parents, to remember that our families come first before anything except God Almighty. And through His guidance and direction, Brent will become the man HE always wanted to be: free of drug dependence and able to live a productive life of his choosing." Sid paused for effect. "Brent, my son.   I hope you can hear me, because I won't fail you again," Sid said as he took a step away from the microphone to blow his nose and wipe his eyes.

Scattered clapping began near the stage and spread like waves through the entire crowd as Sid stood meekly on the platform. Lorie moved forward from her position behind Sid's left and squeezed his shoulder reassuringly. Sid turned and gave her his most pitiful look. "Thank you," he mumbled to Lorie and then again in the microphone so that all the attendees could witness his humble show of gratitude.

Twin Sins

CHAPTER 27

When Leona entered the reserved parking area at Waterfront Park, Brent guided her to a vacant handicapped parking space near the front of the Town Center.

"We don't have a handicapped tag," she said in a concerned voice. "We can't park here. Besides, the entrance to the rally is over there where the balloons are," she explained as she pointed to a spot some fifty feet away.

"I know, but it's only for a minute. I used to come here as a boy. There's a lobby on the second floor of this building with meeting rooms off to the side. The walls facing the harbor are solid glass. Would you please go up there and pinpoint where my father's podium is set up? We'll park closer once you've got a good idea of the setup. I won't have to walk as far if I know exactly where I'm going," Brent requested in a weak voice. "Just leave the car running. This will only take a second," he reassured her.

Leona did as she was told. As soon as she disappeared through the large doors, Brent got out of the car. He gingerly walked to the driver's side of the treasured SL500 and opened the door. As soon as he situated himself in the driver's seat, he slammed the gear shift in reverse and backed out of the handicapped space. He stomped the accelerator with all his strength, sending the car full speed ahead toward the balloon-lined sidewalk that would lead him to his father.

* * * * * *

Slick was still looking around from ground level at the side of the stage.   His watch showed 2:23 p.m., and he could feel his heart beating faster and harder.   He reached into his pocket and pulled out a Percocet (compliments of Leo).   He stuck it in the back of his throat and dry-swallowed it without thinking.   He'd gotten used to that particular ingestion process, unfortunately.

Scanning the crowd for anything suspicious, Slick took note of a tall man in a campaign tee shirt who looked agitated.   He wasn't smiling as he watched Sid on stage.   Instead, the volunteer looked from side to side as if he expected something to go wrong.   *Maybe he's a security guy?*   Slick thought the man looked more apprehensive than excited like the other volunteers. Slick instinctively started to move through the onlookers toward the suspicious man when he heard the rumbling of a motor coming from the nearby parking area.

He paused in his pursuit for only a second, long enough to see his mother's ghost-like figure standing beside the dubious looking volunteer.   "Moms, what are you ..." Slick mumbled softly, noting that she was motioning for him to come toward her. "Moms?" Slick muttered as he sprinted toward the image only he could see.

Seeing Slick Silvio start running in his direction, Big Al tried to move quickly out of sight.   He darted between people who were glued in their spots watching as Sid recovered his emotions on stage. Big Al reached in his pocket and wrapped his right hand around the igniter cell phone.

* * * * * *

When Leona got to the second floor of the Town Center, she was shocked to see Val Taylor standing in front of the tall glass windows. Val was peering down at the stage where her husband stood addressing the rally attendees. Val knew Sid was giving a dramatic heart wrenching oration about something. The audio of the speech was not transmitted through the Town Center, so Val could only guess that Sid was apologizing for the recent Taylor media blitz.

"Lying Bastard," she said as she shook her head. She turned abruptly to find Leona standing a few feet away.

"Aren't you our maid?" Val questioned. "What are you doing here?"

Terrified of Val, Leona stammered, "Your ..your son. Mr. Brent. He wanted to surprise Mr., uh, the Senator," she stuttered.

"Brent? Brent's here? But how could he ..." Val started to say as she looked through the high window to watch the horror unfold in slow motion below.

* * * * * *

Carmen and Adam were standing at the farthest edge of the assembly, watching Sid's speech from the opposite side of the venue as Caroline and her group.

"Maybe this guy's different than we thought," Adam said to Carmen as she watched Sid blot at his eyes.

"Adam, you are a complete sucker. I don't know why you were selected for this job. You overdo it when giving a person the benefit of the doubt."

"I guess that's why they put us together, Carmen. You're the polar extreme of me when it comes to sensitivity and empathy. I suppose they think we balance each other out."

Carmen laughed, but then her facial expression changed as she blurted out something Adam didn't quite catch.

"What?"

"Look out!" she screamed as she shoved Adam hard.

* * * * * *

When Slick caught up to Big Al, the volunteer was moving hastily toward the area where Caroline and her group were sitting.

"Hey!" Slick screamed, causing everyone nearby, including Caroline, to raise their heads to see a frantic Slick. "Oh, God," she said as she put her hand across her mouth. Teddy watched his Aunt who was clearly in distress, and launched from his position in an effort to help Slick.

Big Al kept moving swiftly forward and so did Slick. Teddy caught up to Slick as both men raced in pursuit of the suspect.

Even as he sprinted, Big Al's legs were tingling with a diabetic alarm. As he struggled to outrace his pursuers, Big Al's hand never lost his grip on the cell phone in his pocket.

Suddenly, something red zoomed past, causing Big Al and his pursuers to momentarily stop in their tracks. They stood as if frozen, helplessly watching the event before them unfold into disaster.

* * * * * *

When Brent's foot hit the accelerator of the small Mercedes coupe, he reached down to lower the convertible's hard top as he launched forward. He cackled as he watched the heavy metal top go half way up in the air and stop, never completing its process to the full downward position. The SL500 looked like a transformer car from the movies with its parachute-like top stuck in mid-air. He laughed maniacally as he erratically steered the strange-looking car down the sidewalk and across the grassy rally venue.

People screamed and scattered in all directions, watching in horror as the small car with the strange top came rapidly upon them. Knocking bystanders aside along with folding chairs and tables, the sturdy little car continued its forward progress regardless of what was in its path.

* * * * * *

Slick lunged for his prey as the man slowed to pull something from his pocket. At the moment Slick's upper body connected with Big Al's knees, they both fell hard on the ground, with Slick landing on his left wrist. Something jarred from Big Al's hand, but he recovered it and pushed a button before Teddy could stop him.

* * * * * *

Sid stood spellbound on the platform, still hanging on to the microphone stand. He couldn't believe what he was seeing. His son…his own son…! Brent was driving straight for him in the one car Sid had treasured more than any other he'd ever owned. *That can't be Brent! That can't be Brent!*

Still perched on the platform with Sid, Lorie realized what was about to happen to her beloved Senator. She screamed for Sid to run, but he didn't budge. She moved forward quickly, managing to push Sid hard enough to send him reeling off the side of the stage. Sheer momentum caused him to roll several feet further away from the platform. Lorie watched spellbound as Sid scrambled to his feet.

Lorie found herself frozen in fear after her unplanned heroic gesture. On stage and in the exact spot where Sid Taylor had been speaking moments before, Lorie stood stiffly. She made no effort to avoid the fate that was meant for the Senator. Her feet may as well have been nailed to the stage.

Lorie stood behind the microphone as though she were about to apologize to the Senator and the attendees for what was about to happen. The last word she uttered was "Sorry."

* * * * * *

Within seconds after Big Al pushed '7' on the phone's keypad, an explosion set off showers of wood, splinters, and pieces of burning paper and debris raining like confetti over the grounds. The SL500 had rammed into the stage at the precise moment the bomb planted underneath the platform detonated. There was nothing recognizable left of either.

When he tackled the perpetrator, Slick fell on his left wrist causing his watch to break. The cracked face of Slick's fake Rolex recorded the time of the impact as 2:27 p.m.

Twin Sins

CHAPTER 28

Val looked with horror as she watched the entire event unfold from her perch on the second floor of the Town Center. Standing a few steps behind Val was Leona, the timid maid who had enabled the unstable Brent to execute his vendetta against the father he loathed.

The moment the car rammed the stage, Val's scream could be heard echoing throughout the entire Town Center building. She lunged toward the window, but the heavy thick glass prevented her from falling through. Instead, she leaned heavily against the layered panes, beating her fists against the transparent partition, screeching as the horror unfolded in slow-motion below. With her weight pushing against the glass, her crumpled body slid down the window until she was in a fetal-like position on the floor.

"Oh, God! What have I done? What have I done?" she sobbed as the stunned Leona stood helplessly by, still in shock after what she, too, had just witnessed.

* * * * * *

When the bomb exploded, Big Al had scampered away from his tackled position on the ground, taking full advantage of the momentary diversion of the blast. While the bewildered Slick jerked his head toward the stage, Teddy instinctively looked back at Caroline, Rick, and Sophia. Thank God the three were still where Slick had instructed them to stay.

By the time his two pursuers had shaken off the shock of the fatal blast, Big Al disappeared into the frantic crowd where multiple bodies were now strewn from the explosion. People were scampering everywhere, attempting to shield themselves from flying debris and potential secondary detonations.   Several unrecognizable voices were echoing the same scream: "Call an ambulance! Call an ambulance."

Realizing his prey had somehow vanished during the panic and confusion, Slick jumped upright and took off toward Caroline and the others. Teddy was close behind him by then.

"Are you hurt?   Are you hurt?" Slick shouted as he approached the group, speaking directly to Caroline.

"We're fine, but are you all right?" Caroline said as she leaped from her chair and grabbed Slick by the shoulders. She instinctively embraced him, tears of relief forming in her eyes.

Teddy headed straight to Sophia, kneeling in front of her chair and grasping both her hands in his. They stared at each other in disbelief—this couldn't have happened!

 Rick remained frozen beside Sophia, scanning the carnage before him in an anxious attempt to spot survivors following the battle-like aftermath. When his eyes focused on Adam, Rick realized he was kneeling above the wounded Carmen, lying on the ground bleeding and apparently unconscious.

Moving like a shot from his sheltered position, Rick found himself standing before the traumatized Adam within seconds. Lightly touching Adam's shoulder in a vain attempt of comfort, Rick watched in dazed astonishment as Carmen took her last breath while Adam held her broken body in his arms.

Adam collapsed in devastated sorrow as he clung to the partner he had admired and respected for so long. Rick shed sincere tears as the death scene unfolded, wondering how

Adam could ever possibly recover from such an unnecessary and unexpected loss.

* * * * * *

Sid lay unconscious several feet from the stage, bleeding from his head. His suit was aflame in several tiny spots caused by flying incinerated debris. Some addled onlooker had the good sense to throw a loose picnic blanket over Sid, causing the severe burns he would have otherwise suffered to be minimized. That particular Good Samaritan was never identified.

* * * * * *

The emergency crews took immediate control of the scene: firefighters worked the areas where small flames were still active, while emergency medical technicians set up a triage area to deal with the injuries they could effectively treat. Multiple ambulances had come and gone, carrying the more critically injured to the nearest hospitals. Small black sheets of plastic were spread over the fatalities—once vibrant individuals who had attended the gathering for a delightful afternoon of entertainment in what had been expected to be a serene, safe setting.

The police were stringing yellow crime scene tape over various sections of the area and blocking public entry or exit from the scene. The stoic lawmen gathered as many uninjured witnesses together as they could in order to interview those who still had coherent thoughts to contribute.

The crumpled Mercedes SL500, with its hard top now blown askew but still hanging onto the vehicle's frame by one steel hinge, sat like a charcoal-colored monster where it exploded on impact with the structure. The driver's seat belt lay loose, also still attached to the frame, having been ignored and unused during Brent Taylor's short trip of doom.

When the untethered Brent was launched from the vehicle, he bounced off the hard top which, in its partially retracted position, gave the impression of a giant parachute. His body ricocheted downward into the middle of the explosion zone, ripping him apart on impact.

The remains of Brent Taylor were scattered over what was left of the stage. Pieces of his charred flesh and bone—mingled with those of the heroic Lorie who had saved Sid Taylor's life that day—could be found within a twenty-foot radius from where the podium's singed and partially-melted microphone now lay.

After the assault, the once picturesque park looked and sounded more like a scene from hell. Sirens, moans, cries for help, wailing, fire, ashes, smoke, and devastation soaked into the landscape like a shroud of evil.   It would be years, perhaps decades, before the park would be remembered as anything other than a kamikaze backdrop for a drug-induced, devil-possessed maniac who tried to assassinate New York's beloved Senator, Sid Taylor.

* * * * *

By the middle of the next week, funerals had already been held for Brent Taylor's three victims.

Three days after her demise, the first service was held for a 43 year old campaign worker named Dorothy Newman, known as Dodie to her family, friends, and co-workers. She was a single mother, divorced since her husband abandoned her over 20 years before, leaving her with two children to rear on her own. A bank teller by vocation, she was well-respected by all who knew her. Her grieving grown children and toddler grandchild attended the funeral, along with several hundred others who either knew Dodie personally or felt the urge to attend as a show of support for New York's incumbent Senator.

The following day, a funeral service was held for Lorie Frasier, the vibrant young campaign worker who rode in the VIP car with Sid to Waterfront Park. Perhaps that day's show of attention to Lorie saved Sid's life. Regardless, she was heralded as a heroine throughout the eulogy given by the Episcopalian priest. Her proud but confused parents stared dumbfounded at a 2'x2' snapshot-turned-portrait of the happy volunteer sitting at her campaign office desk with a smiling Sid Taylor standing behind her chair.

Carmen Ryan's body had been flown back to Tennessee where her parents still resided. Adam assisted Carmen's family with the arrangements for transport, and accompanied her body to the Nashville airport where a hearse delivered her casket to a small funeral home in Murfreesboro. There, a private grave side service was held with only Adam and Carmen's immediate family in attendance. Compared to the circus-like atmosphere of the other victims' media-covered memorials, Carmen's ceremony was low key and solemn.

* * * * * *

The entire town was up in arms by all the publicity surrounding what was erroneously deemed as "the car bomb" incident. Forensics was still investigating; but, in the minds of most people who survived the afternoon, the car driven by the

Senator's son had been wired with an explosive that detonated at the moment the car crashed into the speaker's platform. To the public, no one except the Senator's lunatic son was to blame. No other theories were entertained.

* * * * * *

Val could hardly bring herself to organize a memorial for her son. It had been almost a week since he perished, but Val had gone into isolation since returning home to what now seemed to be a shrine to Brent. Everywhere she looked, she saw his image. Every thought she had ended up somehow connected to Brent. Her guilt was eating her alive.

Have I ever done the right thing for Brent? God knows I tried. If it hadn't been for my insistence, he would have attended local private schools, filled with both girls and boys. But, I was so afraid that Sid's bad influences would rub off on him...make him so much more insecure than he already was...I was afraid for Brent to live under the same roof with him. Brent was so sensitive, and he needed to be understood, not bullied. Sid would have killed Brent's spirit!

Then Val would torture herself more: *Brent, why didn't you tell me how you felt about your father? You never uttered a word about hating him, and you must have truly despised him! Did you feel the same way about me? Please, God. Please don't let him hate me, too. All I ever wanted was for you to love me, Brent. I needed you to cherish me!*

* * * * * *

Sid Taylor had been hospitalized immediately after the Port Jeff tragedy and remained in an induced coma during the first four days he spent in the Intensive Care Unit.

He had suffered a significant blow to the head when the bomb exploded less than twenty feet away from him. He also received superficial burns on his legs and arms, but it was his traumatic brain injury that landed him in the hospital.

After he was admitted to the hospital's neurological unit, Sid's doctors discovered that his brain was building up fluid, creating pressure on the tissue inside his skull and causing his brain to swell. A shunt was successfully implanted in his brain to drain off the excess fluid.   After several days, the procedure was deemed successful, and Sid was considered 'out of danger.'   Still, he remained under the hospital's care for another few days before being discharged from the facility to recover at home.

Ever since his traumatic injury he had not uttered a single word.

* * * * * *

The makeshift hospital room located on the second floor of the Taylor mansion had all the latest gadgets and medical equipment that any wealthy person could buy. Sid had attendants and nurses present in shifts providing him with 24/7 medical care. He also had physical therapists working with him daily to ensure he maintained his balance and kept his muscles active.

He had the finest "soft" meals prepared for him, but he found he had little or no appetite. He had a television set mounted above the foot of his bed, including access to all the premium cable channels. He had Netflix, HuLu, Prime, and other streaming sources—more than enough to keep the bedridden man entertained for hours upon end.

But he never saw Val. *Could she have gone to visit the family in Italy? Was she supposed to do that this year?*

He couldn't remember where Brent was . *Oh yes. Brent's away at school. He's at Georgetown,* he thought he remembered.

There's so much I can't recall. I think we must have been having a picnic at Waterfront, because that's what Brent always used to want to do when he was home. I saw his face, so I know he was there. But where was Val? Was she with us? It must have been a family gathering, but all I can remember is something about Brent losing his phone.

A frustrated Sid leaned back in his bed and allowed the nurse to fluff his pillows and tuck the covers snugly around him. He wanted to talk, but he couldn't form any words. His tongue and jaw wouldn't cooperate. He wondered if whatever happened to him affected his brain. Otherwise, why couldn't he remember anything of importance?

The nurse smiled at her patient. "There you go, Senator. Can I get you anything?" she asked pleasantly.

In the exaggerated fashion of a charades game, Sid lifted his bandaged arm and pretended to write in the air.

"Sir?" the nurse struggled to understand.

Sid lifted his other hand and pretended to write on his palm. He looked at her eagerly, hoping this time she'd get it.

"Oh, you want to write something! That's wonderful. I'll call the doctor, and I'll get you a pad and pen. I know the doctor will be thrilled to find out you're ready to communicate!"

As the nurse scurried out of the room, Sid closed his eyes and tried to recall how long he had been sick, or injured, or whatever the hell was wrong with him. *And where the hell is everybody? Where the hell is Val? Where's the household staff?*

Maybe the maid he once saw dusting the piano would venture in and talk to him. He thought she resembled a scared rabbit, but she seemed like a nice young person.

Sid fell asleep trying to remember the young maid's name: *Leanna? Lenora? Leona?*

* * * * * *

The debts that Val had incurred should have already been paid off. She had received some collection calls on her cell phone that more than frightened her. She wouldn't call the messages threatening, but they were pretty damn close. The man had gotten progressively nastier every time he'd called to remind her about her tardy payment. Val tried to explain that an emergency had come up—that she had lost her son, and her husband was hospitalized—and she couldn't get all the money together for a few more days. She could meet him and present every single dime owed to him on Friday, but not before. That was when several of Sid's investment dividends paid off, and their joint bank account would be more than flush when those deposits hit. She planned to avoid touching her own secret stash for this particular debt.

The frustrated man allowed her until Friday to come up with the entire $500,000 payment before something more tragic would befall her family. He told her that she should realize who she was dealing with. She smiled when the man made that remark.

*You don't know ME, asshole. I don't care who you think you are. **I am** more powerful than you could ever hope to be.*

She didn't breathe a word of that out loud.

Twin Sins

CHAPTER 29

The limousine pulled up at precisely noon on Friday, stopping a few feet away from the entrance to St. Charles Hospital, the medical center where the critically injured victims of the campaign rally bomb were taken. Val instructed the driver to pull around into the parking lot to wait. She indicated her business inside might take a while, but she would call him on his cell phone when she was ready to leave. The driver obliged, and soon the car disappeared to the far side of the building.

Val moved nervously through the lobby, her eyes darting from face to face as she tried to locate the person she was there to see.

"Hello, ma'am. How is your husband?" a familiar voice said from behind her. Val turned to look into the face of a middle-aged man dressed in turquoise scrubs and matching surgical hat. His sandy hair and matching brows made his green eyes shine like emeralds against his lightly freckled skin.

"Much better, Doctor," she replied. "Perhaps there is a consultation room we could use for a private chat about his prognosis?" Val asked anxiously.

"Right this way, please," he said pleasantly as he led her to a room not far from the lobby.

Ushering Val inside and closing the door behind them, they settled in opposing chairs, sitting with less than two feet of space between them.

"Do you have the package? My co-workers aren't as patient as I am."

Digging in her large purse, Val pulled out a manila envelope and worked with the gold brads holding it firmly closed. She folded back the flap and flashed the visible contents toward the Doctor. He peeked inside and smiled. He reached for the envelope, but Val jerked it away. He frowned with impatience.

"Before you get your grimy hands on the money, there are a few things I need to say first," Val retorted, scowling like an unsatisfied customer.

The Doctor leaned back in his chair and motioned for her to proceed. "I'm listening, but make it fast."

"First, all you were supposed to do was heighten Brent's addiction to drugs, not humiliate him. You exploited my son on film and spread it all over the place—even on the national news, for Christ's sake!"

The Doctor sighed. "That was most unfortunate. I know for a fact the national release of that video did not happen while the film was under our control. And as far as the sex went? My partner wanted to have some fun while he had a 'captive' audience. All the domination sex was his idea, not mine. As a matter of fact, he said you were fine with his techniques. Since he was the only contact **you** chose to use, I never had the opportunity to check in with you personally for precise instructions. I had to assume everything that was done was with your explicit approval."

"My **APPROVAL**? Are you insane? My goal was to get my heavily drugged son home, care for him, help him withdraw and recover, and then get us both safely away from my husband! Brent was supposed to love me for rescuing him, not despise me for torturing him. I **never** approved of the kind of cruel tactics you used during his kidnapping! I certainly didn't intend to ruin the reputations of the entire Taylor family! I ought to keep my damn money, since you two obviously took it upon yourselves to change the plan!" Val was livid, but the Doctor tried to calm her down.

"Didn't we achieve the goal you were looking for? We did our part."

"Maybe too well," Val said as she gave in to defeat and relaxed her stiff posture. "Now I'll never know if Brent truly loved me or hated me. Either way, he's gone now—drug addicted junkie or precious, loving son—doesn't matter anymore."

The Doctor began to feel sympathy for Val, but remained stoic until she recovered from her sudden surge of self-pity. He sat unmoving, waiting for her to break the awkward silence.

Suddenly she stood and thrust the manila envelope toward the Doctor. "Here. Take your sinful money. We won't be talking again ... ever."

As he took the money, he couldn't help but wish the haunting memories of that terrible few days could be erased from his mind. He, too, believed the Dominator had gone too far, but it hadn't been the Doctor's job to supervise. All he was supposed to handle was the drugs and the nutrition of the young man. He had done that part well, if he did say so himself.

Reeling his thoughts back into the present, he stuffed the envelope in the elastic waistband of his scrubs as he left the small room shortly behind his benefactor. The Doctor headed for his locker to stash the money he would soon divide among the Dominator, himself, and the limo driver who had made Brent's abduction a success.

* * * * * *

When Sophia dialed Adam's cell phone, she was surprised that he had answered from his office in New York. She was unaware he had returned to work without letting her know.

"Hello, Sophia," Adam replied blandly to her greeting.

"I didn't realize you were back in town, Adam. I am so very sorry about Carmen. Rick told me you two had called off your engagement, and I can't help but think I had something to do with that. And now, this...I don't know what to say except I'm sorry."

"Thank you," he answered without emotion.

"I was calling to check on you. If you need anything—maybe even just someone to talk to—I'm here, Adam. If you want company for dinner sometime, I'd be more than happy to join you whenever you're ready."

Adam smiled very slightly. "I do appreciate that, Sophia. I imagine this must be hard for you, too. Just give me a little time to sort things out, would you? It's true we ended our engagement, but Carmen hadn't taken time to move her things out of the apartment. I'm struggling with that."

Sophia sighed. "Adam, would you like some help?"

"No, Sophia. Not from you. Not right now. I'll get it done. When everything is boxed, I'll ship her belongings to her parents in Tennessee. I can take care of it alone."

"All right, Adam. But if you need anything, just let me know. I'll be right here," Sophia said as she hung up the phone.

* * * * * *

Thomas was adjusting well to Key West. Before he had gotten up the nerve to request a change of location, he had done some research about southern Florida. He decided on the Keys as the ultimate, once-in-a-lifetime all expense paid vacation.

When the airline tickets were delivered to him in Boston, he was ecstatic. Deciding not to waste any time, Thomas planned to do last-minute shopping for beach clothes once he arrived at his exciting new destination.

Since arriving in the Sunshine State, he had made several new friends. Some of them were gay couples, but most were like him. Alone. Lonely.

Thomas was initially booked into a motel, but he didn't like the atmosphere. He found himself a charming bed and breakfast and checked in. The two proprietors were single males; but according to them, they weren't attached. Thomas endeared himself to them when he began to join them in the kitchen twice daily to help prepare the scheduled meals the establishment served its guests. In between sightseeing and beach combing, Thomas expanded his assistance to tidying up the common areas, plus he made his own bed every day. The proprietors were thrilled.

Both of the owners told Thomas they'd help him get established if he ever wanted to relocate to Florida permanently. For once, Thomas seemed to fit in somewhere. He felt at ease there, and he was fascinated with the relaxed atmosphere of Key West, as well as its happy-go-lucky inhabitants.

But, would Sophia want to accompany him and live in the Southern most part of the country?

She was, after all, the one bright light that shined consistently in his bleak life.

He would profess his adoration to Sophia when he got back to New York. That would only be a few more days, and he was a patient man. He believed she would enthusiastically agree to a change of scenery, especially if she felt the same way about Thomas as he did for her. Why wouldn't she? He was her most loyal admirer—surely no one else on earth could ever be more loyal.   And she seemed to like him so very much, provided flirting and laughing with him was any indication of affection.

Thomas hummed a show tune as he prepared a large Cobb salad for the bed and breakfast guests, bursting into full song as he flipped slices of boiled egg across the mound of green leaf lettuce that filled the huge wooden salad bowl.

* * * * * *

Surprised by the phone call, Juliana looked puzzled when she heard what Val had to say.

"I just don't think I can do it. I just can't sit through a formal memorial for Brent," Val managed to explain through periodically spaced sobs.

Juliana listened sympathetically as Val sniffed and blew her nose on the other end of the phone.

"It's all my fault, you know. If I had just been a better mother …"

"Val, listen to me! This is NOT your fault! Now, shush. I don't want to hear you say that ever again! Understand?" Juliana said sternly.

"But ..."

"No 'buts,' Valentina. You are so much stronger than this."
Juliana tried hard to soothe Val, but she couldn't find the right
words.

Val continued to sniffle. "Do you think it would be appropriate
to just have a private gathering to honor Brent? I don't want to
face the public right now. Sid can't. Would you get in touch
with the mortician and see what can be done in the way of ...
of ... retrieving his ashes? We have a family crypt, and the
family can meet there to put the urn .... Oh, God! I can't
believe I even have to say these words!" Val started bawling
again.

Juliana didn't know exactly what to say. Awkwardly, she
agreed to handle all the interment details, telling Val not to
worry about anything else. When they hung up, Juliana was
relieved. The event would be much simpler now.

The best thing about a private memorial ceremony was there
would be no expected post-burial gathering at the DeLuca
mansion, which had always been the custom after family
funerals.

Additionally, they would never have to see Sid Taylor's face
again. Once Brent was settled in his final resting place, Val
would be the only Taylor welcome inside the DeLuca mansion
while Lucinda was reigning lady of the house.

* * * * * *

The restaurant was crowded, but Caroline and Slick managed
to get a rear corner table that gave them a hint of privacy.

"I'm telling you. There are suspicious things happening with DeLuca Enterprises. I feel it in my bones," Slick said as he picked up a glass of water and downed it.

"Is that your mother talking, or do you honestly feel that way?" Caroline chided.

"Hey. Don't knock my mother. Moms was spot on at that rally. If she hadn't motioned me away from where I was standing, I wouldn't be here to talk about it. She was standing right behind that weird guy, too. If he didn't have something to do with that bomb, why'd he run when he saw me coming toward him? I tell you, Caroline, it's all connected."

"Don't get upset, Slick. I believe you. I really do. Sounds like I owe your Moms my eternal gratitude," Caroline smiled as she lifted her glass of wine in a toast.

Slick was overcome by her sincerity. "Caroline, I feel ..."

Before he could finish, Caroline interrupted him. "I know. You feel grateful that your mother was there to guide you. So do I, Slick. Now why don't we order something before I starve to death. It's been a long day," she said, changing the subject before the conversation could turn too serious.

* * * * * *

Sid's attending physician came into his room at dusk, bringing with him a small dry erase board and pens. Smiling at the patient, the neurologist greeted Sid with a wide smile.

"Senator, I hear you're ready to communicate. That's very good news."

Sid shook his head as he reached for the small white board and pen. He wrote in a shaky fashion, having a hard time holding the pen steadily in his hand.

VAL ?

As the neurologist read Sid's message, his grin weakened. "I'm afraid your wife has become rather reclusive since the accident. Don't worry, though. Physically she's fine." Erasing the message with his hand, the doctor hesitantly gave the blank board back to Sid.

Sid furrowed his brow, not fully comprehending what his physician had just told him.

Once again, Sid managed to scrawl another question before he flipped the board toward the doctor.

BRENT ?

The neurologist cleared his throat before he answered. "Do you remember seeing Brent recently?"

Sid nodded and wrote more.

PARK ?

"Yes, he was at the park. Do you remember what happened at the park, Senator?"

Sid shook his head and closed his eyes, expecting the worst. When he opened his eyes, his physician had disappeared from the foot of his bed. Sid overheard him speaking on his cell phone outside the room.

"I may need a counselor here within the next half hour. Could you send someone over to help me break the news to the Senator about his son?"

The noise that came from Sid's throat sounded like a wounded animal. Still not able to voluntarily form words, the grieving father had no trouble howling a deep guttural noise that caused the hair to stand straight up on his doctor's neck.

CHAPTER 30

When Big Al's cell phone rang at 2:00 a.m., he knew better than to ignore it. A call that late could only mean one thing: Uncle Joe was unhappy, and he couldn't care less about the time difference between Italy and New York.

"Uncle Joe?" Big Al whispered into the phone, getting out of bed gently and moving stealthily into the guest bathroom in the hall. If he woke his sleeping partner, there would be additional hell to pay.

"You imbecile! You only had one job! You killed the wrong Taylor, you fucking idiot! Sid Taylor is still alive!"

Big Al tried to control his mounting anger, which was mixed with a healthy dose of fear. "Uncle Joe, the package activated at the right time. How was I to know that his druggie son was gonna try to mow down his daddy? There was no way to know that."

"You think I'm gonna pay you for **THIS**? You think you're gonna get a big slice of the Bellini pie for fucking up a simple assignment? You shoulda had control of the situation from the start. Jesus, Mary and Joseph! Am I gonna have to do this myself? That man is **still** breathing, and that's a problem," Uncle Joe roared into the phone.

Big Al took a deep breath, trying to silently count to ten to gain control of his emotions. "Look, Uncle Joe. I can still get to him. I'll handle it if you still want the cocksucker taken out."

"Dammit, boy, that's what I just **said**!" Uncle Joe shouted. "Handle it, or you'll be the next assignment I give to somebody!"

The cell phone went dead in Big Al's hand, and he stared at it with astonishment. "Bastard," he yelled at the phone, lobbing it across the small bathroom into the bathtub.

"Al, honey? You all right?" came a soft feminine voice from the bedroom.

"Yeah, go back to sleep. I just dropped something in the bathroom. Sorry, baby," he answered with fake concern.

"'K," responded the 24-year old hooker who had been shacked up with Big Al ever since the Port Jeff rally. He had paid her to run his errands, bring in food, and keep him company while he laid low for a while.

So far, no one had contacted him—with the exception of Uncle Joe.

* * * * * *

A few weeks had passed since the "Port Jeff Tragedy," which was the newly coined phrase used by the media when referring to the bomb incident.

The forensic team had discovered that the car driven by Brent had not been wired to explode; rather, a sophisticated incendiary device had been planted under the stage platform at about the same spot where the microphone had been located. It was designed to activate by depressing a remote control switch, using wireless technology. Even though this discovery had been reported to all media outlets, the public still chose to erroneously refer to the explosion as a car bomb.

* * * * * *

While Sid was still recuperating, Val Taylor transferred their joint liquid funds into her secret bank account and safe deposit box. To avoid the automatic notification to the Internal Revenue Service of large bank withdrawals, she siphoned $9,900 daily from their joint checking account, and the same amount from their money market, savings, and other accounts—all from different banks. Their accountant had insisted that they maintain their large accounts with different institutions because of the FDIC insurance aspect. She didn't know the difference, and she didn't care. Right now, she was only concerned with increasing her own wealth and stash of cash.

Considering Sid's current incapacities, it was a cinch to convince her attorney to draw up a Power of Attorney form for her to take home to Sid for signature. Val had forged Sid's name so many times, no one would know the difference between his original signature and the perfect one she often imitated. They looked alike, and no one ever questioned her. The challenge would be getting the form notarized. However, the funeral director who had been so handsomely paid to handle Brent's memorial service was more than happy to assist Val with that task, free of charge. Anything to help, he had told her.

The difficult part was almost over. There were still some of Sid's investments to be liquidated; also, she had several of her own stocks and bonds she hadn't yet decided what to do with.

Maybe I should hold on to those, just in case, and *only take care of Sid's assets now while he's still bedridden. No one's going to question those transactions, especially if I say that the money will be going to the victims of the Port Jeff Tragedy. They'll think I'm a saint for wanting to help those people. It'll be a shame when the victims never see a penny of that cash, but I'll be long gone before anyone asks about how the money was distributed.*

She smiled as she called for her driver to take her on her morning rounds to the banks.

This shouldn't take much longer. Before Christmas, this should all be over.

* * * * * *

Thomas had been back at the DeLuca mansion for a while, but Sophia had not visited her mother or grandmother since he'd returned from his vacation. He anxiously watched the driveway every evening, hoping that the elusive young woman would make an unexpected visit to her family, or maybe drop by just to see him.

Trying to keep busy and avoid the obvious questions about his time away had made Thomas feel somewhat stressed. However, he wasn't able to avoid a visit by Mr. Silvio, who showed up to interview Thomas the day after he returned from Florida.

The man told Thomas to call him "Slick," but Thomas found the name distasteful. Instead, Thomas continued to refer to the interviewer as "Mr. Silvio," which seemed to make the examiner uncomfortable.

As Thomas stood staring through the sunroom window toward the swimming pool, he recalled the session with the investigator:

Mr. Silvio: Would you please describe what you witnessed between Ms. Giordano and Senator Taylor the night of the fundraiser?

Thomas: I've already told Maureen and Mr. Rick what I saw. Why do I need to explain all this to you, as well, Mr. Silvio?

Mr. Silvio: I've been retained by the family to look into the alleged attack, because we would all like to resolve this issue and close the file, so to speak. I'm sure you're aware that there was no police report or doctor's visit, so there is very little to go on here. In fact, you are the only person, besides Ms. Giordano, who has come forward as a witness who could help us understand what happened.

Thomas: I see. Well in that case, I would truly like to help Miss Sophia. She is a very special lady to me... and all the other staff members.

Mr. Silvio: Yes, she's a fine young lady. So would you please start from the beginning? Any little detail you can remember might be significant, so think carefully.

Thomas: All right. I remember walking to the kitchen, but Maureen was off doing something so she wasn't present.   We were all so busy that night, you understand. Anyway, I stepped into the sunroom and saw ... what I saw. You know.

Mr. Silvio: No, please describe it to me. I would like to hear it in your own words.

Thomas: Right. Well, I saw the Senator lying on top of Miss Sophia out by the pool. It was ghastly, and I turned away.

Mr. Silvio: He was lying on top of Miss Sophia, you say? Could you tell if he had fallen on top of her, maybe? Maybe it wasn't the kind of attack we've all assumed it was?

Thomas: He was squirming around, as if he was … you, know…having sex with her. She didn't appear to be moving, but I'm not sure about that. At first I thought it was a mutual, consensual …uh, thing. But the more I think about it, I don't know how that could have been the case. Like I've said before, I couldn't bear to watch it. I walked away.

Mr. Silvio: Did you see Miss Sophia again that evening after the encounter?

Thomas: No. I understand she came inside later and collapsed on the floor. Maureen took care of her after that.

Mr. Silvio: When did you find out Miss Sophia had collapsed?

Thomas: I don't remember. It must have been some time later because Maureen sent me a text, asking me to let Mr. Rick know he should join them upstairs in Miss Sophia's bedroom. I suppose it was then.

Mr. Silvio: One other question, if you don't mind. Since Miss Sophia is so special to you, why didn't you want to know the extent of her injuries as soon as you found out she had been attacked?

Thomas: Well, uh. Of course I wanted to know. But I am a member of the household staff here, sir. My first obligation was to ensure the house event continued to run smoothly. Our employers treat us as who we are: members of their staff. We are not part of the family, as much as we might like to think we are. We are not given that kind of information directly from our employers—it's none of our business. Besides, Maureen would have informed me later; and, of course, she did.

Mr. Silvio: I understand you immediately left to visit your family on an unscheduled holiday? In Colorado, was it?

Thomas: Yes, I have relatives there, and I have an open invitation to join them for a skiing holiday. Considering all the stress we've been under here lately, it seemed like a good time to take them up on the invitation.

Mr. Silvio: Thank you, Thomas. You've been very helpful.

Thomas couldn't remember everything he said to the private investigator, but he believed he had told the story perfectly— the way it was supposed to be presented to anyone who snooped around. He hoped that he would hear nothing more from Mr. Silvio, praying the whole mess was behind all of them now.

* * * * * *

Standing in Caroline's office doorway, Slick cleared his throat to get her attention.

"We've got to stop meeting like this," Caroline chuckled.

"Good morning, beautiful lady," Slick announced as he walked briskly toward her. He bent down to kiss her on the cheek as she beamed with pleasure.

"Thank you, Slick. Sit down and have a cup of coffee with me. I was just about to look over my schedule for the day."

"No coffee for me, thanks. I've already had a couple, and too much of that stuff makes me jittery." He chewed his gum rapidly.

Slick sat across from Caroline's desk, indicating he was there on business. "I can't get past the interview I had with the DeLuca's butler, Thomas. There's something just not right about what that guy says. Forget the fact that he kept averting his eyes up and to the right, never looking straight at me. It was like he was imagining the whole thing. I know, avoiding direct eye contact is not a sure indicator of lying, but it's something to think about. Anyway, this was more about **how** he said what he said versus **what** he said. His story lacked a lot of detail. But the way he talked about what happened was like he was trying to picture something he was making up, not remembering."

Caroline watched Slick carefully. "Are you sure you haven't had any visions about this, Slick? Has your mother visited you recently?"

"Caroline, please! I wish I had never told you about that stuff."

"Why, Slick? I'm a believer now. Until you explained everything—basically proved it to me—I wouldn't be asking you those sorts of questions. I really want to know if you've had any other premonitions, especially now." Caroline got up from her desk and walked around to stand by Sid. She touched his shoulder briefly and stated, "I believe in you, Slick. I know what you're capable of."

Slick nodded, still not convinced that Caroline hadn't been making fun of his gift. "There is one detail I **know** he lied about," he replied, "and that is when he found out about Sophia's attack. He said Maureen told him when she texted to go find Rick. That's not true according to what Maureen said. The first they spoke of it was when out of the blue Thomas asked her how Sophia was doing when he came into the kitchen hours later. That's suspicious in itself."

Caroline looked concerned. "Very clever, Mr. Silvio. Very clever. The plot thickens."

CHAPTER 31

There was a touch of some nasty virus running rampant through the DeLuca Enterprises administration building. So many employees were absent because of the widespread illness that several temp agency employees had been hired to fill in. Both Rick and Teddy had stayed tightly closed up in their respective offices, paranoid that walking through the halls and offices unnecessarily would expose them to needless health risks.

Sophia had been braver ...or more careless...than her two executive co-workers. She wouldn't allow herself to stay caged up behind her desk. Instead, she freely visited the DeLuca office staff, held meetings with several different groups, and frequented the corporate break room where she drank her tea out of rinsed mugs that had been left in the dish drainer to dry. She believed if her immune system wasn't strong enough, she'd get sick regardless. Why become a prisoner to potential germs?

A few days later the virus episode seemed to have passed through, and staff members began returning to work feeling much better.

However, Sophia began to feel something less than perfect when she found herself bent over the toilet in her office's private half-bath. Thankfully, she was alone when she threw up her breakfast. She wiped her face with a wet cloth, swished around a healthy dosage of mouthwash, and straightened her clothing.

When she made it back to her desk, she scanned her calendar for any important meetings scheduled for that day and the next. Satisfied, Sophia gathered her things and headed for the door.

As Sophia passed by her administrative assistant's desk, she instructed the woman to clear her calendar for the next two days. Further, she directed that if anything important came up, her assistant was to make sure Rick filled in during Sophia's absence.

Now that she had her next two days covered at work, Sophia felt relieved to leave the building without explanation to anyone, especially Rick or Teddy.

* * * * * *

Boomer hadn't expected to hear from Big Al Bellini again, at least not so soon after he had delivered his recent order. Boomer initially thought Big Al wanted another customized order, but he soon found out he wanted that and more.

"You up for making a little more cash, Boomer?" Big Al asked.

"Depends. What do I gotta do for it?"

"This one's easy. I need a little extra something that you could whip out in no time, given your skills. You might have what I need made up already, considering how you spend your spare time," Al said as he watched Boomer light a cigarette.

"In addition to that little item, all you gotta do is tail someone for a few days. Don't even have to do it full time. I just need to know the mark's comings and goings. Like I said, it'll be easy. I'll give you $5,000 a day until a reliable pattern can be established.   But this can't take more than five days, max. Capisce?"

"Piece o'cake. Yeah. I can handle that. Gimme the name of the mark and let's get started," Boomer eagerly responded. "And I got a few little items ready-made for your other request. You can pick out the one you want."

"Good. Can you start the tail today? Full day's pay for your first half day's work?" Big Al teased.

"Just point me in the right direction, boss," Boomer laughed.

* * * * * *

Stopping by the Walgreen's on the corner a few blocks from her home, Sophia went inside to get a bottle of Tylenol, some Pepto-Bismol, and a few other sundry items. She prayed whatever was gripping her from the inside was going to pass within a few hours. She knew she had been somewhat reckless, expecting the virus to bypass her just because she deemed it so. But, apparently her good intentions didn't trump her immune system this time.

When she arrived at the penthouse, she stared at the shiny name plate on the door. It still said "DeLuca." It had never been changed all these years. *Guess I really should get that changed to Giordano,* she thought fleetingly as she pushed the door open.

Walking straight to the master bedroom with drug store bag in hand, she went immediately to her chest of drawers to pull out her favorite flannel pajamas—the pair she always wanted to wear when she felt under the weather.

Taking them with her to the bathroom, she laid her PJs across the spa tub and placed the Walgreen's bag on the edge of the vanity nearest the commode. Sophia sat down slowly on the commode, pulling her dress pants free from her legs as she sat.

She tried to grab for her pajama bottoms, but they were slightly out of her reach. Instead, she spontaneously grabbed the Walgreen's bag sitting on the edge of the sink, emptying its contents on the adjacent vanity top. Sophia picked up the one item she had bought on impulse and ripped open the packaging before she had a chance to change her mind.

* * * * * *

By now, Sid Taylor was wheelchair-dependent, able to get around inside his house with limited assistance from his attending staff. He was no longer tethered to cords, tubes, or the tangled tendrils of various medical devices.

Broad bandages still adorned his arms and his abdomen, but they were all but invisible under his pajamas and robe. He looked healthy enough, but he still hadn't found his voice. In a leather pouch attached to the side of his wheelchair, he carried a pad and pen, just in case something important needed to be communicated.

The elevator that Val had insisted on adding to the house was finally getting some practical use. Sid had always avoided it, believing he needed the limited exercise that using the stairs would provide his aging body. Now, he was thankful that Val had the foresight to have installed the expensive addition. Without it, he would have been restricted from going downstairs, forced to live and work in the second floor prison cell that Val had deliberately designated as his hospital room.

Damn her. She tried to keep me upstairs, out of her sight. She thought I'd be too weak to ever come downstairs, but her own pride ruined that plan. If she hadn't insisted on that elevator—like the one at the DeLuca estate—I'd be stuck up there even now. HA!

He wheeled himself into his downstairs office, picking up the remote and clicking on the television as he passed behind the leather couch. He muted the volume and turned on the closed captions. Sid had finally learned the value of silence.

When the phone rang, it startled him. He waited, wondering if Val was somewhere in the house. Even if she was there, she wouldn't show her face to Sid. He hadn't seen her or heard her voice since he was injured.

He heard someone clearing her throat, looked up, and locked eyes with the young maid whose name he had tried to remember once. He smiled.

"Senator, sir? Your banker is on the line. Is there something I can tell him for you?" Leona asked.

Sid looked confused. He hadn't initiated any banking transactions for weeks, and wondered why a bank representative would be calling him at home. Especially now. Sid shrugged, then nodded to Leona. He waved her toward the desk and pointed at the phone there.

Leona smiled, understanding his meaning. She spoke into the extension phone with confidence. "Sir, please hold while I switch phones. I will put you on speaker so the Senator can hear what you are saying. He hasn't regained his voice yet, but he writes his responses on paper. I can read them back to you, if you like?"

She listened carefully, then switched the phones so that the banker's voice was heard clearly through the speaker phone on Sid's desk.

"Can you hear me, Senator?" the banker asked.

Sid nodded. Leona replied, "He hears you, sir."

"This is awkward, Senator. There is some information I can only share with you, and it's impossible to handle it in this manner. You understand, I hope," he tried to explain.

Again Sid nodded and Leona responded for him.

"Sir, are you able to travel yet? Is it possible you could visit us here at the main office of the bank?"

Leona didn't need to read Sid's response to answer the banker. "No, sir. Senator Taylor is not able to leave the house yet." Sid gave her a 'thumbs up' gesture for answering appropriately.

"Well, then, are you accepting visitors?" the worried banker asked.

Sid nodded. Leona told the banker he would appreciate such a visit.

"Great. We need to talk as soon as possible, sir. Would this afternoon be convenient?" he asked and Leona relayed "yes" when Sid nodded.

"Wonderful. Let's say two o'clock. And if your wife is available, she should be there, too. Oh, and would you verify your home address for me? We can never be too careful nowadays."

Before Sid could write anything down, Leona told the banker the address of the Taylor home. Sid had wanted her to ask him what the address on file was, but Leona didn't give him enough time to write that down.

I guess we'll find out what all this fuss is about this afternoon when the banker shows up. Val might be here then, and she might not. I don't know if she'll agree to sit in the same room with me, even if it does involve her precious money.

* * * * * *

Teddy rushed past the desk of Sophia's administrative assistant and opened Sophia's office door. The office was empty. Her desk was cleaned off, and the lights were out.

Turning to the smirking assistant, Teddy asked, "Where is she? I've got some information she needs to hear."

"She didn't tell me where she was going, but she asked that I clear her calendar for today and tomorrow," the woman responded in a sharp tone.

"Who's in charge, then? Is it Rick?" Teddy asked impatiently.

"Yes, I've already informed Mr. Giordano that he's to handle the business while she's away."

Teddy didn't like feeling left out of the inner circle. Without another word, Teddy marched to Rick's office, bypassing the vigilant administrative assistant assigned to him. Saying nothing, Teddy opened the door and entered without permission or invitation.

"Where's Sophia?" Teddy bluntly asked Rick.

"I have no idea. She didn't say anything to me, just sent her snooty secretary over to tell me I had to fill in for her. I've only known myself for a few minutes. Why? What's up?" Rick answered.

"Nothing, except I have all the approvals necessary for Sophia to run for Congresswoman this November.

Everything's in, signed, sealed and delivered. Now all we have to do is launch her campaign!" Teddy said excitedly.

"Fantastic!" Rick said. "Come here, old buddy! I knew you could do it." The two men embraced in a congratulatory hug in the middle of Rick's office.

"Sophia's gonna be amazed that you pulled this off, Teddy," Rick commented.

"It's not hard if you know the right people. You taught me that, Rick."

Slapping each other on the back, the two continued rejoicing by drinking shots of single malt scotch.

"It may not be late enough to drink, but it's always the right time to celebrate," Rick toasted. Teddy responded by adding, "Cheers!"

* * * * * *

Her eyes were wide, and her mouth remained open for almost a minute. She read the instructions once again just to be certain she had performed the test correctly.

"Oh, God. Oh, God. Oh, God," she kept repeating as she looked at the direction page and the blue cross that had formed in the middle of the stick.

"Oh, God!" she exclaimed finally, standing up from the toilet. "I gotta call somebody!"

She started to walk forward, but her panties were gathered around her ankles. Struggling to get them up, she stood there momentarily. She grabbed her pajamas and ran to her bed. She jumped in the middle of the king-sized comforter, thinking as she landed, "too rough, too rough." Laughing aloud, she realized that she was genuinely happy for the first time in years.

"Who to call? Who to call? Adam, I'll call Adam."

Stopping after punching the first three digits on her cell phone, she realized that would be the wrong call to make. She needed to think the situation through carefully. She should understand all the ramifications of an unplanned pregnancy before she made the news public. She couldn't be hasty. She had to be smart before anything else.

She'd curl up for a while in her flannel PJs and rest. She had been exhausted lately, and now she understood why.

Need time to think. Later.

For once, I wish I could react to life events like a normal person instead of having to be a pawn in someone else's game.

Twin Sins

CHAPTER 32

Adam Woodson finished packing up the last of Carmen's personal belongings, stacking the boxes in the corner of their small living room until he could ship them off to Tennessee.

Several of Carmen's things were not suitable items to forward to her parents, such as magazines, toiletries, a few ragged tee shirts, and old shoes. He either tossed those things in the garbage or bagged them for delivery to the local thrift shop. He had carefully selected what remained behind as special keepsakes he would treasure. He and Carmen had spent many years together working for the same employer. The last three of those years, they had posed as an engaged couple.

He poured himself a beer, feeling as though he'd finally accomplished something constructive with his free time. He had been neglectful of the apartment, not bothering to make up the bed or even change the sheets. He could still smell the scent of Carmen Ryan on the pillowcases. The towels she had used the morning she died were still draped over the glass door of the shower.

His feelings for her were hard to define. She wasn't wife material—that he knew. He wasn't jealous of her when she flirted with other men. He had always thought of her as a sister, or perhaps a 'partner in crime,' as she so often jokingly referred to herself. He loved her like a sister, or a relative, or maybe even a roommate who merely shared the rent and the utility bills like any good roommate would.

While he drank his beer, his mind wandered to Sophia Giordano. True, he had thought he loved her, but now he wasn't so sure. They had never fully experienced a dating relationship together, and once upon a time that was his dream. In retrospect, he had been with Sophia intimately…passionately… so perhaps he had just imagined he was in love with her when it was actually only the afterglow of their encounter that mesmerized him.

Sighing with frustration, Adam tried to focus on how he would get through the next few days or weeks without feeling the deep pain of losing his dearest friend, Carmen.

* * * * * *

The front door opened and slammed shut. As usual, Val's arms were filled with bulging shopping bags, so she had to use her body to push against the door to make it close.

Leona met her in the foyer and attempted to relieve Val of her heavy load of merchandise. Realizing who was trying to help her, Val snapped at the young maid. "Leave me alone. I don't ever want to see your face again, you murderer!"

Appalled at Val's outburst, Leona cowered and tried to back out of Val's immediate presence. "Why haven't you been fired?" Val screamed after Leona had disappeared from view.

Sid heard the tirade from his seat behind the desk in his nearby office. He shook his head as he closed his eyes and thought about his grieving wife.

I understand what's setting Val off, but damn! Deep down she's such an evil bitch! Somebody ought to put her out of her misery.

* * * * *

A little after one o'clock, the doorbell rang repeatedly at Adam's apartment. He had fallen asleep in a living room chair, several empty beer bottles punctuating the area rug around his seat. Startled, Adam sat straight up when the doorbell continued to ring.

"Coming," he shouted as he shuffled in his house shoes toward the front door. He tried to see through the peep hole, but the visitor was standing too far to the side. Adam took a chance and opened the door without any idea who would be standing outside his door.

"I hope this isn't a bad time," the visitor said.

The color drained from Adam's face as he begrudgingly ushered his employer into his unkempt apartment.

∧ ∧ ∧   ∧ ∧ ∧

Sid wrote a note to Val, carefully wording the message so as not to piss her off. Based on the limited information he had from the banker who called him, it seemed important that Val attend the scheduled meeting set for an hour later in Sid's office.

His note said simply:

> THE BANK IS SENDING SOMEONE TO TALK TO US TODAY AT 2:00. WE WILL MEET IN MY OFFICE.
>
> SOMETHING HAPPENING WITH OUR ACCOUNTS THAT NEEDS ATTENTION OF BOTH OF US.
>
> DON'T BE LATE. IMPORTANT

He folded the paper and sealed it in an envelope. He despised doing it, but he rang the small bell on his desktop that had once been placed there as a decorative accent. Immediately, Leona stuck her head in the door to see if she could help him.

"Can I do something for you, sir?" she asked meekly, still sniffing back her runny sinuses that had been set off by the tears she had hidden from the irate Val.

Sid could see her distress. He motioned for her to come to the side of his chair. She obeyed.

Reaching for his pen, he wrote her a note on the pad he kept by his side.

SLIDE UNDER WITCH'S DOOR

He handed the envelope to Leona, smiling broadly as he lightly touched her hand.

Leona broke out into a grin, then chuckled softly. She nodded to Sid, agreeing to complete the task he had requested. Sid winked at her as she left to deliver the envelope as he had instructed.

* * * * * *

"First, let me say how sorry we were to hear that Carmen was killed while on official duty. It is always heartbreaking to lose someone with whom you've worked so closely, but time will be your friend when it comes down to it," the well-dressed man said. "We have, of course, provided well for her family. I know that was a concern of yours after the unfortunate event happened. As far as they knew, their daughter was employed by the Civil Service as a Customs Official or some such nonsense." He chuckled, amused at himself.

Adam found nothing funny about his employer's comments. He stared at him instead of providing a verbal response.

Clearing his throat, Adam's employer resumed the one-sided conversation. "So, now. Let's get right to it. Carmen sent detailed status reports routinely to the team, outlining what she had already discovered and what she was on the brink of uncovering. Honestly, we have enough information now—with your affirming testimony about your joint efforts—to stop the Bellini crime family and the New York-based DeLuca Enterprises from operating illegally. We have sufficient evidence to send every member of the entire corporate structure to prison. All that's required is your substantiating testimony, of course, since Carmen is now... uh, deceased." He leaned back on the couch and crossed his legs, awaiting Adam's response.

"This is not the time. This is surely not the place. **This** was our home that I have to dismantle, all alone. Everything here has Carmen's breath on it. I can't deal with that part of the job right now. Things are still too raw," Adam whispered, head in hands.

The man stood, pausing briefly before moving toward the front door. "I'll come back another time, Adam. And by the way, you are aware that the Agency provides counseling to their operatives who've been through trauma such as yours? You might want to give them a call and arrange for an appointment."

The man quickly exited the apartment, sprinted to a waiting black sedan, and was whisked away to catch a private plane.

* * * * * *

When the doorbell rang promptly at 2 o'clock, Leona looked carefully at all the foyer doorways to be certain she wouldn't run into Val Taylor there. No one appeared to be stirring near the entry, so Leona opened the door.

"Welcome, sir," she said as she stood aside to allow the well-dressed man to enter.

"Thank you, miss. I have an appointment with Mr. Taylor," he smiled.

"Yes, sir. He is expecting you. Right this way," she said as she led the gentleman to the doorway of Sid Taylor's home office. After he entered, Leona shut the door behind him, leaving the two men alone. The maid disappeared into another part of the house.

Not able to stand and certainly not capable of speaking, Sid Taylor's eyes widened with anxiety when he looked into the hauntingly familiar face of his visitor.

"Surprise, eh?" Big Al said as he took a seat in front of Sid's desk. "You know, you should have to reimburse me for all these duds, Sid. I had to spend a pretty penny to look the part of a respectable banker," he chuckled.

Sid began breathing fast, having trouble catching his breath from the panic he was experiencing.

"No need to get all worked up, Sidney. I'm just here to talk, but I was hoping I could have a few minutes to chat with your lovely wife, Val. Is she here in the house?" Big Al asked with a fake smile plastered across his face.

Sid didn't move a muscle.

Big Al chuckled again. "Don't piss your pants, there Sid. You better not try to roll that chair around here either. I already know your position on gun control. It's a safe bet you don't have one. Lucky for me, I always carry."

Sid squeezed his eyes shut, hoping this whole thing was a bad dream.

Big Al leaned back and lit a cigar that he pulled from the breast pocket of his new vest. "I'll bet you're wondering why I'm here, don't cha? Well, as soon as the little missus comes in here to join us, I'll explain everything in full Technicolor." Big Al laughed at himself. "Maybe Technicolor isn't the right word, but you know what I mean. I'm especially fond of vivid reds. So...why don't I go find her so we can get this little party started, eh?"

Rising slowly from the chair, Big Al was almost upright when the door to Sid's office opened. Val waltzed in, refusing to look Sid Taylor in the face.

"Please excuse my tardiness. I wasn't aware of this meeting until seconds ago. Seems someone slid a note under my door that had escaped my view until now. I'm Valentina Taylor. And you are?" she asked politely.

"I am a long lost relative, Miss Bellini, here to talk to you about your finances and life choices," Big Al stated pleasantly as he kissed her extended hand.

"Well, you're certainly a gentleman. Do I know you? You look vaguely familiar to me," she said innocently as she seated herself adjacent to Big Al's chair. In a maneuver to ignore Sid, Val turned her chair sideways, directly facing the visitor. She positioned her seat parallel to the front edge of Sid's desk, allowing for only an occasional peripheral glimpse toward her revolting husband.

* * * * * *

Adam sat in the middle of his living room floor, surrounded by overdue bills that he had ignored for the past few weeks. His laptop was sitting on a wooden coffee table with his online banking page staring back at him from the bright screen.

Carmen, you would never have let the bills get behind, would you? He somberly picked up the first envelope he touched. It was from the cell phone company and he stared at it blankly. It reminded him that Carmen's phone line was also billed through the account they shared. He threw the envelope down on the floor, wondering what was preventing him from rising from the pit of grief.

When the doorbell rang again, Adam shook his head. *Son of a bitch! Why won't that bastard leave me alone?*

Angrily rushing for the door, Adam was ready to assault his employer for pestering him again. He yanked the door open with a scowl.

Sophia stared into Adam's face which was contorted with anger and rage.

"Uh...maybe I should come back some other time," she managed to say, afraid to make any movement until she knew what had caused Adam to be so irate.

"Sophia. I...I'm sorry. I thought you were someone else," he said, embarrassed by the furious way he had jerked open the door.

"Are you sure, Adam?" she asked cautiously.

"Yes, of course. Come in. I'm sorry." He led her to the living room, again embarrassed by the mess he had surrounded himself with.

Sophia stepped around scattered envelopes and empty beer bottles, finding a clear spot on the couch to sit. "I'm sorry I didn't call first, but this was a spur of the moment decision. I was afraid if I didn't just do this when I had the nerve, I'd never manage to get it out."

Adam was still standing near the coffee table. "Decision? What decision, Sophia?"

She motioned for Adam to sit down.

"Adam, I have some things to tell you."

He continued to stare at her, not responding to her or giving her encouragement. He didn't want to play twenty questions, especially not today of all days.

She cleared her throat, then hesitantly smiled. "Adam, I'm going to have a baby."

Twin Sins

CHAPTER 33

Val looked blankly at Big Al, who had seated himself again in the chair across from where Sid sat in his wheel chair behind his mahogany desk.   Sid's face was still a canvas of whitewash, appearing ghostly as he grimaced uneasily.

"So, you said you're a long-lost relative? Of mine or Sid's?" Val chattered.

"Of yours, Valentina. I'm surprised you don't remember me."

She continued to peer into Big Al's face, and finally a hint of recognition came to her squinting eyes. "You must be Uncle Joe's grandson! What a pleasure to finally meet you! And you're a banker, too!" Val chuckled as she thought she had Big Al pegged.

"Not exactly, Valentina. But you're close. Uncle Joe sent me here, though. He has a message for your husband, but I think he'll be pleased that you're here to get it, too."

Val looked confused, but continued with her fake pleasantries. "Well, of course. How is dear Uncle Joe?"

"He's feisty as ever. In fact, it's because of money that I'm here," Big Al hinted.

"Well, it's about time he made some decisions about the fortune he's sitting on. I'm surprised he even remembered to include me ... us, that is," Val remarked as she looked at Sid's pale face for the first time since the "Tragedy at Port Jeff."

"Sid, are you all right?" she asked as soon as she saw his expression of terror. She started to stand, but Big Al reached across her and barred her from rising.

"What is the meaning of this? What are you doing?" she asked, stunned that anyone would purposely touch her.

"Sit down, Val. You two need to hear every word I say today. Then we'll figure out what to do with you," Big Al barked, pulling a handgun from his waistband and pointing it directly at Val.

Val slowly eased back into her chair, eyes focused straight on the man who claimed to be her distant relative. *Now I recognize him. He's the head of the crime family here in New York…the Bellini crime family. I think his name is Alphonso. OH GOD! He's here to kill us!*

Big Al smiled at Val, watching her mentally solve the puzzle of his identity. "You can call me Al, you know. Long time, no see," he chuckled as he watched her squirm.

* * * * * *

It took more than a few seconds for Adam to comprehend what Sophia had revealed to him. When he finally understood, he wordlessly walked out of the room, making Sophia believe the unexpected news she shared was a grave disappointment to him. Deep down, she'd hoped he would be overjoyed with excitement. Apparently, that was not the case. Sophia dropped her head and began to weep.

Moments later, Adam reentered the living room, carrying a wine glass in each hand. He extended a glass to Sophia, keeping one for himself.

"To the baby," he said as he reached forward to toast Sophia's glass.

"Adam, I can't have alcohol now," she innocently answered.

"It's juice, Sophia. I've got the alcohol, you get the apple juice," he smiled. "Cheers."

"Oh, Adam, I'm so glad you're happy," she said as she quickly stood to embrace him.

* * * * * *

"Well, get on with it then. Say what you're here to say," Val commanded her visitor.

Big Al stood up, taking a spot a few feet away from both the Taylors so he could watch them simultaneously.

"Well, Val and Sid," he started, nodding in recognition to both, "the thing is, for years, Uncle Joe has been very disappointed with the Taylor branch of the family. You, in particular," he said as he pointed at Sid with the barrel of the drawn gun. Sid clenched his eyes shut, not able to respond verbally. He started to move his arm toward his pad to write something, but Big Al stopped him.

"Don't touch anything, Sid. You don't want to alarm anybody, do you? You might make me pull the trigger before I'm ready."

"For God's sakes, Al. Sid can't talk. He just wants to write something," Val surprised them both as she defended her husband.

"Nope. He doesn't get to say anything, and if you don't stop interrupting me, I'm gonna have to shut you up, too," the big man snarled.

Being unaccustomed to taking orders, Val pursed her lips in obvious disdain.

"As I was saying, Uncle Joe doesn't understand why you've consistently ignored his…shall we say, 'requests,' to push legislative actions he's suggested for you to endorse, Senator Taylor. You've turned a blind eye to his orders, and you've gone rogue. You've done this now for too many years to count. You realize if it hadn't been for him and the family, you would never have won the Senate seat to begin with."

Sid dropped his head, tears of regret rolling down his cheeks.

"Now, he could let bygones be bygones, but Uncle Joe is getting old and tired. He's given you a free pass as a part of the family for a long time now, finding other ways to keep the business growing without your political help. It's been a struggle for everybody, I know.

"But now, Sid? You really aren't needed anymore. You've forced the family to find other ways to prosper. Another branch of the family has become more valuable than you ever were or could ever be again.

"Of course, it's a shame that losing your only son and your deteriorating physical condition have made you so despondent that you'd consider ending it all just for a little everlasting peace, eh?" Big Al waved the gun back and forth between his two targets.

Val's anger was growing. Her narrowed eyes squinted in disgust as they ping-ponged back and forth between her relative and her husband. She wasn't sure which man she hated more at that moment.

Big Al laughed and focused on Val. "You think you're innocent in all this?" he directed his words to her.

"Sid, let me tell you what your loving wife's been up to."

The Senator raised his head and looked squarely into Big Al's wild eyes.

"Stop!" Val shouted from her seat, starting to rise and lunge toward Big Al.

He was across the space in seconds, knocking Val back in her chair as the side of his gun connected bluntly with her jawbone. "I told you to shut up, bitch!" he screamed at the shocked woman who was now sprawled awkwardly across the club chair. She touched her bleeding cheek as she gathered herself up and sat meekly again in her assigned seat.

"Now, don't make me do that again, Valentina," Big Al warned. Straightening his jacket and adjusting his grip on the handgun, Big Al continued with his revelation.

"As I was trying to say, Valentina has been a naughty girl. Sid, did you know that it was Valentina who arranged to have your son kidnapped from a night club and taken to a desolate location, only to have him pumped full of heroin? Were you aware of that, Sidney?"

Val's eyes were wide with terror. "That's not true..." she started to say, but when Big Al took a step in her direction, she cowered backwards.

"Tell him, Val. Tell him what you did," Big Al insisted.

"How did you find out?" Val cried, still drawn into a partial fetal position in her chair.

"Do you think anything like that gets past the family? You're a fool, you know. You think you can arrange something like that and the Bellinis wouldn't know? HA! Every member of that crew is loyal to the Bellini family. Uncle Joe knew everything—before your son was ever taken! You're a fucking idiot, Val," Big Al smirked.

"Sid, I … I never…," Val started to explain, but Sid closed his eyes, refusing to look at her.

"Yeah, Val. Try to explain it away. But you don't get it, do you? You were trying to hurt your son so he'd be dependent on you, right? Turn him against his father and make him feel loved and safe with you? Well, what you caused was your son to go off the deep end and interfere with Uncle Joe's plans. It was really tragic when Brent rammed that car into the stage that I'd already set to blow," he chuckled.

Sid's eyes opened wide, suddenly recognizing Big Al as the man he'd passed in the parking lot at his campaign headquarters—the 'banker' was the menacing but familiar face he spotted standing near the back of the rally crowd. Chills ran down his spine as he began to realize that the explosion wasn't because of Brent, but was the sole responsibility of the threatening man standing mere feet away from Val.

Sid squirmed more in his seat, suddenly trying to find his voice. "Uuhh," he managed to get out, causing maniacal laughter to erupt from Big Al.

"Cat got your tongue?" he laughed even harder. "So, Sid? Whatcha wanna do, huh? You want me to kill her now, or do you want to hear the rest of the story? I can assure you, you'll find it even more interesting."

The veins on Sid's forehead looked as if they were dancing. He was clearly agitated now more than he was afraid.

"Well, I'll tell you anyway. She's been withdrawing all your money from every bank account you have, old boy. Your loyal wife has been liquidating your assets behind your back. She's been stashing cash away so she can make a clean break. Looks like she wanted to leave you high and dry, and honestly, I can't blame her. You're not much of a man now, and I'm guessing you never were. Otherwise, Val wouldn't have run around on you for all those years."

Big Al looked at the broken-spirited Val, and asked, "You wanna tell him about your affairs, or should we just let that go?"

Val wailed, not able to respond with anything other than moans and sobs.

"Well, I guess it's time we ended this little chat session. I wish I could say it's been nice, but well … you know."

Big Al cocked the handgun and aimed it at Val. He briefly glanced at Sid and smugly asked, "Would you like to do the honors? I'll help you pull the trigger."

Sid shook his head and pointed to his own chest.

Big Al looked surprised. "You wanna be a hero now? Don't worry, you'll get your turn." He laughed again, this time turning to give his full attention to his cowering female target.

"Uncle Joe sends his love," Big Al announced as he pulled the trigger.

Sid screamed an unintelligible sound as he watched his wife crumple, sliding out of the chair she had tried to cling to before her death. Scarlet smears were painted on the chair's surface as her bloody clothing swiped across the fine leather. Val's lifeless body slithered to the floor in a pitiful heap.

"Now, your turn, Sidney," Big Al announced. He turned slowly toward his target, watching Sid's eyes race back and forth between the shooter and the door. Sid had spied the doorknob turning as soon as the first shot rang out, but he had no hope of rescue.

"Sir?" Leona said as she peeked in the door.

"Come on in, little lady. I was expecting you to join us," Big Al said in a welcoming tone.

Leona took baby steps towards the group. As she circled slowly around Big Al to join Sid behind the desk, she looked down at Val's bloody body. She noticed Val's eyes were still open, frozen in shock. Leona moved carefully as she stood behind the Senator, watching Big Al's every move as he pointed the gun in their direction.

"Maybe I should make you the same offer I made to Sid, little lady. You want to do the honors here? You wanna kill old Sid there?" he asked as he relaxed his aim and waved the gun in the air.

"Uh… what?" Leona said.

"Here." Grip first, he extended the warm gun toward the maid. She reached for it hesitantly, her stoic expression morphing into one of surprised delight.

"Come over here next to me, dear. Your aim will be better from here, and you won't get anything on you," Big Al instructed.

Leona slowly approached Big Al, holding the gun in both her hands as if she were afraid to touch it. Finally she looked at Sid, who sat stiffly in his wheelchair, expecting Leona to make a move to save them both.

"Ok, take a deep breath and aim the gun."

Leona closed her eyes as if in silent prayer. When she opened them, she smiled broadly. Suddenly, she took steady aim with the gun, but the weapon wasn't pointed at Sid. Leona shot the dead body of Valentina Taylor twice more.

Big Al laughed as Leona joyously looked up at his face. Big Al beamed with satisfaction.   "I always hated that bitch," Leona laughed.

Sid's eyes grew wide with horror as he watched Leona swerve the gun past Big Al and take aim at him.

Leona had been the only staff member Sid had ever befriended, and he struggled to wrap his mind around what she was doing.

Seconds later, Leona discharged the weapon again, striking the invalid Sid in the heart. She raised the gun and fired another round in his forehead.

"Double tap. Isn't that what you always taught me, Al?" Leona said proudly. Big Al kissed her on the mouth as they congratulated each other on their successful conclusion to the afternoon meeting.

Big Al slapped Leona's shapely behind before he turned to leave. "Now, go make your phone call, sweetheart. Uncle Joe will be so proud of you!"

Twin Sins

CHAPTER 34

Lying atop the unmade bed, a fully-clothed Sophia cuddled awkwardly with Adam Woodson. Admittedly, Adam felt uncomfortable spooning on the sheets that had not been changed since Carmen passed away. However, earlier when Sophia declared she felt faint, he hadn't had any choice in the matter. Sophia had already headed straight for the bedroom.

"This feels so much better, Adam. Thanks for letting me lie down for a minute."

"I'm sorry I haven't done a better job with the housekeeping. I've been a little out of sorts, I guess," he tried to explain as he lovingly rubbed her forehead.

"I can only imagine. It's been a horrible few weeks." Sophia paused briefly. "There was some personal drama in my life recently, too. It was tragic, actually; but nothing like your loss. That's the other thing I was trying to get up enough nerve to tell you about."

Adam sat up quickly, causing Sophia to turn her head to look backwards at him to see if he was all right.

"Wanna go for a ride, Sophia? I need to get out of this apartment. Too much good news-bad news happening in this place. I feel like I'm on a roller coaster, and I could use some air," he announced as he sprang from the bed. "Let's go get a late lunch somewhere. It'll only take me a minute to get ready," he said before she could respond. He trotted off toward the bathroom to start a shower.

Trying to be sympathetic to everything Adam was mentally processing, Sophia got up and slowly made her way back to the living room. While she sat on the couch, she looked absently around the small room. Her gaze stopped at Adam's laptop, sitting on the coffee table in front of her with its enticing open screen.

She could tell Adam was already in the shower, so she took a chance and swiveled the computer screen to face her. Seeing his bank balance displayed prominently on the open screen, it didn't take a financial wizard to realize that Adam was much more affluent than she had originally believed.

The import/export business must be extremely lucrative these days. Sophia smiled as she returned the laptop to its original position on the coffee table.

* * * * * *

After calling 9-1-1, it took less than fifteen minutes for the police to arrive in full force at the Taylor residence. An entire caravan of marked and unmarked cars—sirens wailing and lights flashing—began pulling into the circular driveway with some cruisers parking on the lawn. The swarm of men and women raced toward the open front door where a solitary maid stood, looking as though she might be in shock. Eyes wide and shaking visibly, Leona had wet tears still running down her cheeks, and she half-bent over sobbing in agony as the first of the policemen approached her.

"Who are you, miss?" he said as he brushed past her to stand inside the threshold. He was barking orders to the other squad members—"cordon that area...watch where you're stepping ...call the chief and confirm it's the Senator's house"— as his eyes remained fixed on the terrified young woman.

"I..I am Leona, the maid," she answered tearfully. "I called you, I mean I called the emergency line," she tried to explain through her sobs.

"Show me the crime scene, Leona. Have you touched anything?" the policeman asked.

"No, no sir. I found them and I called. I called immediately," Leona said as she led the policeman toward the Senator's home office.

She intentionally burst into the room ahead of the policeman. "See, here's the gun..." she began as she reached for the discharged weapon.

"No! No, don't touch ..." he yelled as the gun discharged in Leona's hand. The bullet went into the hardwood floor, and Leona dropped the gun as if it were scalding metal.

"Oh, God! I didn't mean ..." she started sobbing again, this time falling to her knees with her head in her hands.

"Miss? Leona? Did you hurt yourself," the startled policeman asked.

"No, no, no. I'm all right. I'm sorry. I didn't mean ...," she started again.

"Just go sit in the foyer. Don't come back into this room until we tell you to, all right? You've contaminated the crime scene, and now your fingerprints are all over the gun. We may not be able to get the perpetrator's prints now, so please step carefully as you go out. Please, miss. Why don't you let the EMT check you for shock or something?" the riled policeman said. "Go on, get out of here now."

"I..I 'm really sorry. I just wanted to help," she cried.

"You've helped enough. Now let the EMT look you over, and stick around to give a statement. If you saw the shooter, we'll need a description. Sergeant Murray out there will be your contact," he said impatiently.

Leona left with her head down, grabbing a tissue from the box on the couch side table. "I said don't touch anything!" the rattled policeman screamed, causing Leona to visibly flinch as she hurried out of the room.

* * * * * *

Lucinda Bellini Norton was growing weaker every day. Constantly by her side, Juliana sat reading or working crosswords to keep her mind occupied. Lucinda had recently taken a turn for the worst, succumbing to a light case of pneumonia that had prompted her to remain indoors and under wraps.

"Mama, can I get you anything?" Juliana asked her mother softly as she closed the book she had been trying to read through weary eyes.

"I don't need anything, Juliana. I think I might take a nap now," Lucinda responded as she adjusted her head on the plump pillow and pulled the comforter under her chin.

Leaning over to lightly kiss her mother's forehead, Juliana pushed aside Lucinda's stray silver curl before her lips touched her mother's soft skin. "Rest well, Mama."

After Juliana closed the door behind her, Lucinda waited a good five minutes before she reached for her cell phone lying on the bedside table.   Dialing the international number of Uncle Joe, she settled back into the comfort of her plush bed while waiting for an answer.

"Lucy. I'm so glad you called. Are you feeling better?" Uncle Joe asked, clearly concerned.

"I'm tired, Uncle Joe. The doctor says I have pneumonia, but it feels worse than that," she struggled to say in her soft voice.

"Well, I'll say a special prayer for you, then," he replied. "And I have interesting news, Lucinda. I think you'll feel better when you hear it."

"Please tell me it's done," she responded.

"Yes, dear woman. It's over. Your sweet Sophia is avenged."

Lucinda smiled with satisfaction. "Both of them?"

"Yes, both. Everything is under control, and you can rest now. Don't worry about a thing. Just get better and soon you can visit again," Uncle Joe said sincerely.

"Thank you, dear Uncle. I can rest easy now," Lucinda replied with gratitude.

"Ciao, Lucy," Uncle Joe said as he ended the call.

Lucinda turned off her cell phone and laid it back in its place on the bedside table.

Within minutes she had peacefully drifted off to sleep with a faint smile remaining on her lovely, angelic face.

* * * * * *

Adam drove like an old man, concentrating on the road ahead and never once exceeding the speed limit.

"Where are we going, Adam?" Sophia wondered aloud.

"There's a small diner on the corner a few blocks ahead. I thought maybe we could grab a quick sandwich and then maybe stroll around Central Park for a little while. We could get the food to go, if you'd rather. We could take it to the park with us and eat outside."

Sophia nodded. "Sounds great, Adam. I could use some fresh air, too."

Twenty minutes later the two were sitting on a blanket taken from Adam's trunk, eagerly consuming their fresh sandwiches and bottled waters. "Umm, this bread is so fresh! How'd you ever find this place?" Sophia asked as she shoved a potato chip in her mouth as an afterthought.

Adam didn't answer right away. "Carmen told me about it. She used to love their chicken salad. Personally, I'm not a fan."

"Oh," Sophia said softly. Taking another big bite of her pastrami on rye, she tried to change the subject. "I'll be happy when fall is in full swing, won't you? Autumn is such a beautiful season."

"Yeah, it's nice in Tennessee now, too," Adam said without commenting further.

"Right. Teddy always talks about the Smoky Mountains. Have you ever been?"

Adam smiled as he thought about his childhood home. "Yes, our family used to go there on vacations occasionally." He paused before he started his story. "I grew up in a small town in middle Tennessee. Maybe you've heard of it? Shelbyville? The 'Walking Horse Capital of the World,' and it's also known as the 'Pencil City?' We don't have much claim to fame, except for those two things; but, we did get some publicity on national news once—or newspapers, anyway—in the 1950s."

He took another bite of his sandwich and chewed thoughtfully.

"What happened back then?" Sophia earnestly wanted to know.

Adam swallowed and took a long gulp of water. "Well, there was this guy who kidnapped a bunch of teenagers—not all at once, though. He stretched it out over three years or so. He had the perfect set up to get the kids, but some local yokel tipped off the police. There was some other stuff going on, too, like police corruption and such. A few years ago, some hometown woman wrote a book about it. I think she titled the book *Buried Sins*."

During Adam's story, Sophia grew more and more intrigued, and she finally said, "So, Adam? You're hometown became nationally famous for kidnapping kids? That's horrible!"

"Yeah, I suppose. But, my grandparents helped solve the case. They're in the book that woman wrote."

"No way! So your family's famous? How'd they help solve it? Were they detectives or something?" Sophia was extremely interested in this part of Adam's background.

"Actually, my grandfather's name was Harry Woodson, and he was a detective on the city's police force. He became the Chief of Police after the case was solved. My grandmother, Eva Cortner, was one of the very first female FBI agents, and she met my grandfather on the case. They're famous back home. Their pictures still hang in the Bedford County Court House rotunda."

"Wow. That's some history. I'm really impressed," Sophia responded. "So what do your parents do? Do you have siblings?" she asked in rapid-fire fashion.

"No, I'm an only child. My dad is a lawyer, and my mom passed away when I was in high school. She died instantly in an auto accident outside Murfreesboro. She was on the way home from Christmas shopping in Nashville."

Sophia didn't know what to say. "I'm so sorry. What a horrible time of the year to lose someone."

"Any time of the year is a bad time to lose someone," he said as he crumpled up his sandwich wrapper and threw it at a nearby garbage can. He stood up and extended his hand to the sitting Sophia. "Let's take a walk," he said as he helped her up. She gracefully stood, grabbing the blanket and wrapping it around her shoulders as they walked arm in arm toward Strawberry Fields.

* * * * *

Sergeant Murray was frustrated and agitated. He'd missed his late lunch, and hadn't eaten anything since 7:30 a.m. His stomach growled an annoying reminder that he needed something to fill the void in his empty belly.

The maid he'd been interviewing was apparently in shock or was a little nuts, because she kept looking around as if she expected someone to jump out of the bushes and attack her. She seemed paranoid and antsy; however, if he'd been in her shoes when she found those two people murdered, he'd probably have shit his pants. That had to be a horrific scene for an unsuspecting young woman to wander into. He figured she'd settle down after a little while.

Sergeant Murray repeatedly asked the maid several crucial questions to which she tried to answer accurately. When he asked where the rest of the household staff was at the time of the shooting, she said she didn't know. She finally revealed the reason she didn't know their whereabouts: Val had given everybody but Leona the day off. Once she filled in the blanks with random statements, her pieced-together answers made sense; but it was so hard getting to that point.

The young woman didn't avoid answering Sergeant Murray's questions, she just never fully provided all the information required to form a *complete* answer. He continually had to fish for additional details to get the full picture. It was tiring and exasperating. For example, Leona eventually explained that she was not given the day off because she had to be there to provide assistance to Sid if and when he needed it. She then mentioned she was his translator. The sergeant finally realized that meant she read Sid's handwritten notes when he wanted to communicate.

She seemed like a she had a screw or two loose.

"Ma'am, please repeat your full name for me. I don't believe you ever stated your full name," he finally asked, trying to fill in the rest of the report so he could send her downtown to the sketch artist.

"Leona Calli. C-A-L-L-I, No 'E' at the end."

Leona looked at her hands and frowned. "Please, officer. Can I please wash my hands? I feel like there is death all over them! I shouldn't have picked up that gun," she sobbed.

"You did what?" the stunned Sergeant asked. He stopped writing on his note pad and looked at her in amazement.

"Yes! I told the other policeman, I didn't mean to do it. I was just trying to help. I had no idea it would shoot itself!" she whined.

"Oh, Jesus! Does anybody else know about this?"

"Yes, the other policeman. He was mad at me when it happened. The bullet is in the floor. I am so very sorry," she began to wail.

"Geez, lady. You've smudged whatever fingerprints that were on the gun, and you've got gunshot residue all over you now. You couldn't have done anything worse in there when you picked up that gun and it discharged," he admonished her.

Oh yes I could! And I did, you idiot! Instead of smiling, she continued producing alligator tears until she finally convinced Sergeant Murray to let her wash her hands.

* * * * * *

The sketch artist looked at his work and shook his head. "Are you certain this is what the shooter looked like?" he asked Leona who had been at the police station with him for about 45 minutes. "Are you positive?" he asked as he held up his work for her to review.

"Yes. That's him. He was short and scrawny, and he had a kind of delicate face, you know?" Leona shook her head as she stared at the drawing in awe. "I can't believe you drew him so well with only what I told you."

The problem was simple. The details she provided prompted him to draw a very strong likeness to a young Brad Pitt, complete with scruffy facial hair and big, clear eyes.

"Ma'am does this likeness resemble anybody else you can think of," he tested her.

Leona squinted and looked again. "Well, he kinda looks like that actor who played in that New Orleans vampire movie, but I'm not sure of his name." She shrugged her shoulders.

"Yes, Brad Pitt. He looks exactly like Brad Pitt," the sketch artist said, throwing down his pencil. "Are you saying that Senator and Mrs. Taylor were murdered by Brad Pitt?" He took off his black-rimmed glasses and rubbed his eyes.

"No, silly. Brad Pitt wouldn't have done that. I'm just saying he looked kinda like him. I think you drew him perfectly," she answered.

"Who? Who did I draw perfectly? The killer or Brad Pitt?" he said impatiently.

"Brad Pitt, of course. The killer looked different."

The sketch artist counted silently to twenty. Calmly he took the Brad Pitt picture and wadded it in a big ball. Tossing it over his head onto the floor, he took a deep breath. "All right. Let's start over. This time, try to be very specific with your details."

Leona nodded. "Ok, his face was shaped like Brad Pitt's, and he had the same kind of eyes," she started.

The sketch artist dropped his pencil and abruptly stood up behind the table. "Let's take a break. I need some coffee…or some bourbon. I need another witness," he exclaimed as he quickly stepped away from the woman who had ruined his day.

Twin Sins

CHAPTER 35

Adam had listened for more than an hour while Sophia recounted the events that transpired during the fundraiser evening. Every emotion she conjured during the telling— whether it was joy, confidence, fear, terror, sadness, or remorse— was relayed so effectively that Adam felt those things, too.

By the time she was finished, Adam sat dumbfounded on the park bench next to her. "Sophia, why have you kept this from me for so long? When I texted you at midnight that night, you answered that you wanted me to hold you in my arms again. This was **after** all this had happened? I can't believe you've kept this a secret all this time! I can't believe I wasn't there for you!"

"Adam, I don't have all the memories back from that night. Teddy and Rick are convinced that it was Sid Taylor. When they told me they had a witness, I wouldn't let them tell me anything more. I shut them out. I didn't want to know who it was. I just wanted to wipe it from my life."

"I don't know who else it could have been, Sophia. If Teddy and Rick initially believed it was Sid, and they continue to say that after a witness came forward, they must be convinced Sid did it."

Shaken from so vividly having to recall the details from that awful evening, Sophia leaned against Adam's shoulder. "I guess it makes sense to me because he's the last person I was alone with by the pool. And he was angry. But, that sounds crazy! He's married to my mother's cousin, for goodness sakes."

"Some people do outrageous things out of anger or drunkenness. I doubt Sid's any different." Adam put his arm around Sophia and pulled her closer.

"What about the baby? This was after we were together. When you told me you were pregnant, I just assumed the baby was mine," Adam stated with concern.

Sophia jerked her head from Adam's shoulder. "Of course the baby's yours! I haven't been with …,"

Adam watched as her expression changed to shock. "Oh, no! I never even gave that a thought! Oh my God, Adam! What am I going to do?" Sophia whimpered.

"Shush, Sophia. It doesn't make any difference who caused this baby to be created, it just matters how we raise him…or her."

"Adam, what are you saying? Are you sure?"

"Absolutely, Sophia. Let's get married and do this right. I always wanted to be a Daddy, and I know you'll be a wonderful Mom," he said as he passionately kissed his new fiancé. His prior feeling of apathy had been replaced with a renewed sense of purpose.

As Adam drew back and looked into Sophia's happy eyes, Adam toyed fleetingly with the idea of divulging his true vocation to his bride-to-be. Instead, he hugged her tightly.

You can't tell her yet. This is your chance to be a father and a husband. Don't blow this because of a job. Marry her, then explain. It'll be easier that way.

* * * * * *

When Leona was released from the police station, she searched for a payphone from which to call Big Al with an update. She finally found one mounted on a yellow drive-up pole in the far corner of a convenience store parking lot.

When Big Al answered his cell phone, the first thing Leona said was, "I gotta get a burner phone if we're gonna keep talking. Payphones are few and far between anymore."

"Won't be necessary. You'll be safely out of the country before we talk again. Got your reservation info yet? It's an electronic ticket, already paid for. You just need your passport."

"I'll be swinging by my apartment within the hour to pick it up and a few things I'll need for traveling," Leona responded.

"Good. The sooner you get out of the states, the better. Before you know it, you'll be walking in the Sicilian sun, plucking ripe grapes right from the vines. By the way, Leona, I left you a little going away gift on the kitchen table in your apartment, I hope you don't mind. Didn't think it'd matter if I jimmied the door since you won't be living there anymore anyway. It's not much, but it's a token of my appreciation…and Uncle Joe's."

Leona smiled. "I can't wait. Thank you, Al. You're so sweet to think of me like that. I'll cherish it always, whatever it is. I'll call you when I get to the old country, okay? And thanks for helping me get this 'internship.' It's been a long three years, but I think I've done a pretty good job for the family."

"You're the best. Couldn't have done it without you. Good luck, and kiss the old man hello for me," Big Al said as he hung up.

* * * * * *

The news of the Taylor murders was blasted everywhere. Vivid, gory pictures were plastered across television screens on all networks, even the dreaded national news. Apparently, someone had removed the tapes from the Taylors' home security system and selectively spliced together the sections showing the dead bodies of Sid and Val. Those horrible pictures were rotating every few minutes across television and computer screens nationwide.

The other sections of the tape—the parts that might have identified the killer—never surfaced. The truncated film clip had been transmitted to the media from the same IP address used previously in forwarding the Brent Taylor video.

Of course, no one owned up to tampering with the system's recordings. That would have been much too easy. The police believed it could have been the killer himself who so blatantly publicized his crime. A few officers suspected the young maid might have been involved in the murder of her employers. However, those officers who had dealt with Leona first-hand were among those still on the fence or leaning against it. They described her as 'scatter-brained' rather than devious or malicious.

* * * * * *

Leona saw the intricately decorated wooden box on the kitchen table the moment she stepped into her small but efficient kitchen. She smiled with delight as she turned it around to inspect the delicate carvings and inlaid ivory that surely must have been very expensive. "Al is so thoughtful," she said aloud as she bent down closer to see the name that was etched in ever so tiny letters on the corner of the lid.

Who is Boomer? That's a strange name for an artist, she thought as she raised the lid. She expected to see the box loaded with candy or perhaps a necklace made of precious jewels. Instead she saw red digital numbers counting down quickly to 0:00.

The explosion ripped through Leona's tiny apartment and launched a great portion of the kitchen wall through the adjacent living room windows. Part of the kitchen ceiling lay on top of the many scattered pieces of bloody flesh and bone which were all that remained of Leona Calli. She died before she ever realized what happened.

* * * * * *

Juliana was in the kitchen chatting with Maureen about dinner plans when a news alert flashed across her cell phone screen. She picked up the phone and read the horrifying news about Sid and Val Taylor's murders.

"Quick, Maureen! Turn on the television!" Juliana ordered.

Grabbing for the remote, Maureen turned toward the corner of the kitchen where a small flat screen TV was mounted. Fumbling, she turned on the set and gasped when she recognized the images filling the screen.

"My God! What is this world coming to?" Juliana cried out. "This can't be real! They just lost their son! My God, this can't be really happening!"

Thomas overheard Juliana's outburst and rushed into the kitchen. "Is Miss Sophia all right?" he asked before he realized the two women's eyes were glued upward to the television news report.

"My word! That's the Senator and Mrs. Taylor being carried out! They're dead! I had no idea this would go so far!" Thomas exclaimed as he watched the screen carefully. He eased himself down on a bar stool next to Juliana at the kitchen counter.

"*What* would go so far, Thomas?" a vexed Maureen asked him. Juliana watched closely as Thomas carefully formed his response.

"That someone would get revenge like **this**! This is unacceptable!"

Both Juliana and Maureen looked quizzically at Thomas. "Do you know something you haven't told us, Thomas? If you do, now's the time to speak up," Juliana said sternly as Maureen nodded.

"No. No. How could I? I just *assumed*," he answered nervously. "It's all so tragic." Thomas sat still for an awkward moment before he slowly rose from his seat. Head held high, he walked stiffly out of the kitchen, making no more comments to either of the perplexed ladies who watched him depart.

* * * * * *

Both Maureen and Juliana rushed upstairs to make sure the bedridden Lucinda was shielded from the crushing news about Valentina and Sid. Neither of them was certain how Lucinda would react to another tragedy within the family.

Both women feared Lucinda's heart might give out if she were exposed to more catastrophic information.

Peeping inside the door, Juliana saw her mother lying peacefully in bed, comforter tucked around her, and a look of contentment on her face. Juliana glanced toward the bedside table, noticing that Lucinda's cell phone was dark and inactive. There was no news bulletin flashing on the screen that she could see from where she stood. She softly closed the door.

"Mama's resting. Her phone is off, I think, so she wouldn't know about Sid and Val. Let's let her rest for a while longer."

Maureen nodded and whispered, "I'll check on her in another hour. She's due for her medicine then."

Juliana smiled and whispered, "Thank you."

Maureen left to check on Thomas while Juliana scurried away to call Sophia and give her the latest news about Sid and Val.

* * * * * *

Rick Giordano peripherally saw the news bulletin flash across the screen of the muted television mounted on his office wall. Since Sophia had left the office unannounced, he had spent the majority of his time dealing with the loose ends of her pending business responsibilities. Hours before, he had lowered the volume of the TV so he could concentrate better on the pile of work she had nonchalantly pushed off on him. It took a few moments before he looked up at the screen, finally registering what he was seeing.

"Teddy! Teddy! Get in here!" Rick screamed, hoping Teddy was close enough to hear him call. When there was no immediate response, Rick picked up his phone and punched the intercom number to Teddy's office.

"Yell-oh," Teddy said in his mocking version of 'hello.'

"If you're not watching your TV right now, you gotta get in here. Fast!" Rick shouted into the phone.

Rather than take the time to figure out what channel or broadcast Rick was watching, Teddy scampered out of his office and raced down the hallway into Rick's.

"What?" Teddy said as his head turned toward the television screen. "Holy shit!" he exclaimed when his brain registered what was unfolding before his eyes.

Rick stood still, mind racing. "They've taken out the whole Taylor family," he murmured. He began to imagine how Lucinda would react when she heard about this. His grandmother had been so frail lately, he wondered if such news might push her over the edge. "Oh, God. The timing of all this couldn't be worse," he muttered.

"What'd you say, Rick?" Teddy asked, turning to look at his best friend.

"I said the whole Taylor family's gone now. Wow!"

Teddy nodded solemnly, turning back to watch the news. "Maybe it's time we reach out to Sophia. I know she was feeling ill, but this turn of events might affect her badly, too."

Rick agreed. "Okay, but I don't know whether to tell her the good news or the bad news first. She still doesn't know she'll be on the ballot in November. Man, everything seems to be happening at once."

"She may already know about Sid and Val, you know. She could've already heard," Teddy warned.

At that moment, Rick's desk phone rang. He picked it up, hearing Sophia's alarmed voice on the other end of the line.

"We were just talking about you, Sophia. Are you feeling better?" Rick asked as he switched the call to speakerphone mode.

Teddy moved closer to Rick's desk. "Hi, Sophia. It's me, Teddy. I'm listening in with Rick."

"Guys, did you see the news?"

"Yeah, we were just watching in my office. Terrible, terrible," Rick responded bleakly.

"I know. I hope Mama and Grandmamma don't go into shock when they hear what happened to Val. Do you think we should go over there and be with them? Help soften the blow somehow?"

"That's very thoughtful. Sounds like an excellent idea to me. Why don't we go over around 6 o'clock. I'll drag Teddy, too," Rick said as he winked at his friend. "We have some interesting news of our own to discuss."

"Sure. I'll be there, and I'll be bringing a guest. Adam Woodson. I'll call Maureen to see if it's all right for us to stay for dinner. Should be an interesting evening," Sophia said. "Oops, another call … it's Mama! I'm not gonna answer right now. I'll call Maureen later and make all the arrangements." She hung up suddenly.

Teddy and Rick looked at each other, puzzled by Sophia's abruptness and also her surprising choice of dinner guest. "I thought Adam Woodson was grieving the loss of his former fiancé?" Teddy questioned.

"Me, too. Even I grieved over her loss a little bit. I can imagine how he must have felt, having been her partner and lover, too." Rick shrugged his shoulders, but dismissed his concerns about Adam as he looked over the pile of paperwork on his desk that still needed attention.

"Guess we'll have to wait till later to find out what Sophia's up to. Meanwhile, back to the grindstone," Rick said dramatically as he resumed his place behind the massive desk.

* * * * * *

Thomas overheard Maureen speaking with Sophia on the house phone, and he did his best to hear every word Maureen said on her side of the conversation. He busied himself in the kitchen where she stood with the phone against her ear.

"Of course, Miss Sophia. We're all anxious to see you. It's been too long since you've visited."

Pause.

"Dinner? Would you want to eat at 7 o'clock or would you like to dine earlier?"

Pause.

"Then 7 o'clock it will be. Party of how many extra? Oh, my. We'll spread out the dining room table, so there will be room for everyone. Do you have any special requests?"

Long Pause.

"Excellent choice, Miss Sophia. I'll make up the best lasagna you ever tasted. And I'll make sure you get the tiramisu you and your Grandmother love so much, too."

Longer Pause.

"It's no trouble at all. I'll let Miss Juliana know you returned her call, and you're all arriving around 6 o'clock. She'll be excited to see you. When I go up to give your grandmother her medicine, I'll tell her, too. I know that will perk her up! See you tonight!" Maureen hung up the phone.

Lingering too long in the kitchen, Thomas tried to look busy near the kitchen counter. Hearing every word Maureen said, he understood that Sophia would be visiting along with some others—probably her brother and his friend. He smiled to himself, imagining what Sophia would say when he told her of his plan to move with her to Florida.

"Well, guess we'd better get busy, Thomas. Why don't you alert the other staff that we'll be having guests for dinner tonight. Miss Sophia and a guest, Mr. Rick and Mr. Teddy will come, as well. I'm not sure about Miss Caroline yet. Miss Sophia wants Miss Juliana to call Miss Caroline to extend that invitation herself. We'll need to set the table for eight."

Maureen hurried past Thomas as she went to the cabinet where Lucinda's medicine was kept.   Noticing that Thomas hadn't moved from his spot, she smirked, "Get along now, Thomas. Chop! Chop! We've got things to do and very little time to get them done!"

Thomas smiled, but still hesitated. "Maureen, I brought a little something back from vacation for Miss Sophia. I was hoping I might get a moment with her to give it to her," he said coyly.

Thomas had purchased a gold letter opener for Sophia to use at her DeLuca office. He hoped she'd think of him when she picked up the gift by the gold filigreed handle. It wasn't extravagant by any means, but it was beautiful, delicate, and sharp, much like Sophia.

"I'm sure she's got enough little trinkets, Thomas. But it was nice of you to think of her," Maureen said, silently thinking that Thomas was a silly old fool. *He must have never been married and had daughters of his own. Nice that he thinks of Miss Sophia that way, though.*

Twin Sins

CHAPTER 36

Caroline had been busy catching up the work she had accumulated during her trip to Italy, including the growing backlog that had naturally followed during the last few weeks of distracting events.

She and Slick tried to get together as often as possible, but she found most evenings she was too exhausted to go out to dinner or set aside a few hours for entertainment. Sometimes she needed an extra incentive to keep from going home and crawling into bed immediately after a long work day.

Tonight, her incentive came in the form of a dinner invitation from Juliana Giordano. She and Slick were invited to dine with the family, including Teddy, at the DeLuca mansion. She hoped Slick felt comfortable enough with her and the Giordanos to attend the dinner gathering at the Southampton estate.

In their budding relationship, intimacy didn't seem to be the first priority on either of their lists. Nowadays, Caroline's thoughts on the topic differed from when she was younger. *The anticipation of winning the prize is often more thrilling than the achievement itself,* she frequently told herself.

Instead, on the few occasions Slick and Caroline had been alone, the main topic of interest was the newest information Slick had uncovered about DeLuca Enterprises. That morning, they had broached that subject once again during their regular early morning coffee meetings in Caroline's office. She thought about the conversation they had only a few hours before.

"Caroline, when I met Carmen Ryan at the rally, there was something familiar about her, you know? I couldn't place her for a long time, but last night I had another vision…sort of a flash memory. This was more of a recall thing, though. Maybe it was a dream? Doesn't matter. I saw her clearly. She was standing in the Court House and she looked over at me while I was reviewing the DeLuca files a few weeks ago. I heard the clerk tell her when I was finished, she could look at the files."

"That's odd. Are you certain it was her?" Caroline wanted to know.

"Yeah. Absolutely. I guess I've been so consumed with the bomb premonition, that particular memory got pushed way back. Anyway, it's probably nothing, but I think maybe I'll start looking into her background, God rest her soul. I'll check out Adam Woodson while I'm at it."

Slick took the last sip of his coffee. "Another interesting item I came across, Caroline, that I think might be the grand slam. There are routine money transfers being sent to the Grand Caymans from DeLuca Enterprises. The money splits into three accounts there as equally divided deposits. Rick Giordano signs off on the DeLuca transfers, but this part is interesting: one of the three accounts also receives periodic transfers from different shell corporations from New York and Italy. I'm still snooping, but I think this may be what we've been looking for."

"My goodness, Slick. You may be on to something. No wonder Rick was so concerned that I had hired a private investigator. Keep digging, Slick. We'll handle whatever it is, I'm sure."

Slick stood up and handed his empty Starbucks cup to Caroline. She threw it in the garbage can beneath her desk and stood to embrace Slick goodbye.

"I can't tell you how much I look forward to having coffee with you every morning, Slick. Thank you for the new routine. It makes my day, you know," she said as she kissed him quickly on the cheek.

"It's worth the trip just to see your gorgeous face, Caroline," he said as he pulled her closer and kissed her with more passion than usual. "This always makes my day."

Slick didn't realize the total impact he had on Caroline who was always reserved and careful with her personal feelings. She had suffered a great loss once before... so many years before that she'd forgotten how it felt to be attracted to another man. For too many years she had harbored the distant memory of her ex-husband and the love they once shared. It wasn't perfect, of course, but whose relationship was?

By the time she realized how special John Sanderson was to her, he was dead—murdered in cold blood. She was the one who had to identify his mutilated body—the one she had partially disfigured in trying to make the coroner think his body was actually that of her murdered brother.

The whole episode was such a complicated mess, but Perry Norton had helped her through it. She would always be grateful to Perry, her future adoptive father, and to Lucinda

DeLuca Norton, Perry's true love. Thank God they had both been in Caroline's life during the crises she endured so many years before.

Reflecting again on the informative tidbits Slick had shared with her that morning, Caroline feared what the efficient private investigator might still uncover while poking around in the DeLuca businesses. There were questions he raised that certainly needed to be honestly answered. She believed that whatever he might find could surely be righted, provided it was within the limits of the law. She feared she might have some tough decisions to make in the very near future.

* * * * * *

When the classic Jaguar pulled into the DeLuca mansion driveway, Thomas stood anxiously inside the sunroom, hoping to get Sophia's first moments of attention and a few minutes of privacy when she entered the house. He had stashed the gilded letter opener in the sunroom behind some potted plants on the sofa table. Expecting her arrival to be the best chance to have her to himself, Thomas planned to be ready at a moment's notice to present her with his special gift.

 He watched nervously as the white car pulled behind the house to its usual parking spot. Thomas's face fell when he saw the passenger door open and a handsome man step onto the driveway. He stared at the man the whole time he circled the car to open the driver's door, reaching in to help a sparklingly beautiful Sophia out of the driver's seat.

Thomas sneered as he saw Sophia look lovingly into the eyes of her escort, appearing more excited than she should have been if the man was only a business associate.   Thomas clenched his jaw as he saw them holding hands while they approached the house.

Thomas turned quickly, hoping Sophia wouldn't notice that he had been waiting inside the glass room, but he was too late. As Adam opened the door for Sophia, she called out to the butler.

"Thomas, wait! Hello, stranger! How was your vacation? I hear you were off to Colorado to visit your family. I hope you had a great time."

Thomas turned and nodded slightly, trying to smile convincingly. "It was wonderful, thank you, Miss Sophia. May I take your things?" he said robotically, trying to maintain his emotional control.

"Yes, of course," she said, as she handed him her wrap and purse. "Adam, let Thomas take your coat. He'll take care of it for you," she remarked.

"Thank you, Thomas. By the way, I'm Adam Woodson. I was at the fundraiser a few weeks back. I'm sorry we didn't get a chance to be formally introduced then, but I remember your face," Adam said politely.

"Of course, sir. I remember you well. You sang for the audience, I believe, and you were quite good," Thomas replied, almost choking on his words.

"What? Did I miss that? I didn't know you could sing, Adam!" Sophia exclaimed as she took hold of Adam's arm. "You've got to sing for me tonight! What did you sing at the party?"

"*Our Song*, by Elton John. I didn't think it was that good," Adam said, slightly embarrassed.

"Oh, Adam. I think we've just found 'our song!'" she giggled as they left Thomas standing alone in the empty sunroom.

Thomas wanted to throw up.

* * * * * *

Slick met Caroline at 5 o'clock at her office so she could drive them both to the DeLuca mansion for dinner. It would be a long drive, and Caroline knew the way so well that she volunteered to take the wheel. That was fine with Slick. He liked watching the scenery, and that was hard to do from the driver's seat.

Once they were on the road, Caroline launched the conversation about his recent findings.

"How was your day, Slick? Find out anything else interesting?" she asked as she set the temperature control on her heated seat.

Hesitantly, Slick responded. "I don't think you're gonna like it much, but yeah. I found out some details about those accounts."

"Really? Well, spill it. I don't like being in suspense," she replied.

"Okay, if you're sure. But like I said, you won't like it much." Slick waited for Caroline to make another comment, but she remained silent and kept her eyes ahead on the road.

Clearing his throat, he began to tell her his findings. "It seems there is a definite connection between DeLuca Enterprises and the Bellini family. Remember that big account I told you about? The third one that gets an equal transfer of funds directly from DeLuca? That's a Bellini-backed account. Money is funneled through that Grand

Caymans account and eventually lands somewhere in Switzerland."

Caroline shook her head in disappointment. "What about the other two? The smaller Grand Caymans accounts? Whose are those?"

"They are separate Giordano accounts. One belongs to Rick, as you probably already guessed. The other one is under the name Sophia Parker Giordano." He paused momentarily. "I'm sorry, Caroline, but it appears that your best friend's two little angels have been ripping off DeLuca Enterprises and lining their own pockets—with the help of the Bellini crime family. Sid might not have been such a bad guy after all, because his name hasn't appeared on anything recent enough to top this."

Caroline saw an exit sign ahead and made her way to the ramp. Once off the main highway, she pulled into the corner of a gas station parking lot and put the car in park. Sid sat stiffly in the passenger seat, having no idea what she was about to do.

"You still want to go tonight, Caroline? We can beg off, you know."

She reached in the console and found a tissue. She blew her nose and took a deep breath. "You can't imagine what I'm feeling right now, Slick. 'Betrayed' doesn't even touch it. 'Angry' doesn't do it, either. I am APPALLED at what those two have done! How could they do such things—to the legacies of their family, their grandmother, and their mother! Juliana raised them as her own when her bastard of a husband died all those years ago. She gave them both FULL REIGN of the DeLuca business. And THIS is how they repay her? Working in cahoots with a crime family that their mother and grandmother worked so hard to distance themselves from?" Caroline wanted to weep, but took control of herself. She took more deep breaths instead.

Slick said nothing for a second, but asked a probing question. "Maybe I shouldn't bring this up, but you yourself just got back from visiting the Bellini crime family patriarch, didn't you? Uncle Moe or Uncle Joe?"

Caroline's head snapped to attention. "NO! Uncle Joe is retired. If he ever did run the Bellini crime family, it'd be hard for me to believe. He's a kind soul. The money he's made for the family is through the legitimate vineyards he's managed. He doesn't keep in touch with those other family criminals. He's so old he can hardly get around. All he does is putter around the vineyards and fix broken things in the house. His biggest joy is a hearty meal. I refuse to believe Uncle Joe—or Lucinda, for that matter—would EVER be able to hide something like that from me. We've all been too close over the years. DeLuca Enterprises is legitimate now and has been ever since Juliana and Sophia took over. I honestly believe that!" she preached. Her emotions broke through the little control she had and she sobbed loudly. "You must be wrong about this! I can't believe what you're saying is true." She grabbed the steering wheel and leaned down to rest her forehead on the leather wheel cover. "God help them. I don't know how this can be fixed," she moaned.

Slick reached over and rubbed her right shoulder in an attempt to console the shattered woman. "Let's go back to your office, Caroline. I can show you my research, and you can see for yourself. I don't think you're going to be able to get through a dinner party tonight with those two present. Here, let me drive," Slick offered as he started to open the passenger door.

"No," she said sharply. "We will do this, and we will be pleasant. This is my first chance to introduce you to Lucinda and Juliana. You need to see what kind of people they are. I wish Uncle Joe could be here so you could meet him, too. But, you'll just have to settle with meeting the ladies."

Caroline sat straight up in her seat, adjusted her seatbelt, and put the car in drive.

"Okay, if you say so," Slick said as he settled back for an interesting evening.

* * *   * * *

Teddy and Rick arrived together, as usual, carpooling from their office in Rick's fancy sports car.

"Why do you buy these things?" Teddy asked as he shifted his weight in the low and uncomfortable seat. "You can't even move."

Rick laughed. "It's to attract the women, Tedster. Maybe you should trade in your SUV for something a little flashier."

"I'm fine in my sturdy, Japanese built work of art, thank you very much," Teddy smiled.

"No wonder you never have any dates, man. Are you saving yourself for someone special back home in the hills of Tennessee? You got a secret double life somewhere in the boonies?"

"Nope. No one special. When I was growing up, I always thought Sophia and I might date someday, but I grew out of that fantasy. She's more like the sister I never had, you know? Sorta like you."

"Whoa, man. I'll never admit to being your sister," Rick chuckled as he pushed hard on the accelerator of the Mercedes-Benz AMG SLC 43.

* * * * * *

Caroline made another unexpected stop on the way to the DeLuca mansion, but this time it was because of Slick.

Caroline was aware Slick was napping after her outburst. She assumed he was making an attempt to stay quiet and let her think through the information he had sprung on her. But soon, through her peripheral vision, she caught his arm jerking. She slowed down and tried to pay better attention, hoping he hadn't fallen into a deep sleep when they would be arriving so soon at their destination.

When Slick started moaning, she became alarmed. *What's wrong with him? Is he having some kind of seizure?*

Caroline pulled off the road as soon as she could find a safe spot. Panicking, she shook Slick's shoulders as she tried to lean as close to him as possible beyond her seat belt restraint.

"Slick!" she yelled, praying to see his eyes opening. They didn't. "Slick! Wake up!" she yelled again, this time lightly slapping his cheek to see if he would stir.

Within seconds, his eyes fluttered open and grew wide with terror. "Caroline, something bad's going to happen tonight. I just saw it! We need to turn around! I don't want you anywhere near those people!" he exclaimed.

Caroline quickly clicked open her seat belt. She stretched across the console to hold Slick in her arms. "It's all right, Slick. You'll protect me. We don't have any choice in the matter. Not tonight. Just stay close to me and we'll be all right. I know we will," she said as she cupped the back of his head in her hand.

"Listen to the Shiska," Slick heard his Moms say from the behind him.

When Caroline leaned back into the driver seat, Slick turned his head to look in the back seat. It was empty.

"You okay now?" Caroline asked tentatively.

"Yeah. I guess so. Between you and Moms, I'm living on the edge these days," he said as he leaned back into the cushy seat. It was almost impossible for him to get comfortable during the rest of the ride to Southampton.

Twin Sins

CHAPTER 37

The mahogany dining table was set elegantly, with Caesar salads already in place atop golden chargers that punctuated the room with a rich splash of class. Maureen had taken special care to place handwritten name cards in the appropriate spots so that the guests would be seated in the best possible arrangement for conversation.

Maureen and Thomas would serve the main course from the buffet, rather than bringing in individual dishes from the kitchen. This modified serving arrangement was implemented via special request of Sophia. Apparently, she hoped that as the evening progressed, the guests would feel comfortable enough to serve themselves second helpings or perhaps dessert, if they so desired. The mood she wanted to inspire was that of a semi-formal family gathering, relaxed but still classic in form.

Thomas stood at attention at the opposite end of the buffet from Maureen. His face remained expressionless as he observed the diners file in and take their designated places in the side chairs. His eyes were trained on Adam Woodson, who casually escorted Sophia into the room and who had the good fortune to be seated next to her.

Juliana, seated at the head of the long table in an arm chair, reigned over the assembly as if she were a queen. Glancing to her right, she scanned the smiling faces of the young people gathered along the table on that side. Nearest to her were Sophia, then Adam, and finally Teddy. Looking to her left, she smiled at the faces of Rick, Slick, and Caroline. Noticeably missing from her empty arm chair at the other end was Lucinda, who remained upstairs to rest. There was hope that she might join them later for dessert, but Lucinda wouldn't commit to a definite appearance.

"Shall we begin?" Juliana asked the anxious diners, all of whom mumbled or nodded their accord. At that, the family members reached for their water glasses, prompting the new guests to follow suit and do the same. Juliana raised her glass and said happily, "To our family, our friends, and our Savior, Amen."

The chorus of "Amens" preceded the small sips of water taken by all in attendance. When the brief prayer-toast was over, Maureen and Thomas stepped forward to fill wine glasses for all the diners as they began heartily eating the salads.

As was the custom, Juliana began the dinner conversation. "Adam and Slick, I'd like to take a moment to welcome you both to our home."

Adam mumbled, "Thank you," as Sophia leaned against his left shoulder, playfully bumping him before she resumed her more lady-like position.

Already chewing on a mouthful of salad, Slick almost choked before he could swallow and respond. "Yes, thank you," he managed to say while Caroline chuckled at his awkwardness.

Moments later, the entire congregation was engaged in separate conversations, laughing and enjoying the progressively relaxed atmosphere.

As Sophia had hoped, Slick stood unexpectedly and picked up his plate. "This is great lasagna, Juliana. I hope you don't mind if I grab a little more?" he said and moved to the buffet without waiting for her permission. He scooped up another serving, then turned toward the diners and politely asked, "Anybody else want some more?" No one took him up on the offer.

Rick stood as Slick took his seat. He tapped his dessert fork against the crystal water glass to get the audience's attention. "Tonight, we've discussed so many tragedies, awful things that have happened within our family lately. But as tragic as those events were, life goes on. I'd like to make a special toast to those family members who have been taken from us much too soon," Rick raised his wine glass and waited for everyone else to do the same. "To Sidney Taylor, Valentina Bellini Taylor, and Brent Taylor. May they rest in peace," he said as the crowd answered with "Cheers" and "Here, Here."

* ** ***

Thomas had slipped into the kitchen to slice the tiramisu into serving portions and place the decadent dessert on individual plates. The buffet had been cleared of the entrée and side dishes, and was now ready to showcase the large tray of authentic Italian delicacies adjacent to the giant silver coffee urn.

As he methodically sliced the cake, Thomas gripped the big knife tightly. *I cannot believe that she is treating me as though I don't exist. I thought we had something special. I don't understand what's happened to the Sophia I thought I knew.*

In an obvious attempt to keep his emotions in check, Thomas took a deep breath before lifting the dessert tray carefully. Balancing the heavy silver cautiously, he glanced once again at the cake-smeared knife. His thoughts were churning as he stared blankly at the enticingly sharp cutlery. *If only I had the nerve.*

* * * * * *

When seven plates of tiramisu had been placed in front of the diners, Lucinda's motorized wheelchair appeared in the wide entrance of the dining room. "Wait for your grandmother," she said in a low and weak voice as she motored toward the dining room table.

Quickly, Thomas removed the arm chair where Lucinda usually sat to make room for her wheelchair to take its place. Sophia jumped from her chair and rushed to help.

"Grandmamma! I'm so happy to see you," she told Lucinda. "I was afraid you were still too ill to join us!"

"Stay back, child. I may still be contagious, but something kept telling me I should at least visit for a few minutes. I haven't seen you in so long, and it was weighing on me," the elderly lady said through watery eyes.

Ignoring her grandmother's warning, Sophia stooped over to kiss Lucinda on the forehead. "I love you, Grandmamma. Thank you for joining us," Sophia earnestly told her.

"What's this? Maureen, what have you prepared for us this evening?"Lucinda asked.

"Tiramisu, Miss Lucinda. I saved you the biggest piece," she chuckled, clearly pleased to serve the eighth slice to the matron of the house.

* * * * * *

Everyone ate their desserts slowly, pacing themselves so as not to finish before Lucinda. Her tiny bites and slow-motion chewing had unexpectedly extended the group's allocated meal time in the dining room.

Rick and Teddy had planned to announce Sophia's approval for a congressional bid after dinner while they enjoyed cocktails. Instead, Rick motioned for Teddy to proceed with the surprise announcement. Teddy nodded and took his turn standing and tapping his water glass to get the crowd's attention.

"Rick and I have good news tonight. It's been difficult to hold it back, but we believe this piece of news will help the family heal and launch us all into a stronger, better future." He paused for effect, and glanced around the table at the various expressions of suspense around the table.

"Let's just say that a member of the family *might* be answering to a different title in the near future," Teddy teased as he locked eyes with Sophia.

"What?" Sophia said as she suddenly turned to Adam. "You *told* them?" she disappointedly asked.

"No! Of course not!" Adam replied, as he and Sophia simultaneously looked back at Teddy, shock all over their faces.

"What?" Teddy said, clearly the one who was surprised. "What are you saying, Sophia? Adam?" All eyes were now on the couple.

After a few seconds to gather his thoughts, Adam stood and Teddy took his seat. Sophia looked embarrassed as she remained seated, wondering exactly what Adam was going to say.

"I don't think I've ever had such an exciting evening. I came here with Sophia tonight expecting to meet her family and friends, and perhaps find the right moment to ask a very important question. But the privacy I assumed I would have doesn't appear to be a part of the grand scheme," he grinned nervously. He looked squarely at Juliana as he continued. "Be that as it may, Mrs. Giordano, I would like to ask your permission to marry your daughter."

Juliana's first impulse was to say "no, I don't even know you," but she looked fleetingly at her daughter's expectant face. She knew she couldn't refuse Sophia this request. Instead, she questioned her daughter, "Are you sure, Sophia, is this what you really want?"

Smiling happily, revealing the softer side of herself that the family didn't often see, Sophia answered her mother with an eager nod. "Yes, Mama. I want to marry Adam. And we'll make you the happiest grandmother ever," she shyly added.

The final comment Sophia made didn't immediately sink in with anyone, but finally Teddy stood to applaud. "Congratulations to Sophia, Adam, and the future blessed event! I'm gonna be a pretend Uncle!"

"And I'm gonna be a 'real' Uncle!" Rick exclaimed.

"Oh, my! You mean I'm really going to be a grandmother?" Juliana asked with tears forming in her eyes.

"That's right, Mama. And Grandmamma will be a great grandmother! Isn't this wonderful news?" Sophia leapt from her chair and embraced her mother. Meanwhile, everyone (except Lucinda) rose from the table and began to mingle, giving hugs to all and wishing good luck and congratulations to the happy couple.

Everyone except Thomas, who had slipped into the sunroom during Adam's speech.

* * * * * *

Slick grabbed Caroline's hand and pulled her out of the dining room into the hallway. He guided her into the foyer and started to ramble. "I feel it coming, Caroline. You need to stay in here. I don't know what's about to happen, but you need to stay here," Slick told her frantically.

"Slick, everybody's happy! How could anything awful possibly happen now?" Caroline looked vexed.

"I don't know, exactly, Caroline. I just know it's coming. There was a wheelchair in my vision, and I could smell coffee. I could hear chatter, and then I saw splashes of blood. I don't know if it has anything to do with Lucinda, or if her chair was just a part of the scenery. All I know is, when she wheeled in, I thought I was gonna lose it. The picture wasn't complete before then," Slick tried to explain rapidly.

"No, Slick. I've got to get to Teddy and warn him. He's my Godson, and I can't let him get hurt if something really is about to happen tonight. This time you won't dump me on the sidelines," she insisted as she brushed past him to join the others.

Slick was frustrated as he watched Caroline hurry back down the long hallway leading from the foyer. As Caroline rushed into the double door to the dining room, Slick saw his mother's image a few feet further down near the hallway entrance to the kitchen. Moms turned her head and pointed away from the dining room, indicating that Slick should be scouting the kitchen for danger. She smiled at her son before her spirit dissolved into nothingness.

When Slick saw Thomas moving hurriedly through the kitchen toward servant's entrance of the dining room, he knew his mother was right.

Twin Sins

CHAPTER 38

Standing near the head of the table talking with her mother, Sophia's back was to the kitchen door that the servants used when bringing food into the dining room. Chatter was rampant all around, with the low hum of good cheer filling the joyful atmosphere.

When Thomas stepped closely behind Sophia, she started to turn to face him but was stopped when Thomas threw his left arm around her neck and held her tightly against his chest. With her back to Thomas and not understanding what his sudden movement meant, Sophia's expression turned from surprise to fear as she felt terror rising within her.

"Shut up, EVERYBODY!" Thomas bellowed as he sliced at the air with the long-bladed letter opener he had planned to give Sophia. "You ALL disgust me! Especially you, *MISS* Sophia!   What a fool you've made of everybody!" he screamed, face contorted and crazed.

"Thomas, let her go!" Rick shouted from his nearby position. He had been standing next to Sophia, between her and Adam, who was still standing, as well.

Thomas jerked the gold letter opener toward Sophia's throat. "No, she has to confess her sins. You need to know everything she's caused. Every bad thing that's happened is because of her selfishness. She has to atone: blood for blood!" he roared in a voice filled with rage. He pushed the sharp tip against the soft skin of her throat and cooed into her ear. "Tell them, dear."

Seeing a flash of movement in Adam's direction, he brought a bead of blood from Sophia's throat.   "Everybody sit down.

NOW!" he commanded the stunned group. No one moved at first.

Everyone scurried to an empty chair, Rick slowly settling into the one Sophia had previously occupied. Adam sat back down in his chair, and one by one the others followed suit, including a petrified Maureen who took Slick's vacant chair.

Thomas didn't bother to take a headcount, concentrating only on his prey who he held close against him for the very first time. He glanced at the elderly Lucinda, who was sitting motionless in her motorized wheel chair. Lucinda's eyes were fixed on Sophia's. "I apologize, Miss Lucinda. I wish you'd stayed upstairs through all this." For a second, he looked as if he was sincerely sorry, but then his full attention turned back to Sophia.

"Tell them, sweet Sophia. Tell them about the night you were so savagely raped," he demanded.

Sobbing, Sophia only said, "Please, Thomas. Stop this. I'll do anything you ask, just please don't hurt us."

"Aren't you thoughtful, for once! Thinking about others ahead of yourself. That's ironic, especially now. I said TELL THEM!" he barked.

Sophia flinched and started to talk. "It … it wasn't Sid. Sid didn't do anything," she cried. Unable to stop her tears, she sniffed trying to keep a stream of clear snot from running onto her lips. "Please, Thomas," she pleaded.

By now the entire audience was spellbound, unmoving in their chairs. Fear and curiosity were strangely comingled among their collective emotions. Caroline sat back, eyes darting between Thomas and the kitchen door behind him. She didn't know where Slick had gone, but she suspected he would appear any minute.

"Am I going to have to do it for you, Sophia? They'd rather hear it from your own mouth. So would I, come to think of it. So, TELL THEM NOW or I'll cut your tongue out and you'll never be able to say another word!"

In anguish, Sophia started to describe what happened to her on the night of the fundraiser. "It was me. I was never raped. Thomas helped me frame Sid," she explained as Thomas pressed the letter opener's point upwards under her throat. "I...I...wanted to get back at him because he hadn't cooperated with Uncle Joe like he was supposed to all these years," she sobbed. She wanted to lower her head to avoid the wide eyes of her audience, but it was impossible the way Thomas held the makeshift weapon against her skin.

Lucinda raised her eyes to meet Sophia's once again. "Uncle Joe?" the matriarch asked.

Sophia squeezed her eyes shut, and a steady stream of tears gushed forth. "Ye..Yes. Uncle Joe. He contacted me years ago...when I first took over the business from Mama. After college but before Rick started working with me. Uncle Joe had a plan to separate the crime family businesses from the legitimate companies, but the illegal businesses never really went away. He kept those going, and we still had hidden interests as a part of the Bellini family. Those companies just didn't show up on our DeLuca official records. Uncle Joe took care of all that. And he helped me run the company and make it successful for all those years. He steered legitimate businesses our way, and he kept the other businesses going on his own. Our books were clean, but we still got kickbacks from the family," she stated and paused briefly. "Do I have to keep going?" she meekly asked Thomas, whose response was a harder press of the blade under her chin.

"Okay. Okay. I convinced Rick to make fund transfers to off-shore accounts in our names, so we each had an account. Some of the money went to Uncle Joe as his portion of the clean businesses he helped us build. Rick knew about the arrangement, and where the money came from. But Rick always wanted our business with the crime family to go away. He was trying to help me get legitimate. Uncle Joe told me if I would help him ruin Sid, he'd remove DeLuca Enterprises entirely out of the organized crime family. We could be totally clean. He said he'd make it look like those illegal businesses were never part of our enterprise. He swore!" Sophia watched Rick lower his eyes in shame.

"I swear! Rick didn't get us into this. He was trying to get us out of the mess I made by wanting to be successful. But Uncle Joe hated Sid so much he would have done anything to get him out of the Senate office and punish him. I never knew he'd end up having Sid killed...or Val, or Brent," Sophia sobbed even harder. "I'm so sorry, so sorry," she cried.

"That's a good start, Sophia. But you haven't told them what you did to me, have you? Go on, finish your confession," Thomas urged her.

"I guess I've always flirted with Thomas. At first it was kind of a joke, at least to me. But when I realized he seemed to be genuinely interested in me, I took advantage of that. When Uncle Joe gave me the option to get back at Sid, it took me a long time to come up with a plan. When it finally came to me, I timed everything so that it would happen when Mama and Grandmamma would be away. I couldn't bear to think of what they'd go through if they'd been here when everything happened. Then I persuaded Rick to throw the fundraiser for Sid while they were away in Italy," she took a deep breath and squeezed her eyes shut again. She continued with her eyes closed, ashamed to see the faces of the congregation.

"I... I ... asked Thomas to hide a tiny video camera in the living room, aimed toward the part of the room near the bar where I knew Sid would spend most of his evening. Rick doesn't know anything about any of this," she interjected before continuing. "I guess we were lucky enough to get a short clip of Sid talking about marijuana and gulping his drink. Before he went to bed that night, Thomas retrieved the camera's SD card and clipped out the unimportant parts. He forwarded the incriminating clip to the local newspaper because I told him to do it. I'd already set up a fake email account for him, and that's how he managed it."

Rick looked puzzled as he asked his question, "But you were hurt! You were bleeding! *We* saw the blood on your leg! You did *that* to yourself?"

Thomas smirked as he nudged Sophia again. "No, Thomas did it."

"Thomas raped you?" Rick stood quickly but Thomas backed up a step, dragging Sophia with him. Rick sat back down, realizing his sudden movement could have caused Thomas to puncture Sophia's throat. "Sorry," he apologized as he sat back down, trying to calm himself.

Sophia sobbed. "There was no rape, Rick. There was never any rape," she bawled.

"But how …?" Rick asked, still very confused.

"Sid passed out even before I made it to the sunroom door. Thomas had slipped something in Sid's last drink to cause him to black out. Sid drank the last few gulps of his whiskey and threw the glass in the pool when I coerced him to argue with me. I moved slowly toward the house, waiting for him to fall, and he did—just like Thomas said he would. Thomas came out from the side of the house, and helped me drag Sid across the pool deck to get him out of sight. Sid's knuckles were scraped up as we dragged him across the rough concrete, which helped make it look like Sid attacked me."

"Geez, Sophia," Adam muttered as he shook his head in astonishment.

"Finish!" Thomas screamed. "Tell them the rest!"

"To make it look like I was attacked, Thomas reached into the pool and retrieved the cocktail glass that Sid had tossed in. It had floated across to the edge and was bobbing on the top step where he managed to get it. I stood very still as Thomas hit me on the back of the head, just hard enough to bring blood but not completely knock me out. He threw the glass back into the pool and helped me smear the blood from my head on the inside of my thigh. Nobody ever looked close enough to realize it wasn't there because of a rape, but as a prop to help sell the story." She kept her eyes closed as long as she could as she stood there helplessly in Thomas's angry embrace. "I really am so sorry," she cried again. "I didn't mean to hurt Thomas, either. I'm sorry, Thomas. I thought if you went away on vacation, nobody would have the chance to question you before you had your story down pat. And I thought you deserved a little pampering of your own, since I had treated you so cruelly—involving you so innocently in something so horrendous. Can you ever forgive me?" she asked, as sincerely as she could.

Thomas relaxed his grip on the letter opener, momentarily distracted from his anger by the sorrow in her voice. He also loosened his left arm that held Sophia against him, hoping that if he shifted just a little, he might get a glimpse of Sophia's sorrow-filled eyes.

Rick unexpectedly lunged toward Thomas with cat-like mobility. Pushing Sophia aside, Thomas raised his arm in an effort to fend off Rick as he grabbed Thomas around the abdomen. Instinctively, Thomas's right hand jabbed downward as he tried to defend himself from his attacker. The gold blade pierced the left side of Rick's back, fatally puncturing his heart. Thomas stood in shock, staring at Sophia's gift buried to the hilt in the blood-drenched shirt of Rick Giordano.

Screams erupted as a troop of armed policemen—spearheaded by Slick Silvio—burst into the room and tackled Thomas to the ground.

Slick hung his head as he spied Rick Giordano, sprawled on the floor with his sister and mother leaning over his lifeless body. "Oh, Jesus! I'm too late! I'm too late!" he sobbed as he fell to his knees. Caroline rushed around the dining room table to kneel in front of him. She embraced him and they cried together. "No, Slick. You saved the rest of us! If Rick had only waited just a few seconds more before he tried to be a hero, you would have saved him, too."

"No, Caroline. I failed. I knew it was Thomas, and I was inside the kitchen listening for a minute. I didn't have my pistol, but I had my phone. I sneaked out the front door and called the police. They told me to wait until they got here to go back inside. They told me they needed me to lead them to the right area. I believed they'd be here soon enough that nobody would be hurt, but I was wrong," Slick bellowed.

"Slick, listen to me! You did exactly right! You saved us. You've got to realize that! If you had tried to sneak up behind him without a weapon, we'd have all died! Including you!" Caroline kissed his tears and sniffed back her own. You're my hero, Slick Silvio," she admitted as she held his face between her shaking hands. "I love you," she whispered as she kissed his lips.

* * * * * *

Lucinda wept as she sat struggling with what she had just witnessed. She had known all about Uncle Joe's participation in DeLuca Enterprises, even the fact that Sophia and Rick were regularly transferring large amounts of money to the accounts in the Grand Caymans. She never condemned the family business the way others had.

What Lucinda didn't realize was how deeply Uncle Joe had woven himself into Sophia's life. He had lured her into doing despicable things that she should never have become involved in. Lucinda knew Sophia wasn't evil, only young and gullible. She had allowed herself to become one of Uncle Joe's many pawns.

Everything had always come easy for her granddaughter, except business success. Uncle Joe had offered the struggling young lady a quick alternative to that particular goal. Greedily, Sophia took it. Apparently, Sophia hadn't realized that once she accepted a generous 'favor' from the family, future demands for payback would forever endure. *Until death do us part,* she thought. Lucinda could certainly relate to that.

Lucinda believed—as did the rest of the family—that Sophia had been attacked and raped by Sid Taylor. She never dreamed Sophia would lie about something so horrible, so demeaning. The pride she once held for her granddaughter was now replaced with disenchantment. But, Lucinda also knew that Uncle Joe wouldn't have depended only on Sophia's act to ruin Sid; Uncle Joe had a whole army of pawns. The elderly woman was wise enough to know that what happened to the Sid Taylor family was a crescendo orchestrated by a whole troop of Uncle Joe's musicians. Sophia would have been the most innocent of all the players. And to top it off, Lucinda had stupidly agreed with Uncle Joe when she realized he was out to avenge Sophia's innocence. Sophia wasn't the only fool in the family.

* * * * * *

Maureen noticed Lucinda weeping silently, still parked in her wheelchair at the end of the dining room table. The loyal cook worked her way around policemen, crime scene investigators, and the others in an attempt to go to the sad matriarch.

"Why don't we get you upstairs, Miss Lucinda. You've been through enough, and you're still sick. Let me get you settled upstairs. If anyone needs to talk to you, we'll let them know you're resting."

"Thank you, dear. I'd like that very much. I would like to have a few minutes to myself to clear my head, if you don't mind."

Maureen smiled. "You bet, Miss Lucinda. I'll get you to the elevator and if you're up to it, you can take it from there to your room."

Graciously nodding, Lucinda allowed herself to be pushed down the long back hallway. When she was safely in the elevator, she looked out the doors to the sympathetic Maureen still standing in the hall.

"You're an angel, Maureen. Take care of my precious girl, please," she said softly as the elevator doors closed between them.

Maureen's hand was still hovering in the air from the "see you later" wave she had given Lucinda. She stared at the closed elevator door for an extra second thinking, *What did she mean by that? Which precious girl?*

Lucinda had been hording pills for some time now, especially those nice white, round ones for pain she'd been prescribed months before. She'd never taken any of them when she had sprained her wrist, believing she could tough it out. She had stockpiled enough of the OxyContin to release herself peacefully from the Bellini grip, and she would do it as soon as she got to her room behind a locked door.

* * * * * *

Everyone had been ushered into the living room while the police, the coroner, and the other officials remained in the dining room, the crime scene. Thomas had already been whisked away in a police car and was most likely being processed by now for Rick's murder.

Juliana sat numbly between Caroline and Slick, each of whom had tried ineffectively to give her comfort. Finally, they all stared ahead, thoughts wandering and sadness mounting.

Across the room was a sorrowful Adam, sitting in a side chair with his head in his hands. Sophia sat on the chair arm, her hand resting on Adam's right shoulder. She had finally stopped crying and sobbing, and gazed with empty eyes at a painting that had adorned the wall since the years when Vincenzo DeLuca lived there.

Finally, the Police Chief entered the room to give them all an update.

"Mrs. Giordano, I am sorry for your loss. The coroner will be transporting your son's body to his office for processing and autopsy. He left his card here for you to contact him when you're up to it. You may want to go ahead and start thinking about his final arrangements. You can discuss where the body should be sent when you speak with the coroner.

"About the assailant, Mr. Thomas Sutton. He told everything to the officer-in-charge, including his part in the staged assault. He repeated what Miss Giordano told you all about the illegal activities she supported indirectly through the crime family, specifically racketeering. Your son, had he lived, would have been considered an active co-conspirator, but perhaps not to the greater extent of your daughter's alleged involvement. Mr. Sutton has agreed to testify to the crimes he heard Sophia Giordano confess while in the presence of all you witnesses. One or all of you may be called upon by the Federal prosecutor to collaborate Mr. Sutton's testimony in the RICO case, when and if it comes to trial."

Sophia leaned across Adam and wept openly. "Adam, help me! What is he saying? Is he going to arrest me?"

Adam unwrapped Sophia's arms from around his neck as the family and the Police Chief watched his next move.

Adam stood and approached the Police Chief. He addressed him by name.

"Chief Carson, are you going to be the one to arrest her?" he asked as he stood eye-to-eye with the Police Chief.

"Not me, son. Her part is under federal jurisdiction," he answered with sympathy.

"I understand," Adam said as he turned toward the mother of his child.

He took a deep breath as Sophia stood to face him. He took her hands in his and said for all to hear:

"Sophia Giordano, you're under arrest."

"What?" shouted Slick as he started to rise from the couch, but Caroline motioned for him to remain seated.

Adam led Sophia to the Police Chief who slapped hand cuffs across the stunned young woman's wrists and started reading Sophia her Miranda rights.

Adam slowly reached in his back pocket and pulled out his FBI shield, holding it up for all to see, including the arrested woman.

Slick shook his head in amazement. "Moms, why didn't you let me in on **this** part?" he said as he looked up to the white ceiling.

Nobody knew what he was talking about except Caroline.

EPILOGUE

She clenched the rails on the hospital bed and let out a guttural scream. Sweat was pouring down into her eyes, her hair wet and matted from the internal heat she radiated from her core. She hardly had time to catch her breath after the pain subsided before another stabbing jolt consumed her again.

"Push, Sophia! Push! Now!" the doctor commanded her, coaching her through her temporary nightmare while he watched the fetal monitor to his right. "Push!"

"I CAN'T," she screeched, exasperated and exhausted. "I don't think I can," she started to whimper when another blast of hard labor hit her.

"The baby's crowning! Just one more good, hard push!" he said, coaxing her to try again, just a little harder and longer.

"UGGGGGGGHHHHHHHHH," she screamed, lifting her head up off the uncomfortable pillow.   Her face turned beet red from straining and holding her breath as she pushed as hard as she could. She lay back suddenly, breathing hard and feeling her heartbeat in her head.

She waited for what seemed like forever in the suddenly silent room. The doctor's head was moving and he was talking, but Sophia couldn't hear what he was saying.

The silence was broken when the newborn took his first big gasp of air outside his mother's womb. "WAAAA WAAAA WHAAAA" came from his strong lungs as the doctor handed off the perfectly beautiful baby boy to the waiting nurse.

"Another push, Sophia," the doctor commanded.

Exhausted, Sophia tried again. This time it was easier, but the effort required her to use the last bit of energy she could muster. She thought she would pass out before the doctor stood up and smiled.

"WHAA WHAA," she heard again.

"The baby has a good set of lungs," Sophia murmured as she tried to take a deep breath to relax her body.

"Yes, they do," the doctor beamed.

Sophia thought he said 'they.' She furrowed her brow as she struggled to comprehend the message the doctor was trying to relay to her.

"You are the mother of twins, Miss Giordano. Identical twin boys!" he proudly proclaimed. "Congratulations!"

Sophia was overcome with confusing emotion as she turned her head toward the other side of the delivery room. There she saw two nurses, each with a baby swaddled in her arms. They began to walk proudly toward the new mother.

"Congratulations," they both said as the crying, squirming babies were presented to Sophia.

They carefully positioned the tiny bundles in Sophia's arms, a perfectly shaped head resting in the crooks of each of Sophia's elbows. The nurses watched as the new mother's face softened when she peered into the babies' tiny faces.

Remarkably, the pain of childbirth was now a fleeting memory. Just like that, a new memory was taking its place. An overwhelming sense of joy exploded inside the new mother like fireworks on the Fourth of July. The feeling was indescribable.

She cradled her sons closely, kissing their tiny fingers, toes, and noses. She swayed side to side in slow movement, attempting to rock the babies while still lying on the hospital bed. The sheets were still damp from the sweaty ordeal of delivery, but Sophia didn't notice.

"Sweet little Ricky. That's what I want you to be called. Ricky, just like your Uncle Rick who saved Mommy's life while you were still tiny in her tummy," she told the son who lay in her right arm. "I love you, precious baby. I will always love you with all my heart," she whispered as she cried happy tears.

"And you! You have to be named for Adam, your handsome father. The man I will always love. Oh, how I wish things had turned out differently. I have so many regrets, but you both make life worth living again," she cried as she cuddled her newborn sons. "I love you both so much."

Both nurses stepped forward and reached for the tiny bundles. "We need to get them cleaned up, measured and weighed, Miss. You need to get some rest, too." one of the nurses declared.

"Do I have to give them up right now? Can't I hold them for just a few more minutes," Sophia pleaded.

"I'm sorry, but the babies need immediate attention and have to be checked by the pediatrician. He's waiting," the nurse explained.

Reluctantly, Sophia allowed the nurses to take her newborns into the nursery where they would go through their own individual examinations. Sophia lay back on the pillow, suddenly feeling overwhelmed by a plethora of rolling emotions: happy, sad, giddy, tearful, and so many more feelings she would never be able to describe in effective words.

The obstetrician came to her side and patted her shoulder. "Good job, Miss Giordano. Your babies appear to be healthy, and you will recover in a few days. During the old days, some women went back into the fields and worked the rest of the day after childbirth. Imagine that," he chuckled. "You're going to be good as new before you know it," he encouraged her.

* * * * * *

In the seating area not far from the delivery room, Teddy Brantley waited impatiently with Adam Woodson to learn any news about the baby's delivery and condition. They were particularly interested in whether or not Sophia would be allowed to visit with them before she had to be returned to her cell at Bedford Hills Correctional Facility for Women.

Caroline and Slick had arrived soon after and waited with the two nervous young men during the last hours of Sophia's long labor. Even though Adam wasn't yet positive he was the baby's father, he paced the floor like an old pro. His nerves were shot, and he frequently revealed his fear of holding a newborn and somehow 'breaking the baby' by accident.

Although Caroline had never had a baby of her own, she found it amusing to watch the two young men discussing how diapers were supposed to be changed. Neither had a clue what they were talking about, which made the conversation even more comical. Meanwhile, Slick kept his head down, and was only there because Caroline made him tag along. He popped a Percocet when no one was watching, hoping to relieve the back pain he suffered from sitting in the hard institutional chairs. A few minutes later, Slick's eyes glassed over as if he were in a trance. No one noticed.

A nurse rushed through double doors and headed straight toward Adam and Teddy.

"Mr. Giordano?" she asked, looking back and forth between Adam and Teddy.

"No. Yes. I mean, I'm Mr. Woodson, Miss Giordano's father … I mean the father of the baby," Adam stuttered. "Is the baby here?"

The nurse laughed at the confusion Adam was trying to clarify. "It's all right, Mr. Woodson. I understand. And yes, the babies are here— both healthy and weighing in at 5 pounds 6 ounces and 5 pounds two ounces, respectively. They're beautiful identical twin boys. Look a tad like their father, I'd say," the nurse teased.

Adam and Teddy stared at the nurse as if she were invisible. Their eyes were blank, still reeling from the surprise announcement that Sophia had delivered twins.

Slick gently punched Caroline in the ribs, and whispered, "I knew that already. It came to me right before that nurse ever said a word."

Caroline looked at Slick, wondering if he truly saw a premonition of Sophia having twins. Shaking her head in wonderment, she turned back toward the nurse. "How is the mother," Caroline thought to ask.

"Miss Giordano is resting, but you can go through those doors and take a right. You'll see the little miracles through the nursery window."

The two young men didn't wait for further instructions, and zoomed past the nurse and pushed through the double doors. Slick and Caroline embraced quickly, kissing each other on the cheek in happiness. They chuckled at Adam and Teddy, watching them stumbling over each other trying to get hastily through the doors for the best spot at the nursery window. Caroline and Slick followed behind at a normal pace, accompanied by the proud nurse who guided them to the nursery area.

"They DO look like me! Look, Teddy. Don't you see it? They have my nose!" Adam exclaimed.

The nurse left the gawking family peering at the infants and went inside the nursery. She lifted one of the babies from its transparent cradle and brought him to the window for the family to see more closely. She did the same with the second baby.

She decided to proceed with the babies' baths while she had the audience of adoring family still at the window. Gingerly pulling apart the snaps of the baby's long gown, she laid the first baby across her shoulder as she put the soiled gown aside. She laid the baby down once more to remove his diaper. The nurse once again picked up the naked newborn while she adjusted the bath water and reached for the soap and cloth.

It was when the nurse turned toward the window the final time that Caroline and Teddy spotted it. They looked at each other in awe, Teddy's mind racing while Caroline found herself wondering how to explain what they were seeing. There was an obvious explanation, of course, but it had been kept secret for almost thirty years.

Teddy's eyes shifted to Caroline, locking with hers as if pleading for help in understanding what he'd observed. Caroline nodded, and motioned for Teddy to follow her outside. Adam and Slick didn't notice them leave; instead, they found themselves captivated by how the nurse so carelessly moved the tiny fragile babies about. They thought she was much too rough, not understanding that real life babies are much sturdier than baby dolls made from papier mache.

* ** ** **

"Aunt Caroline, that baby has the same red diamond birth mark as I do!" a panicked Teddy told her. "I swear I never had sex with Sophia! I swear it, Aunt Caroline. You've got to believe me," Teddy pleaded with his Godmother.

"I do believe you, Teddy. There's an explanation for what you saw. I've tried to put off telling this story, and I thought maybe I'd never have to share it. But it's time. You, Sophia and I need to talk privately. Let's see if we can get the nurse to let us have a few minutes alone with Sophia. Just us. Okay?" she smiled comfortingly at Teddy.

"All right, Aunt Caroline. But I don't want Adam to know about my birthmark until we get everything cleared up. I can't imagine how this can be explained away, but I hope you're convincing."

* ** ** **

When Adam went to talk with the hospital laboratory personnel about securing a DNA sample for the paternity test, Slick accompanied him at Caroline's suggestion. The minute Adam and Slick departed, Teddy and Caroline darted toward the nurses' station to request a brief visit with Sophia.

"She's not due to return to Bedford Hills Correctional until the morning, so I don't know what it could hurt. There's a police officer stationed outside her door, but I'll introduce you as her family. It shouldn't be a problem. Oh…and one other thing, Miss Giordano is handcuffed to the bed rail. It's a security requirement when we treat inmates."

Caroline swallowed hard, not expecting Sophia to be chained to the bed. "We understand. We'll try not to be too long."

After gaining the guard's approval for admission, Teddy entered the room first, followed by Caroline a few steps behind.

"Hey, there. You awake?" Teddy whispered. Sophia had her back turned to the door, so it was impossible to know.

"I'm awake," Sophia said as she turned over as far as she could. Only one arm was cuffed to the bed rail, thankfully.

"Have you seen my little babies? Ricky and Adam?" Sophia smiled broadly. "They are the most beautiful babies. I never imagined they'd be so beautiful. I thought newborn babies were all wrinkly and shrunken like a …I don't know…lizards or something," she laughed.

"They are both absolutely gorgeous, just like Mommy," Teddy chimed in.

"Thank you for coming. I know you didn't have to, but I'm still glad you're here. Where's Adam?" she asked.

Teddy answered, "He's gone to the lab to arrange for the paternity test."

Sophia's smile started to droop. "I don't blame him for not believing me when I said he was the only partner I had. It was true, though. This test he's so fired up about taking will prove it."

Caroline smiled and patted Sophia's hand. "I'm sure it will, dear. But there is something I need to tell you and Teddy about events that happened around the time you all were born. I wish Rick could have been here to hear this. I know he was always curious about this time period, too. But, regardless, you both have a right to know what happened in 1994—the year you were born, Teddy. And Rick's birth year, as well."

Caroline and Teddy pulled up straight backed chairs to the edge of Sophia's bed so they could all be comfortable while the story unfolded.

"Okay. I'm going to tell you the story about the kidnapping of a baby who was never officially located by the police. But the baby was never lost."

"You're talking in riddles, Aunt Caroline. Just tell us whatever it is." Sophia requested.

"Right. Assuming you haven't held the babies long enough to inspect them closely, at least one of them has the same exact birthmark on his lower back as Teddy." Caroline stopped talking to see Sophia's reaction. "Don't you find that odd?"

"Why should I? Lots of people have birthmarks, Aunt Caroline. So it looks a little like Teddy's. So what?"

"My dear, it is *exactly* like Teddy's little red diamond marking! This one is passed down through generations. It's precisely the same one."

Sophia shook her head. "You are confusing me, Aunt Caroline. I never slept with Teddy. It couldn't be genetic."

"I'm about to say something that you won't believe at first, but after you hear the whole story you'll understand." She paused for a moment, looking back and forth between Teddy and Sophia.

Taking a deep breath of courage, Caroline started the story. "You two are sister and brother. Rick and Teddy were fraternal twins. Teddy was the one with the birthmark that exactly matched his father's, Lorenzo. And now the birthmark reappears on a male child of Giordano descent. Sophia, it is the Giordano birthmark that one and maybe both of your sons were born with. It's there because of *your* Giordano blood."

Teddy's brow wrinkled, and Sophia started to laugh. "No way, Aunt Caroline. That's ridiculous. You're saying Teddy is my biological *brother*?"

"Yes, and I assure you, it's true. Here's what I know: My ex-husband, John Sanderson, came home from work one night in 1994, driving through a raging snow storm. So John takes his usual exit to Hicksville, but he meets a car coming head-on, going the wrong way down the ramp. The other vehicle missed hitting John's car, but crashed into the guard rail. The impact knocked out the two adults who had a baby in the car with them. Before anyone else arrived at the scene, John grabbed the baby from the crashed car and took him to his house—the house we used to share when we were married.

"John thought God somehow had a hand in this discovery because of John's college buddy, Doug Brantley. Doug had called him that very morning, upset about how he and his wife lost a baby a few weeks before. Doug asked John about how to replace the dead baby, legally or illegally. He was desperate, because his wife had been heavily sedated ever since the baby died of SIDS. She didn't realize her baby was gone, and Doug feared she'd die of a broken heart if she ever knew the truth."

"This is complicated," Teddy said. Sophia agreed.

"Long story short, the baby John rescued from the wreck was Teddy—or rather, Francesco Lorenzo Giordano, III—that was your birth name. Teddy, you had been kidnapped a few hours before by Vincenzo DeLuca's crew to pay off a gambling debt owed to him by Dr. Lorenzo Giordano, your father. DeLuca's crew had staged a robbery at the doctor's house, but they randomly took only one of the twin babies. They left the other infant, as well as the toddler sister who was asleep in the house. The children left behind were you and Rick, Sophia.

Teddy, of course, you grew up in Lenoir City, Tennessee. If you haven't figured it out by now, your father, Doug, was the school buddy of my ex-husband, John. When you were less than a week old, John drove you all the way from New York to present you to the man who raised you as his own miracle son. Your mother gradually came out of sedation and accepted you as her own biological child. The real Teddy Brantley was buried in the woods behind your parents' home. Your dad buried him.

I have to warn you two. Not everyone knows the whole story. For example, Teddy's mother in Tennessee—Stella—still doesn't know anything about the switch. It would crush her to think that she never gave birth to you, Teddy. We have to promise she will never know that. We can't speak of it until Stella eventually passes away. It's the most respectable and humane way to handle this, I think.

"You're probably wondering about your real mother, aren't you, Teddy? Sophia? Cathy Parker Giordano was a beautiful woman, so elegant and classic. But when one of her 3-day old sons was kidnapped, and her guilty husband didn't seem very concerned about whether the police quickly recovered the child, she slowly succumbed to alcohol. I'm sure that was the way she numbed her grief. In an alcoholic stupor, Cathy killed herself using a knife from her own kitchen counter.

"You probably don't know that your father, Dr. Giordano, helped save Lucinda's life, and that's when he met Juliana. They eventually got married, trying to build a new life around Rick and Sophia. It wasn't until a few hours before Lorenzo died that he was told where his abducted son was. A few hours later, it was believed he fell overboard on a cruise ship. His body was never recovered.

"Juliana doesn't know that Teddy is really the kidnapped Giordano baby, and I don't believe we should ever reveal that to her. She only knows Teddy is my Godson. I gladly accepted that responsibility and cherish my part in your life. My ex-husband's insurance proceeds helped support you, Teddy, while you were young and growing up in Tennessee. I managed those funds until just recently, when they were finally depleted.

"There are so many other twists and turns to this story. I wish we had time to discuss them, but we don't, at least not today. But I promise I'll find a way to record everything that happened during those days. Maybe I'll write a book and title it *Sacrificial Sins* so you can learn every detail about everything that happened to us during the winter of 1994." She laughed as she stood up from her chair.

"I'm going to wait for Slick outside. Perhaps you two want to talk privately for a few minutes? I'm sure you have a lot of questions to ask each other," Caroline told them. She blew Sophia a kiss as she exited the room.

"Wow. So you're my little brother, huh?"

Teddy shrugged his shoulders. "Hell of a way to find out, don't you think?"

Sophia nodded. "So that birthmark you have is a 'Giordano' birthmark? You plan on changing your name?"

"Nope. That would crush my mother. And since we pledged not to tell her my true identity, I don't think it'd be wise. Guess I'll just let that secret stay hidden for a while longer.

"Hmm. Probably best. But now you will inherit part of the Giordano fortune."

"I don't want it, Sophia. I'm not planning on staying in New York for much longer. I want to go back home to the South. Things are simpler there, and the people are nicer, you know? They say things like, 'Bless Your Heart' and 'How's your Mama' ... you know, friendly, nice ways of communicating. Gentle and kind people. But, I haven't decided for sure, yet."

Sophia nodded. "I understand. And by the way, Teddy. I never got to thank you for working so hard to get me on the election ballot for the Representative seat. I'm so sorry, Teddy. You should have run in my place."

"Nah. I never wanted to be in politics. I might have turned into another Sid Taylor," he joked.

"No way, little brother. Come here and give your big sis a hug," Sophia smiled and outstretched her one unshackled arm toward Teddy. They embraced tightly and allowed their hug to linger. When they broke away, Teddy headed straight to the door and never looked back.

* * * * * *

Adam ordered an expedited paternity test so that he could know as soon as possible if the children were his. When the results confirmed his paternity, Adam and Caroline worked through all the legal requirements to ensure Adam Woodson was listed on their birth certificates as the father. Soon after, with expert assistance from Caroline, Adam was legally awarded permanent custody of the twins while Sophia remained incarcerated for the next twenty years.

* * * * * *

About the same time as Adam was awarded custody of the twins, Big Al Bellini finally came out of hiding, surfacing at JFK airport for his long flight overseas.

When Big Al arrived in Italy, Uncle Joe sent a car to the airport to pick him up and deliver him safely to the Bellini compound in Marsala.

"Uncle Joe!" Big Al exclaimed as he entered the foyer of the main house, driver standing closely behind him toting two big suitcases.

Uncle Joe came out of the kitchen and smiled widely. "Al, good to see you! You've earned yourself a seat at my table in perpetuity. Come. Have a drink with me to celebrate." Big Al followed the old man into the kitchen, taking a seat at the wooden table while his uncle retrieved glasses and a bottle of wine.

"This is the best. Right from our own vineyards," the elder Bellini stated, pouring two generous servings of Sangiovese.

"Excellent," Big Al remarked after he sniffed the wine and took a sip. Uncle Joe nodded as he joined Al at the table.

"Don't think I'm insulting you, Al, but did you tie up all the loose ends from your last job?"

Big Al took another sip of wine before he answered. "If you mean are the witnesses eliminated, yeah. I took care of Leona the day she gave that fake sketch to the police. The other two assistants were from my own crew—the doctor has been working with the family ever since he was a resident. For years now he's been patching up our boys, and makes more from us than he ever will as a legitimate practitioner. And the limo driver? He's my own driver. He works directly for me. Those two? You don't have to worry, eh?" he laughed as he emptied his glass and set it down hard on the table.

"But what about the handsome man you hired to lure the Taylor boy out of that bar?" Uncle Joe queried.

Big Al shook his head. "Oh, yeah. I forgot about him. He never made it back to New York that night. Seems he had faulty brakes or something equally disturbing. The van he was driving went over a cliff," Big Al chortled, then broke out into full laughter.

Uncle Joe laughed along, and shook his head. "You thought of everything then, right Al?"

"Right, Uncle Joe. There weren't any problem witnesses left around after the bomb went off at the campaign rally, either. Everybody that we need to worry about was killed that day," he proudly responded.

"You didn't keep any souvenirs that could tie us back to these unfortunate events, did you Al?" Uncle Joe asked, trying to qualm the queasy gut feeling he had that something or someone would come back and bite them in the ass someday.

"Naw, just the leather mask. I couldn't keep the red contacts in my eyes for very long. I hated that leather jumpsuit, too. It was too damned hot. All that stuff got burned up. Everything except the leather head piece. Made me feel like a superhero or something. I put it in my safe deposit box. You know, a little something to wear on Halloween sometime," Big Al laughed and reached for the bottle to pour himself another glass of Bellini Vineyards' finest.

Uncle Joe's mind was working fast. He finally gave up and decided Big Al had covered the most important bases.

"So Al, did you remember to bring me what I asked for?" Uncle Joe said as he faced him and smiled mischievously.

"How could I forget? I've kept it close the whole time," Big Al smirked. He reached into his pocket and pulled out the trinket. "Wear it in good health, Uncle Joe," he said as he handed him the gold Rolex that once belonged to Sid Taylor.

* * * * * *

Within a few weeks, Adam Woodson had adapted to being a single father with two newborn babies under his exclusive care.

Even though he immediately requested and received an extended temporary leave of absence from his FBI position, Adam dreaded going back into that particular job.

Eventually, he made the difficult decision to hand in his resignation and planned to move back home to Shelbyville, Tennessee. Adam's attorney father, Henry, was elated when he heard the news. He looked forward to having his son and grandsons at home with him in the big empty house on Cannon Boulevard.

After arriving in Bedford County, Henry convinced Adam he and the boys should permanently reside with him in the family home, discouraging Adam from moving into a 'substandard rental.' The elderly man offered to hire extra help for the babies while Adam looked for a steady job. Adam couldn't refuse his father's generous offer.

Soon after, Henry informed Adam about an opening he'd heard about for a detective within the Shelbyville City Police Department. Coincidentally, it was the same job Adam's grandfather, Harry Woodson, started out in during the 1950s.

When Adam went to the interview his father had arranged, the Shelbyville Chief of Police hired him on the spot.

Henry Woodson, Esquire, couldn't have been prouder of his remarkable son, Detective Adam Woodson.

* * * * * *

It took Teddy Brantley a little while longer to figure out what he wanted to do with his future. With Juliana's assistance, DeLuca Enterprises dissolved its corporate status and liquidated its holdings—under the watchful guidance of the federal government, of course.

When all was said and done, Juliana was paid handsomely. The money she had already inherited from Lucinda, plus the liquidation returns she reaped, pushed her well into the multi-billion dollar wealth category.

Teddy was also generously rewarded for his loyalty, expertise, and perseverance through the corporate dissolution process. When he walked away from his Senior Vice President-Chief General Counsel position at DeLuca, he was paid almost fifty million dollars after taxes. He had enough time and enough money to spend the rest of his life doing what he loved—hiking the majestic mountains of Tennessee.

When he left New York, Teddy's first stop was in Lenoir City, Tennessee, where he modestly grew up with his parents, Doug and Stella Brantley. He arrived at the brink of autumn, his favorite season.

After he pulled up in the Brantley driveway, he surprised his parents when he opened the door to his silver Lexus 350 SUV and stood silently surveying the house he loved.

"Teddy! Teddy, my baby!" Stella exclaimed as she ran down the porch steps to greet her boy. "We didn't expect you so soon," she said as she fought back her happy tears.

Doug Brantley meandered out on the porch, still standing partially inside the house as he peered through the screen door he held open.

"Doug, get out here! It's Teddy!" Stella exclaimed to her husband who was still squinting in the distance to identify the unexpected visitor. He smiled broadly and let the screen door slam behind him, making his way slowly down the steps.

"My boy! Teddy, you're looking good for an old bachelor. Glad to see you made it, son," Doug said proudly as he reached to shake Teddy's hand. Instead, Teddy pulled his father close to him in a warm embrace.

"Dad! Mom! I can't tell you how glad I am to be home," the prodigal son replied.

* * * * * *

For Thanksgiving that year, Caroline and Slick rented an eight-bedroom ski mountain resort house in Gatlinburg, Tennessee for an entire week. They invited Juliana Giordano, Teddy, Doug, and Stella Brantley, plus Adam Woodson, his father Henry and, of course, the twins.

Caroline planned everything carefully, insisting that the guests come prepared to ski if they wanted, or perhaps just relax next to the wood burning fireplace in the huge great room. Housekeeping and catering had already been arranged during their entire vacation, so there was no concern about cleaning or cooking. Everyone was invited to celebrate and not worry about anything. All they had to do was be present at 6 o'clock the Saturday evening after Thanksgiving. Everyone agreed.

The holiday was perfect, and so was the weather. A light coating of fluffy snowflakes shrouded the mountains and tall pine trees around the house. The roads were slick but not necessarily treacherous. By 4 o'clock Saturday evening, Caroline and Slick left the resort and gave explicit instructions to Juliana to get the rest of the group to the designated meeting spot that only Juliana knew.

At 5:55 p.m., Juliana led the caravan into the parking lot of the "Angels Altar," a well-known wedding chapel located in the center of Gatlinburg. When the group entered the small sanctuary, Slick was waiting at the door. Dressed in a black tuxedo and looking quite dapper, his grin reached fully across his exuberant face. As each guest filed in, Slick handed out boutonnieres to the gentlemen and corsages to the ladies. For the babies, he held two blue pacifiers adorned with blue lace ribbons. His new 'authentic' gold Rolex watch, a gift from his bride-to-be, glinted in the candlelight that radiated within the chapel.

When all the guests were seated, Slick slipped behind the closed double doors at the rear of the sanctuary. As the organist started to play the wedding march, everyone turned as the rear doors swung open to reveal the bride and groom. Arms looped together, Slick and Caroline slowly walked down the aisle to the waiting officiate.

Caroline couldn't have been lovelier in an elegant wedding gown made of delicate lace, shiny satin, and embroidered pearls accenting the long and delicate train. She wore a simple necklace—a small heart-shaped blue sapphire— which was the only precious possession Slick had to give his bride-to-be. It had been his mother's.

Caroline was stunningly beautiful and extraordinarily blissful as she and Slick took their vows, becoming husband and wife that evening before God and their cherished family.

Even Moms attended, standing near the front so she could get a good look at her son's new bride and the heirloom sapphire adorning her neck.

* * * * * *

A few months after the wedding, Caroline and Slick moved into the residence that had once been the Oyster Bay home of Cathy and Lorenzo Giordano. It had been vacant ever since Rick Giordano's death. Juliana and Sophia wished the house could somehow remain in the immediate family, and could never bring themselves to put it up for public sale.

Caroline and Slick had been looking for a home in which they could start their newlywed lives together. So, when Caroline and Slick asked about buying the house, both Juliana and Sophia were elated and readily agreed to the sale.

Together, the newly married couple began to update the appliances and change out the older carpeting in the bedrooms to match the beautiful hardwood in the other parts of the mansion. Inheriting her mother's decorating flair, Juliana helped Caroline choose new draperies, linens, and fresh paint colors for the walls. What was once known as the Giordano house was now being referred to as the Norton-Silvio estate.

Late one night after a long day of renovation work, Slick lay in bed next to his sleeping bride. He had started to doze off when he heard clinking noises coming from somewhere in the house.

Tiptoeing down the hallway, he heard the noise again…then subtle laughter from what sounded like multiple people.

He grabbed an umbrella from a nearby closet and proceeded to inch his way down the dark corridor. Suddenly, he dropped the umbrella as he peered through the kitchen doorway, shaking his head in amazement at the scene before him.

"Ah, Raymond! Won't you join us in a glass of bubbly?" Moms asked as she clinked glasses with her new friends.

"Moms, what are you doing here? Rick? Is that you?" a stunned Slick uttered in surprise.

"Yes, it's me. And I want you to meet my real mother, Cathy, my biological mother. She died right about where she's standing now." Cathy smiled as she took a step backward and looked down. "My mother has been filling me in with stories about my father and my family, something Aunt Caroline never got the chance to do." Rick smiled at his mother's happy image as she leaned toward him and slipped her arm through his.

"I've wanted to talk to him ever since… well, you know," Cathy explained. "And I've yearned to talk to Teddy, too. I needed them both to know that I never gave up on them, just on myself."

Slick's mother reached toward Cathy and patted her arm. "Dear Cathy, you'll spend eternity with Rick, unveiling the past and watching the future as it unfolds for Teddy."

Slick moved cautiously out of the doorway and toward the kitchen counter. With shaking hands, he poured himself a short glass of champagne. "I can't believe this. I just can't believe this. Are **all** of you going to share this house with us? I thought Caroline and I could start fresh—alone. Geez, Moms."

"Now, now, Raymond. Mind your manners. Besides, Cathy and Rick have a right to be here just as much as you do. It's still the Giordano house as far as they're concerned," his mother admonished him.

"What about you, Moms? You don't have a stake in this house," Slick retorted.

"Yes, I do, Raymond. **You're** here," she chuckled as the spirits of Rick and Cathy joined her with soft laughter.

Without warning, the overhead light flashed on. Caroline stood at the kitchen door staring in Slick's direction.

"Caroline, I can explain…," Slick started.

"No need," she responded, walking toward the spot where Slick had been standing in the dark. "Just pour me a little champagne, and I'll join you."

Her husband complied, handing her the glass and watching her face with interest.

Caroline took a sip and stared at Slick in suspense. "Well? Don't be rude, Slick. I already know Rick, but aren't you going to introduce me to these two charming ladies."

Slick gulped. "You can **SEE** them, too?"

"Afraid so," she answered. She turned to raise her glass toward the spirits in a gesture of welcome."

" Oh, Geez!" Slick muttered, dropping his glass on the kitchen tile and abruptly fainting.

"He always was fragile," Moms said as she moved toward Caroline to embrace her new daughter-in-law. "Welcome to the family," she told Caroline.

"Thank you. And by the way, you looked beautiful at our wedding, Moms," Caroline teased.

Moms squinted as she looked questioningly at Slick's new wife.

"Actually, I've been seeing and hearing you ever since I put on your beautiful sapphire necklace, Moms." Caroline laughed as she winked at her new mother-in-law. "Nice to finally get an official introduction."

Slick was stirring and opened his eyes slowly. He focused on Caroline's face above him when she peeked across the counter and looked down where his collapsed body lay on the floor.

"Caroline, have I been sleepwalking?" he asked as he slowly propped himself up on his elbows.

Before Slick made it off the floor, the faces of his mother, Cathy, and Rick merged next to Caroline's face above him. All four of them peered down at him with big smiles.

"You got a good one here, Raymond. She's got the gift," Moms enthusiastically told her son— right before he fainted for the second time that extraordinary night.

ABOUT THE AUTHOR

Twin Sins is the third work of fiction in the **Sins Volumes** written by author, Mary Elizabeth Gaines.

Her first novel, *Buried Sins,* is a standalone mystery set during the 1950s in her hometown of Shelbyville, Tennessee. Her second book in the series, *Sacrificial Sins*, is set in New York during the 1990s and is the prequel to *Twin Sins,* her newest release.

Mary lives in Knoxville, Tennessee with her husband Sam. She enjoys spending as much time as possible with their children and grandchildren, as well as playing with the family dogs, Amos and Gypsy. Mary is an avid reader, a music enthusiast, and she loves vacationing at the beach.

Twin Sins

For more information about Mary and her suspense novels, visit her website at
<u>marygainesbooks.com</u>

Please Join

Mary's FaceBook Group Page,

Mary Gaines Books.

SPECIAL ACKNOWLEDGEMENT

Sandra F. Crowell

Sandi, you have inspired me to write and publish all three of my books. For that, I am eternally grateful.

You've motivated me with your constructive criticism and honest feedback, helping me learn to boldly create suspense and intrigue. You taught me the difference in developing a simple story versus a real brain teaser. My biggest challenge has always been trying to stump you—the ultimate Rex Stout fan! I've rejoiced every time you couldn't imagine how my plot would end because if YOU couldn't figure it out, not many other readers would be able to, either.

Dear lady, you've reminded me that our hidden gifts are often something much different than the career skills we hone throughout our working lives. After I retired from my desk job, I never dreamed that I would write anything, much less a series of novels. Thank you for the encouragement and inspiration you gave me to tackle the improbable and make it a reality.

My sincere thanks to my former UT classmate, my beach vacation buddy, and my treasured friend of more than thirty years—Sandi with an "i".

I will never be able to repay all your kindnesses.

-Mary-

ACKNOWLEDGEMENTS

Jennifer D. Carr and **Lisa S. Ferris:** Thank you both, darling daughters, for making me believe I can do anything I set my heart to do. Of course, that is the lesson I always hoped you would learn from **me**! LOL! Regardless, your editing help and positive feedback have added so much to this experience.   I love you both, and will treasure you and your loving hearts always. I am so very proud of each of you!

-Mom-

From one old married couple to another.......

Joe W. Finch and **Rosemary S. Finch:** You two are the epitome of generosity, selflessness, and loving kindness. For all three of my books, you have both honored me by reviewing, commenting, and helping me through those little snags that are often left unnoticed in the pre-publishing phase of writing a novel. Sam and I salute you both, and we are proud to count you among our dearest friends. You have blessed us with your insights and candid assessments. You are awesome promoters! We are so grateful that you have re-entered our lives, and look forward to many more years of true friendship.

-Mary & Sam-

Samuel L. Gaines: You already have my admiration, friendship and eternal love. Once again, you have my acknowledgement for your tireless efforts during the weeks it took me to write *Twin Sins*. Thank you for being my sounding board, my plot co-conspirator, and my grammar policeman. *Twin Sins* is a better book because of you.

Not everyone is as blessed as I am to have someone like you as a partner in life. Your unfailing support for my writing is only one of the many ways you make me feel special every day.

Sam, the lines I dedicated to you at the end of *Sacrificial Sins* say it best, and I will always mean every word:

> *"If you live to be a hundred,*
>
> *I want to live to be a hundred minus one day,*
>
> *So, I never have to live without you."*
>
> — *Winnie the Pooh* - A. A. Milne

Sam, you are and forever will be my Soul Mate. I love you.

-Mary-

Twin Sins

AND last but never least…

To

All my wonderful readers and followers,

The loyal members of my FaceBook Group page,

And

All who support struggling new writers everywhere,

Thank You

Mary Elizabeth Gaines